The Fix

Also by Lisa Herrington

The Beach House
Dixieland
The Fix
One Starry Night

The Fix

Lisa Herrington

Writerly House Publishing

THE FIX

Published by Writerly House Publishing
www.WriterlyHouse.com
www.LisaHerrington.com

This is a work of fiction. Characters, names, places, and events are products of the author's imagination. Any similarity to events or places, or real persons, living or dead is purely coincidental.

Copyright © 2017 Lisa Herrington
First Published May 2017

All rights reserved. No part of this book may be reproduced or transmitted in any form or by any means, electronic, mechanical, photocopying, recording, or otherwise, without written permission.

ISBN: 978-0999062609

10 9 8 7 6 5 4 3 2 1

For G. G. & J.

Chapter One

RYAN GENTRY SLOWLY DROVE the winding road around Maison-Lafitte Lake, taking in the cypress trees and live oaks that shaded the drive. These trees, with their knobby roots, called knees, and the ones with large winding branches, gave the area character and helped set the small water town apart from other vacation destinations nearby.

The small town of Maisonville had virtually gone unnoticed until the late sixties when a group of young professionals from the city started buying property and settling their wives and children there for the summer months. Some remodeled old homes, but many tore down existing structures and built houses to fit their needs.

It was then that Maisonville had its largest population, and covenants were quickly established to keep the town from growing any larger. Currently, there were four hundred permanent residents, many who spent their childhood vacations at the lake and then later brought their children for the summer months. The town was enjoying a sort of renaissance.

A large group of retirees lived there year round, and they were a social group, getting together as often as possible, which gave a boost to the downtown shops and restaurant. Most the retirees used the nickname Renaissance Lake for the area because living there felt like a new beginning. Things had never looked better as they refurbished their homes and spent endless hours perfecting their lawns and flower beds.

It was turning into a retirement haven, but that quaint and peaceful town also lured young adults looking for the same type of paradise, which was why Ryan Gentry called it home. Unlike other towns in the area and the large city on the other side of the lake, Maisonville only opened itself up by hosting a few distinct festivals and by allowing rentals exclusively during the months of June and July.

Maisonville was a beloved area, and outsiders were always curious to get a peek inside the extraordinary town.

It was rare for homes to be sold because they were passed down to family members or relatives of friends. Therefore, property was usually at a premium with newer homes and condominiums on the east side of town and older homes in need of restoration on the west side, split in half by a perfect little downtown. Running north and south was the large lake and the famous bridge that ran twenty miles over water into the bright lights of the city.

Ryan lived and worked on the west side of town. He owned a small company that specialized in old home rehabilitation, and after repairing a few places for others, he began slowly acquiring homes himself. He was becoming well known in town for single-handedly rebuilding Westside, the name given to the area by locals.

He loved Westside and spent most of his vacations there as a kid with his sister and their Uncle. They swam and played water sports all summer long, and he'd hoped he would end up living here.

He was especially happy at the moment because he'd finally talked the owner of his favorite property into selling to him. Tracey McHenry had inherited the large white house at the bend of the lake thirty years ago, but he left Louisiana after college to live in Maine and never returned. He swore he couldn't take the heat, but he wouldn't budge on the property until Ryan kept at him.

Ryan sent pictures of the pier falling into the water along with the vines that had overtaken the solarium. It was one of the oldest homes in town, and he dreamed of restoring it to its original stature. He couldn't believe it was finally going to be his.

Well, it would be his when he sold his latest project house so that he could afford the steep asking price. He couldn't wait to see the look on his sister's face when he told her. Reagan had encouraged him to start his own company and had invested a considerable amount to get him started. He was excited to pay her investment off, several months ago, but understood his working capital was strapped until he sold another property. He needed a buyer to fall out of the sky that week so he could buy the house.

He was in the middle of the steepest curve around the lake when he suddenly slammed on his brakes to avoid hitting a car that had stopped on the road. It was late afternoon, and with the tree cover, the old beige colored Subaru wagon was difficult to see. He quickly turned on his flashers and ran back behind his truck to throw down three orange cones and a flashing light.

Damn tourists were going to get someone killed with their site-seeing.

"What the hell are you doing, stopped here in the middle of the road?" he yelled, trying to locate the driver.

"Just looking around," said a woman standing on the other side of the car.

"A ninety-degree turn is a great spot to stop your car. I almost hit you," he said sarcastically as he rounded the car to see a pretty redhead wearing a sleeveless blue sundress and sandals. She was peering over the slight drop off at the edge of the road. When she turned around, he could see she had black marks on her forehead and cheek where she must have wiped her dirty hands.

She blinked her brown eyes several times, and he immediately could see she was trying not to cry. He then noticed she had a flat tire and when he looked over the side of the road, he could see her spare tire had somehow rolled down the steep hill several feet.

"Stay here. I'll be right back," Ryan said and jumped down the incline to rescue her roll away spare. Without talking to her, he returned and began to change the tire.

"Thank you, but I know how to change a tire," she said, and he stopped and stared at her. She stepped toward him, and he held up his hand.

"I got it," he said.

He had it done in ten minutes and then when he lowered the car with the jack, her spare went flat, too. He shook his head and walked back to his truck to get an air compressor. "When you have your oil changed, you should always have them check the spare tire for air."

"I just bought it, okay?"

"The tire?"

"The car, genius."

He looked at her and then at the car. He may not be a genius, but they didn't match. She was wearing sandals that cost a fortune, and there was a purse on the seat of her car that cost more than the car. He knew because Reagan had the same bag and brand of shoes.

He held his hands up and then nodded at her. "You're good to go now. I wouldn't drive too far on that spare. It looks pretty old."

She avoided his eyes but nodded as she headed for the driver's door. She whispered "Thanks" before she got in and sped off.

City girl.

He hated the city.

❦

Sydney Bell hurried into the driveway of the small real estate office. It was just off the downtown area, and she was thankful it was easy to find. She shook her head and wiped the black soot off her face and hands. Of course, she would have a flat tire since she was already running late for the real estate agent.

Houses here didn't last long, and she knew she might not get another chance for a place here for quite some time. Four months ago there had been a condo on the lake that went up for sale, but there was a bidding war, and she lost out to another buyer.

The house she was seeing today wasn't on the market officially —yet. She'd been driving around the area and stopped in at a small diner for some coffee and overheard a waitress there talking about it. She didn't care what it looked like but hoped she could afford it. She desperately needed out of the city and hoped to find a place in Maisonville. She'd sold her late father's house and then her luxury car, the only thing she got in the divorce, and was ready.

Now she just needed to talk these people into selling to her.

She smoothed down her dress and plastered a smile on her face as she walked into the office to meet Will Fontenot.

It didn't take long for her to win Will over. He was a nice older man and a sucker for a pretty face with a sob story. She'd told him that her father had passed away before he was able to retire in Maisonville, but it had always been his dream.

She was going to hell for lying and for using her dead father as a reason to earn sympathy. Then again, she was desperate and if she could have asked her father, she was certain he would have given her permission to do it.

She wiped her eyes lightly with a tissue as Will drove her around the lake and toward Oak Cove. "I know the owner personally. His uncle and I were best friends, and I'm certain he would approve of you," Will said, making her smile.

The drive on the west side of the lake was mesmerizing. It was curvy like the other side, but the road was closer to the water. A canopy of beautiful trees with moss shaded the area while the rippling water sparkled nearby.

Will appeared just as excited to show Sydney the house as she was to see it.

"You should have seen the place before it was redone. It hadn't been lived in for over twenty years, and had the same décor that it did when it was built in the early fifties," Will explained, talking the entire way over to the house.

Sydney was getting nervous as she listened to him talk about how old the property was and how terrible it looked. She wasn't sure she would be able to afford the place already, but if she had to hire someone to do repairs, she would be in a lot more trouble.

They pulled onto the street, and she noticed a giant tree growing right in the middle of where the road should be, but instead, the road adjusted around it. Then at the end of the street, there was a circle, with two houses side by side. There was plenty of land on either side of the houses for more homes, but there were perfectly spaced trees everywhere. There was also a fountain on one side, and the grounds were enclosed by a white picket fence. It looked like a private park. She wrung her hands as she realized both of the houses looked very nice and really expensive.

"Are you sure that's it?" Sydney asked as they pulled into the driveway on the left.

Will looked disappointed. "You don't like it?"

"It's beautiful, Mr. Fontenot. I just don't think I can afford this place," she said.

"The porches and garage make it look bigger. Come on. You'll see. Besides, we can make a lower offer. You never know."

Will turned off his car, and she followed behind him as he went to the front door and opened it. She paused to look at the details of the porch. It was beautiful. Someone had taken their time and hadn't pinched pennies there. The spindles were painted white while the hand railing had been rubbed in a black stain to match the wide boards on the decking. It was stunning against the white house.

When she stepped inside, there was a small mud room with shelves to the left and a bench underneath. She slipped off her sandals and followed behind Will. Immediately, she noticed the open floor plan. She was standing in the kitchen but could see the dining room, then the living room, and large glass doors that looked out onto a beautiful deck, pier and the lake.

No way could she afford that house.

She exhaled and then bit her lip so she wouldn't cry. All the time she spent worrying about the house selling too fast before she got there or it being in complete disrepair was a waste. She should have known that it would be out of her league. Most people wanted to live there. It's why Drake insisted they spend their summer vacations at Maison-Lafitte Lake: it was expensive and exclusive.

"I'm sorry, Mr. Fontenot. I've wasted your time," she said, walking toward the front door.

He gently held out his hand to stop her. "Don't you want to see the upstairs or go out on the back porch? It has an amazing view of the lake." He smiled at her and gently led her to the staircase. "The owner is motivated and wants to sell this quickly."

Sydney nodded and walked upstairs to see the spare bedroom with bathroom, laundry room and then the master bedroom with an attached bath. There was a smaller version of the downstairs glass doors on one side of the master bedroom, and it led out to a wide second story balcony.

Without speaking, she looked at the closets and checked out the attic, knowing the house was too much for her.

When they walked back downstairs, she followed Will out onto the deck and then pier and looked over to see the large boathouse next door. The house was for families, and she didn't have one of those anymore. She wiped her eyes with tissue again, and this time the tears were for real. She turned her head so Will wouldn't see her and was startled when he spoke standing closely behind her.

"Come now, Miss Bell. Let me go inside and make a call."

She nodded and then watched as Will walked inside already on the phone with someone. He was gone for thirty minutes, and Sydney sat on the end of the pier with her feet hanging over the water. It was a beautiful place. If her boys could be here, they would already be in the lake, swimming and laughing. She wiped her face quickly and swallowed back the emotion. She shouldn't have tears left, but she did. She had to toughen up and make a go of things. She was on her own. It was time. She had a plan, and she would find a way to make it happen.

She heard Will clear his throat, and she jumped up to meet him at the glass door. He had a strange look on his face, and she couldn't tell if he was angry or sad. Something was wrong.

"You okay, Mr. Fontenot?" she asked, nervously.

He slapped a smile on his face and nodded at her. "He's a hard-headed bastard."

"The owner?" Sydney asked.

Will kept grinning, but she knew he was mad. "Yes. He's home but won't come meet you. He said to send him an offer."

"Is that bad?"

"He does usually meet the prospective buyers, but don't let that get to you. We'll go straight to my office and see how eager he is to sell."

Chapter Two

THE DELUGE OF RAIN WAITED until the moving truck was scheduled to arrive and then drowned any hope Sydney had of a smooth move in day.

She'd paid a little extra for them to arrive that morning; that way she'd be finished by the time Ryan returned home next door.

He was the jerk who had helped change her tire the first day she came to town and the owner who reluctantly sold her the house. She wasn't certain how Will talked him into it, but Will said he was a family friend and that must have mattered to Ryan. Of course, he could have simply been motivated by the cash offer. It took the money she had from the sale of her father's large home and the sale of her Mercedes wagon for her to afford the beautiful cottage. It was more than she should have spent but way less than the place was worth.

Ryan shook his head during the closing, avoiding looking at her the entire time. Will said he was perpetually grouchy, but she knew he was unhappy about selling to her specifically. She acted sweet and told him how much she loved the house and promised to be a quiet neighbor. However, during the hour-long meeting, Ryan didn't say more than a few words to her, but he managed to slip the word "genius" into the conversation at least five times.

She couldn't help it, sometimes words popped out of her mouth before she could stop them. She'd wished she hadn't been snarky and called Ryan a genius that day on the roadside, especially after he changed her tire, but she couldn't take it back.

It didn't matter. He didn't have to like her. She would prove she could be a good neighbor and ignore him back.

As the moving truck turned onto her twisted street, she realized the truck was much bigger than she remembered. Most of her belongings had been from her father's estate and picked up from a large storage building where there was plenty of room to maneuver. There was a lot less room on her new street that had large oak trees that had taken up residence a hundred years before the houses were built.

Ryan had made sure these incredible trees, along with the one that partially divided their driveways, weren't disturbed during the remodeling of their houses. Instead, they were showcased in the landscape with up lighting.

As the rain pummeled down, Sydney ran to motion the truck in front of her house, hoping she could keep them from driving on Ryan's perfect grass. More importantly, she had to protect the tree limbs that dipped down to the ground before twisting back up to the sky.

She was wearing shorts and a t-shirt but thankfully thought to throw on her green rain boots and matching raincoat before she ran out there, waving her arms. She shook her head as she considered how mad Ryan had acted toward her already, and she'd just gotten here. She had to protect that tree.

The truck barely made the turn around the tree in the middle of the street and then ran partially into Ryan's yard before making the sharp left into hers. Sydney suddenly realized they didn't see her and she was narrowly missed by the truck as she ran up the stairs onto her porch.

Screeching the brakes as they hit the wooden steps, Sydney braced herself as the entire porch groaned and shook. The driver then reversed a few feet before throwing the truck into park and sliding out of the driver's side door to look at her.

The rain slowed down but didn't stop. Sydney cut her eyes at the driver when she realized his truck not only blocked her driveway but was stretched precariously across the street and Ryan's drive, too. The driver had completely trapped her in and the rest of the world out.

"Who put those steps there?" The driver laughed and then lowered his eyes at her, daring her to say anything.

Sydney didn't care how he looked at her. She wasn't going to accept his behavior. "Look at my steps! Look at my porch! No one would take that turn at forty miles an hour in clear weather. What were you thinking?" she yelled.

The scruffy man's eyes turned to slits. "Look, lady, I have three deliveries today. Either you want your furniture, or you don't. Let's get on with it, or I'm going to take care of my other customers, and you can get your stuff tomorrow."

He thought he'd made a good point. After all, what could she do? He had her stuff, and she needed help to unload it. She was alone, and he could make things easier or harder for her. He gave her his most arrogant grin and watched her walk to the truck door and climb partially inside the cab before she jumped back out. She then walked past him, and he watched her curiously as she strutted up the steps to the porch and into her house, slamming the door.

The other man in the truck stuck his head out. "Chuck? Um, she took the keys."

"She what?" Chuck asked.

"Keys to the truck. She took 'em."

Chuck made a sound like an animal snarling. "Why the hell didn't ya stop her, Alan?"

"Why didn't you stop her?" Alan mumbled, as he sat back down to keep dry and slammed the door shut.

Sydney returned holding her cell phone. "Are you going to call

Mr. O'Malley or am I?" she asked, ignoring the growling sounds he made and his red face.

She clearly had no regard for her own safety. Chuck marched right up to her and glared into her eyes. "Now why the hell would I call my dad?"

Sydney was on her tiptoes trying to appear bigger as she argued with the driver.

"You know why, and --."

They were interrupted by a loud pickup truck horn blaring on the other side of the moving truck.

"No," Sydney muttered. It was Ryan. What was he doing home?

The driver turned to look as Ryan walked around the front of the truck and toward Sydney's porch. Ryan gave a short wave to Alan and then slowly walked over to the steps where Sydney and Chuck looked like they were about to brawl.

"Ms. Bell," he said, and nodded his head her way. "What have you done this time?"

"I haven't done anything, and this is none of your business," she said defensively.

The driver grinned. "We were having a little chat, and she took the keys out of my truck."

Ryan looked at the bowed porch and crooked steps and nodded his head. The driver added, "I may have bumped her steps when I made the turn, but it was raining like hell."

Ryan looked closely at the steps and then walked up on the porch. "No reason to cry over spilled milk. I can patch that up in no time." Ryan smiled at the driver. "Need some help with that furniture?"

"No. I, uh, wait, Ryan. I need to call his boss." Sydney stammered as Ryan stepped in to take over.

"No need to call Mr. O. Right, men?" Ryan asked the movers as they opened up the back of the truck and got ready to hand down furniture.

"But--." Sydney wanted to disagree, but the look Ryan gave her made her stop.

"You direct traffic, and we'll haul things inside," Ryan said and nodded his head until Sydney gave up and nodded back.

It didn't take long for them to unload her furniture and boxes. Then Ryan thanked them and walked them out of the house to their truck. Sydney's anger had calmed down through the rain, sweat, and tears of moving her belongings into the house. It was clear she no longer had a family and certainly no kids by looking at her things. She sat down on the couch, thinking about her boys.

Before she could get misty eyed over them, Ryan walked back in the front door without knocking.

Sydney stood up and looked at him. "Thank you," she said, but as she barely got the words out of her mouth, Ryan was in her space.

"What the hell were you thinking?" he scolded her.

She wanted to yell back at him, but she was exhausted and more than a little shocked at his behavior. She avoided his eyes as she whispered, "What?"

"I drive up and, of course, there is a moving truck blocking the entire street and my driveway. You're standing there in your little girl rain boots and coat, about to start World War III with two ex-cons! Are you looking for trouble?"

Before she could answer, he threw his hands up in the air.

"Or maybe you just don't understand the concept of peace and quiet. You certainly don't know how to keep the peace. Don't tell me you don't know that O'Malley's movers are ex-cons recently let out on parole, including Mr. O'Malley's oldest son, Chuck. Hell, some of the guys he hires just have day passes from jail to work and then return at night." Ryan eyed her. "Surely you knew that was the reason they were so much cheaper than everyone else. Besides, did you get a good look at that Alan guy? I'm pretty sure he was *on America's Most Wanted* a few years back."

Sydney held back the tears that threatened to spill down her cheeks. She'd spent most of her money buying the house and was simply grateful to have found an inexpensive moving company. There was no question about O'Malley's because they were her only option.

She refused to admit she didn't know about the workers being ex-cons. She was having a hard enough time keeping her wits and not looking foolish around Ryan. She couldn't remember the last time she'd slept more than a few hours. The lack of sleep coupled with the stress of moving, how much she missed her boys and now for the umpteenth time, the disapproving words of her only neighbor, she found herself without words. That didn't happen often.

Ryan stopped and stared at her, probably disappointed that she wouldn't fight with him. He seemed like a man who liked to argue. He then turned, grabbed his rain jacket and stalked out her back door.

She watched as he stormed across her back deck and jumped across to his side and then into his house. As soon as he was out of sight, she slumped back down to the couch where she let her tears take over. She sobbed over missing her children. No matter what Drake had said in court, they were her kids. She cried over the end of her marriage and the idea of being alone. She then cried over her new lake house and how she could ever afford to live here by herself. Then she finally cried because she was just so flipping tired.

Ryan slammed the door as he stomped into his house. What the hell was he thinking? He wanted to buy that great property around the bend, but he could have waited a few more weeks to get his list price and a different buyer. How did he allow Uncle Trey's best friend, Will, talk him into selling at such a deeply discounted price? He shouldn't have listened when Will told him she was alone and needed help as a single woman who was recently divorced. It was business and not personal.

Ryan had rules, and when he stuck to them things were fine.

In fact, the only time he ever had a problem was when he skirted around these rules. Now, instead of a nice quiet retired couple that might invite him over for a beer every now and again, he was stuck with her.

He slammed his hand down on the counter. He didn't have anything against Sydney for being a woman. His sister was his closest friend. He loved women. He enjoyed the way they smelled, their soft skin, sweet voices and especially how they felt in his bed, but he couldn't handle the complicated ones. His life was simple, peaceful and quiet. He fixed houses, not people.

Ryan walked to his fridge and grabbed a cold beer. It was ten in the morning. He paused, looking at the clock and then put the beer back into the refrigerator. He went into his garage and picked up the drill and charger that he'd forgotten that morning and then went back to work.

Driving back toward his current project house, he calmed down, and then his mind went back to her. Sydney Bell. So, she was going through a breakup. Everyone had been there. It was tough, but you do what you have to do and move on. It had been ten years since he'd dated anyone seriously. His girlfriend had sent him a Dear John letter while he was overseas, and he simply went on with his life.

He shook his head and smirked. He'd moved on as often as he could without getting labeled a womanizer. Now in Maisonville, he was considered a confirmed bachelor, and life was good. Women wanted to reform him, and some just wanted a notch on their own bedpost.

Sydney would get over the whole thing easier if she would simply find someone to come home with her. There were plenty of men who would take one look at her and step up to the challenge. In fact, Ryan had helped more than a few divorcees in town. He ran his hands through his hair and tightened his jaw. He had a weakness for redheads, but she was not his type.

First of all, she was his next door neighbor, and he believed in the rule, don't screw your neighbor. No, she was not going to happen. He was going to have to stop coming to her rescue. She either was helpless or had the worst luck of anyone he'd met, and he'd made the mistake of jumping in three times already. That was just stupid. He should have made a U-turn and avoided their street until that moving truck was gone, but O'Malley's movers were from the next town over and had a reputation. He'd had a fight with Mr. O'Malley's son, Chuck, some time ago and understood wherever Chuck went, there was trouble. Then he saw her standing on her tiptoes, arguing with that mouth-breather.

It was a wonder the bastard hadn't taken a swing at her or worse. Ryan couldn't let that happen even if she had let her mouth overrun her ass. He had to step in. He couldn't just let the freaking animal at her. Besides, the creep would have just come back later to make her pay for causing him trouble with his old man.

Not on his watch.

That was his neighborhood, and he wasn't going to let anything disturb the quiet nirvana he'd created at the lake. Ryan reached up and squeezed the bridge of his nose as he parked his truck. He would make sure Sydney Bell understood the rules again. He'd torn that house down to the bones and built it back up to the perfection it was today so that he could have an exquisite neighborhood. She wasn't going to ruin that, and he was going to set her straight.

He wasn't there to watch over her. Her tears had made him queasy, and he had to bolt before he offered to help her with anything else. She could learn a thing or two from him about healing herself with alcohol, women or a nice loyal dog. He laughed. *Maybe not women.*

Ryan spent the rest of his day working, but he didn't have the stamina that he'd started with earlier. He couldn't get his new neighbor off his mind. He was going to have to go out tonight so that he could avoid her. He needed female company to get that woman out of his head.

It was late when he returned home. He dropped his things

into the garage before he walked into the kitchen and grabbed a beer. He barely made it before the sunset and hurried to sit outside on his large deck. It was his evening routine. Before dinner, he would sit outside and watch the sun go down over the lake with his feet propped up. It was his form of meditation, which his therapist had ordered, and it helped his stress slip away.

Tonight he couldn't get Sydney off his brain. He should go back and give her a piece of his mind, but he remembered the look she had given him when he left. Instead, he paced the deck a few times and then leaned back on the railing, where he realized he could see into her great room.

There she was on that tiny sofa of hers. Ryan saw her body shaking as she cried uncontrollably.

He set his beer down and turned to pace the deck again. He was an asshole. He was a straight shooter, and he knew that sometimes it came off rude.

Not sometimes.

He shouldn't have yelled at her. He should have just walked away after those movers left, but that bastard Chuck had said some crap about her before he got into the truck, and it got him worked up. She needed to be careful. A woman living alone had to be more aware of the vibe she gave off around men like that.

Ryan walked back over to look in on her. She appeared to be sleeping now, must have cried herself to sleep. He wiped his face and finally had a seat on one of his outdoor chairs, propping his feet up.

He had fallen for the lake the first time he came here to visit his uncle.

Uncle Trey was married for a few years, but eventually divorced and didn't remarry. He loved to fish, play cards and tell jokes. He was the perfect uncle. Ryan's sister would talk their mother into letting them spend most of the summer with Uncle Trey. It was during those summers that Reagan learned how to play poker and used the skill to pay her way through college and law school. She was ridiculously smart and sort of his hero.

She lived in the city, but getting together once a month for dinner was the most she could manage with her work schedule. He wanted her to share the house their uncle had left to them, but she refused and signed the deed over to Ryan. She then turned around and bought the first house he rehabbed before anyone else had a chance to buy it.

Reagan had told him that was what he was born to do. She supported his military service but was the only one who saw the damage it had done to his soul. They rarely spoke of it, but when he returned from his final tour of duty overseas, she hired a therapist and sent a car each week to make sure he went.

He did it for her. At least, in the beginning, that was true, but by the end of three months when he felt like a normal person again, he realized he had done it to heal himself. He'd been up close to some of the earth's most despicable criminals that put not only his life in danger but sacrificed their wives and children in order to protect themselves. His unit had prevented more than a dozen large-scale attacks on the U.S. and three allied countries. It took eliminating entire families to stop many of these events, and for a long time, he couldn't process any of it.

Reagan saved his life with that therapist, and he wasn't sure she understood that, even today.

He stood up. He couldn't think of any of that right now. It was dark, and he was starving. Tonight Miss Lynn's Diner served meatloaf, and he'd planned to eat out, but now he didn't want to be around anyone else. Instead, he went out and picked up a pizza to eat at home alone.

He was drinking another beer and eating two slices at a time from the box as he sat on his porch when he saw the light turn on next door.

He slid his chair into a dark corner, pretending he hadn't been watching for her. Then he settled back to continue eating.

Sydney was up.

Chapter Three

IT WAS DARK WHEN SYDNEY finally peeled herself off the couch. She had puffy eyes and swollen red lips and was sure she looked as badly as she felt. She avoided the bathroom mirror when she went in to wash her face.

After finger combing her tangled hair back, she looked at herself. She may be alone, but she didn't have to act like a wilting flower. She had married at nineteen and instantly became the stepmother of four young boys, although none of them ever referred to her as a "step". She had seldom been around children, and yet she jumped into that situation with her head held high and a ton of love in her heart. She hadn't been afraid. She'd known she could figure out how to take care of them and give them what they needed.

It was time she found her backbone and started acting like her father's daughter. She was strong and smart. She could do it. She could handle anything.

Sydney thought about the divorce and how the judge had denied her even visitation of the boys. She couldn't handle that. They were like the air she breathed, and she thought she would die without them. But she hadn't died. Only felt near death. Now she had to get her life in order because she would get to be with her boys again. And she didn't need Drake, some ignorant judge, or even the jerk next door's approval.

She shrugged out of her t-shirt and shorts and turned on the shower. A hot shower would make her feel better. She stood under the steaming water and thought about Ryan. What was wrong with him? She was a nice person and other than Drake, who turned out to be a cheating scum-bag, she usually got along with everyone. Well, except for the movers today. What was wrong with her? She was usually great at diplomacy. She could turn most people's frowns upside down. She thought about her boys again and closed her eyes. Was their dad's new girlfriend good to them?

Sydney turned the water off. She couldn't do that again. She had to pull herself together. It had been seventeen months and four days since Drake had kicked her out. The divorce was final six months ago. She'd attempted to reason with him to let her see the boys. When he wouldn't be rational, she fought him in court. She had fought, and she had lost, spectacularly.

She wrapped herself in a towel and walked into the bedroom. She looked at the mattress leaning against the wall next to the bed frame. There were boxes of clothes and one with bathroom items. Those things were what her life amounted to after twenty-eight years. She looked at the strewn items again and decided she wasn't going to deal with any of it tonight. She could sleep on the couch and wake up fresh tomorrow. She tightened the towel around her body and headed for the kitchen.

One thing about the lake was when the sun went down, it was a lot darker than the city. She searched for the light switch in the kitchen and finally found one over the sink. It wouldn't take her long to get something to eat because she hadn't done any grocery shopping. It was difficult to do for just one person, and since the divorce, she'd mostly existed on junk food she could pick up at convenience stores. She looked at the counter: a bag of chips and a box of donuts. Donuts sounded good, and she pulled one out and bit into it, leaning against the counter as the buttery dough melted on her tongue. Her stomach was grateful, and she took two more quick bites, moaning over the sweetness. Something caught her eye outside, and she went to look out the glass doors.

She could see a few lights shimmering off the water in the distance. It was beautiful, and for a moment she was mesmerized watching the twinkling lights that belonged to a far off boat and a house around the bend of the lake. She finished her donut and then glanced over at Ryan's house. It was completely dark.

Sydney licked the sugar off her fingers and took a deep, comforting breath. The view from her back door and deck were exactly what she needed. It calmed her in a way that nothing else had in months.

Whether it was the quiet ripple of the water, the darkness lit up by the slight moon and stars, or the peaceful sway of the trees in the night air, she wasn't sure, but the lake helped her soul. She nodded, reassuring herself that it was where she belonged and then turned to walk back over to the couch to lie down.

She pulled her quilt over her towel clad body and snuggled up to her neck in the material. She lay there for three hours, thinking of her sweet boys, then the messy divorce until sleep finally rescued her.

S*unrises* on the lake felt like a new beginning, and Sydney smiled, looking out at the varied colors of the early morning sky. As she stretched and sat up, she realized somewhere during the night she had lost the towel that she'd had wrapped around her body. She saw it crumpled on the floor and sidestepped it as she got up and walked completely naked upstairs to her bedroom.

She wasn't modest, but she hadn't lived alone and quickly glanced out the large glass doors, past the balcony, to make sure there wasn't anyone watching. The world outside was still, and she turned to look at herself in the mirror propped up against the wall that hadn't been attached to her dresser yet and took a hard look at her body. She'd lost fifteen pounds since the divorce and was softer since she hadn't kept up with her workout routine or even ran in weeks. She ran cross country in high school, and it helped her in more ways than her shape. She'd given it up for yoga and Pilate's classes because Drake told her running wasn't very attractive. She shook her head and looked at her small breasts. He didn't like those either, but they were perky, and she refused to change them. She turned to the side, running her hand across her flat stomach that hadn't been affected by her newfound donut addiction. Then she turned to look at her backside, which was smaller but still round. She shook her hips and grimaced when she saw her bottom jiggle. She would have to start running as soon as her things were unpacked.

Her father had been a large man, but Sydney mostly took after her mother, Abigail. She took a deep breath and was thankful she hadn't completely taken after Abigail.

Sydney rummaged through the wrinkled clothes in her suitcase, throwing dresses on the floor. Her wardrobe consisted mostly of beautiful dresses and heels but also casual ones that could be paired with slip on shoes as she towed the boys to sports practices, music lessons, and play-dates. Those clothes didn't feel like her anymore, and she dug until she found some of her workout attire.

Donning loose yoga pants and a tight top, Sydney went into the bathroom to brush her teeth and hair. She twisted her hair up into a loose knot on top of her head and watched a few shorter pieces fall around her face as she wrapped a wide elastic band around the bun. Her red hair shimmered with gold and brown highlights. She had inherited the thick red hair from her mother and her brown eyes from her father. She was the perfect combination of her parents, and when she looked in the mirror, she often thought of them.

She smiled, thinking of her sweet father as she washed her face and added some lotion and mascara to finish off her routine. That was as much effort as she'd given herself lately, and it would have to do. She had a house to unpack, and right now she could use some caffeine motivation.

She went into the kitchen and dug out her coffee pot and searched through a box to find some ground coffee. She had some dry creamer in the box, but she couldn't find any sugar. She frowned at the idea of drinking coffee without sweetener and then smiled, remembering the donuts. She could simply take a bite of donut and then a drink to balance her need for sweet coffee.

She stepped out onto her deck with a cup in one hand and a donut in the other. She would have to buy some furniture for that deck one day. One day when she had a job. For now, her built-in seat would have to do. She headed across the deck and down to the pier and sat on her bottom to look out over the water.

When she finished her donut and most of her coffee, she took some deep breaths and thought about her yoga and Pilates classes. She'd taken those classes with several of the other mothers she'd befriended at her kids' private school. Friends who would only talk to her when she was part of the mom club. As soon as she and Drake broke up, the other moms didn't return her phone calls.

She stood, placing her cup on the wooden rail and then stretched up to the sky. With a few more deep breaths, she could feel her body loosen ever so slightly, but it motivated her to drop to the wood decking into two more positions that would help energy flow freely through her body. She didn't need those fake friends anymore. The discipline and stamina she'd learned from those classes would stay with her forever, and soon she would return to running and be stronger than before.

As she slid back into her final pose, Sydney caught Ryan sitting on his deck, watching her. He didn't pretend he was looking at something else, just kept sitting there as she had her arms wrapped around her ankles with her bum in the air. Surely he didn't have a problem with her quietly doing yoga on her own pier or deck in the mornings. She refused to deal with his negative attitude today. She was going to take her fresh start that morning and make some positive changes. She grabbed her cup and headed up the pier toward her house.

Before she went inside, she turned to him and did a quick bow, but she didn't utter a word. She avoided his eyes but could see him out of her peripheral vision as she turned to go inside the house. As soon as she closed the door, she giggled at the puzzled look on Ryan's face. He totally didn't understand her, and she couldn't explain why, but that made her really happy.

Chapter Four

SYDNEY WATCHED RYAN leave for work most days at eight and return home at seven. He never spoke to her or payed attention to her in any way except for the mornings she did yoga and the one time she didn't park in her garage. Her car didn't start easily, and she had to turn the key ten to fifteen times before it would choke back to life. That particular day, Ryan came outside just as the engine turned over and shook his head before going back in.

How could he be so rude?

The entire town of Maisonville was full of sweet, considerate people, and she had to buy the house next door to the only person who wasn't.

He was ridiculously good looking and appeared to date a different woman every other night. He would come in and sit on his deck or at the end of his pier and drink a beer or iced tea and then go out to dinner, returning with some random female. Then the woman would strip out of her clothes right there on his back deck or they would stumble inside to the living room before going at each other.

Sydney tried not to watch, but it was mind boggling how he charmed so many different women. She didn't see anything charming about him. The few interactions between them had left her wanting to strangle him. No, she didn't understand him, and what was up with all that promiscuity? She'd only slept with one boy in high school, which was a major fail. Then there was Drake. They were married for seven and a half years, but he never acted really hot for her. He was too busy or too tired, and honestly, she just enjoyed curling up next to a warm body after a long day with the kids.

Casanova next door seemed to be hot for everyone. Everyone but her. It wasn't like she was looking for a date anyway, but what was wrong with her? She pulled the band out of her hair and let it tumble down her back and shoulders. Maybe he didn't like redheads. She wiped her eyes. He probably didn't like sad redheads.

She had to find something to do so she wouldn't think about the boys starting school without her. The twins' birthday was in two days, and it would be another one she didn't get to celebrate with them. She struggled to think of the wonderful birthdays they'd had together, but she couldn't stop the heartache when it enveloped her.

※

RYAN WATCHED as Sydney rearranged the furniture in her living room for the third time. He'd spent the better part of three weeks eating his dinner on his back porch in the dark, watching her. Now and again he had company, but as of late he declined so he could watch her. She was the most confusing woman he'd ever seen. She moved things around until she had them just so, and then started over again, with her arrangements.

He would watch her until she ate her dinner around eleven, which was a donut or some equally unhealthy snack food, and then she cried herself to sleep on the couch. Didn't she have a bed? He remembered how those movers threw things into her bedroom without even setting the bed rails up. She most likely couldn't move those heavy items on her own. It had taken two men to move them into the house.

He would help her if she would just ask. He shook his head because he knew better; he'd pretty much told her not to bother him. She'd taken to drinking her coffee and crap breakfast on the end of the pier most mornings at sunrise, and then she'd stretch and contort her body into some impressive moves as he watched. She never spoke to him, but she would nod his way before she went into her house and started crazily rearranging things again.

Ryan would go to work, and for the rest of his day, he would think about her and how it bothered him watching her painfully get over her break-up. She rarely went out and hadn't visited the bar in town like the other singles. He didn't understand why she worked so hard on her house and constantly cleaned up when she didn't have any guests coming over, and she didn't go out to meet any new people. She stayed there in her little fortress and rearranged furniture, usually crying as she worked.

Ryan kept himself busy with work and was finishing the house a half mile around the bend of the lake from his own so that he could focus on his favorite and newest project, the White House, next. He walked out on the deck to look at Sydney's house. Was she in there, still rearranging that living room furniture, or was she finally organizing the bedroom alone? He shook his head worrying about her dresser or headboard falling on her as she attempted to move it by herself.

Damn, that woman was irritating!

He finished cutting a cabinet box and then headed inside to install the last piece of custom kitchen cabinetry.

It didn't fit into place.

Ryan pulled the cabinet back and looked at the wall as if it had changed. He then looked at the cabinet, thinking about the measurements he had taken and applied. He was meticulous and didn't make careless mistakes. At least when he was focused, he didn't make mistakes. He had to admit that his focus and routine were gone ever since Sydney Bell had moved in next door.

He carried the cabinet back outside where he'd set up his workstation today on the deck. He looked across the lake to where Sydney was most likely worrying herself to death over hanging a picture or arranging her small appliances. She was distracting the hell out of him. Why wouldn't she speak to him in the mornings when she finished her yoga and went back inside the house? She saw him and nodded, but still wouldn't say hello or good morning. That beat up car she drove barely ran, and when her alternator started failing he went outside to help her, but it started, and she rolled her eyes at him before pulling it into her garage. He would see her jogging as he headed out to pick up dinner or watch her walking into her house after her run, but still she never said a word.

After helping her multiple times, would he actually have to be the one to talk first? Didn't she feel responsible for extending courtesy to him now? In general, women usually walked up and talked to him. Even most of the men would eventually sit and have a beer with him. Hell, she was his neighbor. Wouldn't speaking to him be the neighborly thing?

Ryan measured the cabinet and realized he was three inches off in his calculations and then was even more frustrated at Sydney. He dropped his measuring tape and ran his hands over his face. This had to stop. He had to confront Sydney Bell and ask what her problem was and why she was ignoring him.

He took a deep breath and stretched. His mind immediately went to Sydney and her yoga in the mornings. He'd gone out with a lot of women, but he couldn't think of one that did yoga. They didn't do yoga, but most of those women still talked to him. Most of the town talked to him.

He shook his head and went outside to look over his supplies. Thank goodness Reagan was coming across the lake to have dinner with him tonight. She would take his mind off Sydney.

Ryan looked forward to dinners with Reagan. He was also looking forward to finishing up the house. He smiled when he saw just enough wood left over to redo the last cabinet. He usually measured so precisely that he didn't have much scrap wood, but clearly, he'd been off his work game for a few weeks and had made a mistake with the order, too.

Happy to finish up by five, Ryan drove home, showered and was ready to head out to meet Reagan for dinner when he saw Sydney sitting outside.

So, she isn't running tonight?

She hadn't run that morning either. That was unusual, and he wondered what was wrong. He went to his back door and watched her for several minutes. She was sitting there with her legs hanging off the end of the pier over the water and holding a picture. She wiped her eyes, and his stomach ached to see her out there alone.

He looked down at his watch. He didn't want to be late, but Reagan was usually ten minutes later than she said, and it wouldn't be a big deal. He walked out onto his deck and closed his door loudly, so Sydney would definitely hear him.

She didn't look his way.

Ryan moved some of his furniture around, making noises that she could hear, but still she didn't pay him any attention. Was she going to make him walk down the pier?

He grabbed a fishing pole and his tackle box and walked down to the end. His pier was a little bigger than hers, and he had built a large boat house to one side. He stood on the side closest to her and baited his hook and threw it out into the water. She didn't even look up. He saw her wiping her eyes again.

He finally pulled the lure out of the water and threw it closer to her, splashing the water slightly onto her legs. She looked over but avoided looking at him.

"Sorry. Did I splash you?" Ryan asked, knowing he did.

She shook her head and cried a little harder.

Ryan reeled the fishing line in as he sat down with his feet hanging over the side. "Are you okay? Wanna talk about it?" he asked, staring at her.

She wiped her eyes again, but when she looked up at him, the tears were still rolling down her face. "Are you talking to me?"

"Yes. Of course. Who else is out here?"

She shook her head. "Sorry. I didn't mean to disturb your fishing." She jumped up and headed to the back door.

He was terrible in situations like this and rarely knew what to say. "That's not what I meant!" he yelled.

Sydney paused with her hand on the doorknob as she heard him walking up to his porch. Just as he caught up to her, she turned to look at him and nodded before she went inside and locked her door.

Ryan felt like he'd been punched in the gut when he saw the anguish on her face. She wasn't doing well and looked like she'd lost weight since she moved in. Probably the garbage she was eating. She needed fuel for her body if she were going to run. That was stupid of her.

He heard his cell phone ringing and knew it was his sister, wondering what was keeping him.

At the diner, Reagan was sitting at a table and had already ordered drinks for both of them when he arrived. She made an exaggerated look at her wrist, where she didn't have on a watch, just to aggravate him. He was seldom late.

He told her about his new irritating neighbor during most of dinner, listened to Reagan tell him about work, and then he repeated the story about Sydney distracting him and making him late for dinner tonight.

Reagan ordered dessert to go and two coffees as Ryan explained his deep frustration with having a stranger as his new neighbor. He then gave his sister hell for not buying the house he had for sale next door instead of the one a mile down the lake.

She smiled and told him they were going back to his place to have dessert and coffee, and he didn't question her as she got in her car to follow him home. He hadn't considered why they didn't eat dessert at the restaurant until Reagan walked into his house and then straight out the back door to his deck. Reagan didn't like being outdoors.

They sat and ate bread pudding with bourbon sauce in silence for several minutes, then Ryan leaned back in his chair drinking coffee and watching Reagan as she smiled his way. "You want to tell me what the hell you're grinning so big about?"

Reagan kept smiling and looked back toward Sydney's living room. "It's just been a while since I've seen you so passionate about anything, little brother."

"What's that supposed to mean?"

Reagan laughed. He truly didn't see himself clearly. "I haven't seen you in five weeks, and for the entire meal that lasted forty minutes, you talked for thirty about the woman who moved in next door."

Ryan sat there, thinking about what she said and then shook his head. "I did not."

Reagan leaned back in her chair. "If you're so bothered by her not speaking, then why don't you speak to her?"

"You don't understand anything, Reagan. I did speak to her. Today." he said. His jaw clenched, and his sister knew he was getting frustrated. He didn't discuss feelings with anyone. She'd hoped the therapist could help him with some of that, and maybe Dr. White did, but she couldn't see it in him right now.

Reagan reached her hand across the table to touch her brother, and he looked at her. "I'm not talking about today. I mean the mornings when you're out here ogling her while she does her yoga. Just say good morning. Or instead of sitting here in the dark like some perv, knock on her door and invite her to eat a decent meal with you."

Ryan rolled his eyes but nodded his head. Reagan wasn't sure he would take her advice, but she could tell he was thinking about it. At least that was a start. She sat quietly watching Sydney's house with him for a while, hoping she would get a glimpse of the mysterious woman who was wearing her brother out.

She knew he worked his way around the single women circuit,

but he never talked about any of them. It would make her very happy to see him settle down with a nice lady. She worried about him being alone so much of the time.

By ten o'clock, Sydney hadn't made an appearance and Reagan needed sleep. She was a woman who needed her eight hours each night or she couldn't function. She headed to her house down the road, promising to stop by in the morning for coffee before she headed back to the city.

Ryan walked his sister out and then headed back to his porch. This was the first night he hadn't seen Sydney stirring around in her place. She was terribly upset earlier, and he needed to know she was okay.

He could knock on her door like his sister said, but he wasn't sure she would answer if she knew it was him. She was clearly mad at him, which he couldn't figure out. Then he remembered her front porch. He had forgotten about it. Could she be mad because he still hadn't repaired it? He had wood flooring being delivered at his project house first thing in the morning, but he could work on her porch the next day.

He was mentally planning his schedule when he saw her walk into her living room in a towel again. Anyone passing by on the water could see into her living room clearly when she had the kitchen light on after dark. He watched her open her refrigerator and then close it. She opened her pantry and pulled out a bag of popcorn but then set it on the counter. Then she looked into her box of donuts. It was empty. She left her popcorn there and crawled under her blanket on the couch and went to sleep. So she wasn't going to eat? Ryan stood up, angry because she wasn't taking care of herself. It was exactly the way he had behaved after he attempted to rejoin civilian life. He didn't want to think about how badly things could go from here. He scrubbed his face and then ran his hands through the top of his hair. He stared at the leftover bread pudding and thought about the catfish dinner he'd had tonight. He could have easily brought her back some food. He should have brought her a to-go box and knocked on her door and insisted she take it. They didn't have to talk, but she could have eaten a regular meal for once.

He sat back down and stabbed the bread pudding with the fork a couple of times. He couldn't fix things tonight, but he wouldn't let it go another day. She needed help, and he knew better than anyone that most the time you couldn't ask for it for yourself. He would handle things differently tomorrow.

Chapter Five

IT WAS SEVEN WHEN REAGAN showed up at her brother's door. She wasn't surprised Ryan was up and had coffee ready, but he also had bacon and pancakes.

"Impressive," she said as she walked in on him flipping a flapjack in the air and then catching it with the pan. "You know I don't eat pancakes for breakfast, right?"

"Are you sure you don't want at least one? They're homemade buttermilk pancakes. I have plain ones and blueberry. I also have real maple syrup," he said.

"Nah. I'll take a piece of bacon and a shot of coffee."

She watched him finish cooking two more pancakes. "Do you have an army coming over this morning? That's a lot of food."

"I thought you might be hungry. I doubt you'll stop to eat lunch today."

Reagan wasn't sure he was doing it just for her. She wasn't a breakfast person even when they were kids, but if he needed her as an excuse, then she wouldn't call him on it.

"You know, Ryan, you might should ask your new neighbor if she would like some food. It would be a shame if it went to waste. I mean, it smells good, and most single ladies don't make breakfast like this for themselves."

"Maybe I will," he said, avoiding her face, and she knew right then that was his intention all along.

She gave him a hug and told him she was stealing his coffee mug before she left. As she closed the front door, she saw Sydney coming up the drive. She'd been jogging and was avoiding looking at Reagan. But Reagan was dying to meet her.

"Hey. I'm Ryan's sister, Reagan," she said, and then stepped off the front porch toward Sydney.

"Oh. Hi. I would've never guessed Ryan had a sister," Sydney said, smiling. She was wearing purple Nike shorts and a black tank top that made her red hair shine. Her face was a little flushed from running, but she still looked pretty, and Reagan could see why her brother was so attracted to his new neighbor.

"I don't get to see him too often. I live in the city and, of course, he's always busy with his rebuilding the community one house at a time thing."

Sydney nodded, but Reagan wasn't going to let the opportunity go. "He does incredible work, doesn't he?"

"I don't really know. I mean, we don't really know each other, your brother and I." Sydney frowned. She looked like she wanted to say more, but held back.

"That's funny," Reagan said. "He had a lot to say about you. In fact, I've never seen him more distracted by another human being in his entire life."

"What?"

Reagan looked down at her wrist. "Oh, look at the time. I'm late," she said and grinned over how befuddled Sydney was by her comment about Ryan. "It was nice to meet you, Sydney. Perhaps the next time I'm in town, we can all three go out to dinner together?"

Sydney nodded but was still processing what Reagan had said. She motioned back to Reagan, who was waving out the window of her car as she drove off.

A few minutes later Sydney had a glass of ice water in her hand and was heading out to her pier to cool down from her run.

She'd ran out of coffee, and the donuts were long gone. She was starved and would have to go out to the grocery for a few staple items that morning.

The minute she walked outside the smell of coffee hit her. She looked over and saw some plates of food on the table on Ryan's porch. He must have made breakfast for his sister, which was funny to her since he hadn't had any of the women he slept with stay over for breakfast.

She put her hand on her stomach as the smell of breakfast food surrounded her, but she managed to walk down to the end of her pier and have a seat. What she would do for breakfast right now would be sinful. She smiled at her thoughts because she would have to steal the food before her neighbor would sit down at a table with her. She giggled at the idea, but her humor wasn't going to make it any easier to sit out here with the delicious smell of food in the air.

Suddenly, she realized Ryan was standing at the end of his deck staring at her. Did he know what she was thinking?

"Good morning," he said as he continued looking at her.

Was he talking to her? She was confused and honestly still baffled by what his sister had said about him being distracted by her.

"Did you hear me?" Ryan asked and again waited for her to respond.

"Yes. Good morning," Sydney said, nervous over the fact they were talking. That usually didn't end well.

"My sister couldn't stay for breakfast. Could I interest you in some homemade pancakes and bacon? Possibly some coffee?"

"Really?" Sydney asked. "Why?"

"What do you mean, why?"

"I was pretty sure you didn't like me."

"I never said that." Ryan looked hurt over the accusation, which only confused her more. She was starving though, and she didn't have any food at her place. No one had cooked her breakfast since her father died.

She looked Ryan in the eyes and nodded. "Okay. Thanks. I ran out of coffee yesterday."

Their back piers were close enough for them to talk, but not close enough for her to step over to him. He motioned for her to walk back up her pier to her deck where her side bowed out toward his. He then reached over with his long arm and held out his hand. It was odd to hold his hand, but she didn't hesitate and let him help her to the other side.

He'd already set the table, and the pancakes looked perfect. "It smells great," Sydney said, staring at the table. He pointed her to a chair and reached over to pour her a cup of coffee from a carafe and then handed her some sugar packets and creamer.

It was a little surreal, but she accepted his hospitality and bit into her pancake like a starving woman. She moaned when she took her first bite and then was embarrassed when he looked at her until he laughed.

"These are really good. You made them?" she asked, taking another bite.

He nodded his head as he watched her quickly eat one pancake and two pieces of bacon. She then sat back in her chair, sipping her coffee.

"Better than donuts?" he asked.

"Nothing is better than donuts."

He laughed, and she smiled at how warm his face looked when he was happy. He really was handsome. Dark hair and gray-blue eyes. He was tall and very fit. He looked like he worked out every day, but as a home builder, she figured it was a perk of his job. It was pretty obvious that he didn't have to try very hard with most women.

"I met your sister, Reagan. She's nice." Sydney said, making small talk. "At first I thought she was another one of your girlfriends."

There went her foot, right into her mouth.

He looked directly into her eyes but didn't comment about her watching him bringing home women. Instead, he looked at the giant plate of pancakes and then slowly ate a blueberry one without syrup as she watched him.

It was unnerving, and she wasn't very good at leaving words floating in the air. "Reagan said she works in the city?"

Ryan nodded his head, and for a minute she didn't think he was going to talk to her anymore. "Yes. My sister's an attorney with Williams, Morrison, and Weisnick."

"I didn't peg her for an attorney."

"She's pretty amazing. She brings in more money than any two of the partners combined. She'll be a partner by the end of the year."

Ryan stopped eating to look at Sydney. She set her coffee cup down and was sitting on her hands, but she looked like she was going to jump out of her seat any minute.

When he finished his last bite and put his napkin on the plate, she reached over and stacked her dishes with his and started cleaning the table. Ryan reached his hand out to touch hers, and she stopped to look at him.

"I've got it," he said.

"I don't mind helping," she answered, standing there like she needed something to do. Ryan reached over and picked up the plates.

"Why don't you carry the syrup and coffee for me?" he said, heading for the back door.

Sydney quickly grabbed what was left on the table and followed Ryan into his house. Once she was inside, she admired his incredible space. He'd decorated minimally with furniture, but the intricate moldings and built-in cabinets were awe inspiring.

They set the dirty dishes into the sink, and he put away the syrup. He watched Sydney as she looked around. She was eyeing the moldings and woodwork, similar to her new home. She ran her hands along the back of a chair that he'd designed and grinned as she approved of the feel of the wood.

She was heading toward the door, and he quickly caught up

to walk her out. "You made those chairs and the table set, yourself?"

He nodded. "It's sort of my thing."

"You're good. Your sister said you were well known for your work and that you're rebuilding the entire community or something like that," Sydney said, deciding whether or not she could make the jump to her deck on her own but hesitated.

Ryan guided her to a spot where the decks were closest to one another and then he jumped and reached back to give her a hand so she could make it across easily. He followed her up to her back door, and when she turned around, he was watching her.

"My sister exaggerates," he said, looking her in the eye. He had a way of staring that made her feel exposed.

"She said you were distracted by me more than anyone else ever before. Is that true?" Sydney asked, not looking away until he answered.

His face instantly flushed, and it made her smile. It was true even if he couldn't admit it.

"I was thinking you needed help putting your bedroom furniture together, Sydney. I know you sleep on the couch at night, and that those movers didn't put the headboard on the rails for you."

"Have you been watching me, Ryan?"

"It's not like I could help it. Occasionally, I sit out here at night. In the dark, your kitchen light illuminates the whole downstairs."

Before he let himself feel too embarrassed, he remembered what she had said about him bringing women home with him. "How about you? You watch me with my visitors?"

"You do more than just visit," she blurted out and then turned her face away.

Ryan laughed and watched as Sydney bit her bottom lip, probably to keep herself from talking. She couldn't seem to keep things from spilling out of her mouth.

He leaned down toward her and whispered, "Looks to me, we're even."

Sydney squinted her eyes at him. "Depends on how often you were watching me."

"You weren't having sex with anyone, so I'm pretty sure I lose this round."

Sydney nodded and then looked up at him. "You sure you won't get mad about helping me move the bedroom furniture? I mean, I've already put the mattresses on the floor." She didn't admit that she'd knocked them over and then was forced to slide them out of the way or step on them when she walked into the room.

When he didn't say anything quickly, she added, "I'm actually comfortable on the couch."

"I won't get mad," Ryan said. "I promise."

Sydney watched his face, because that sounded like his version of an apology. Why some people couldn't simply say they were sorry didn't make sense to her, but actions were better than hearing the words.

"I'm here most of the time. So whenever you feel like coming over," she said. "I mean, you know, to do the furniture. No rush, just whenever you feel like it." She was shuffling back and forth, and it was obvious she wasn't used to accepting help.

"I have to get to work this morning. There are a couple of deliveries I have to be there for, or I would do it now. How about tonight? I'll be home early, around four or five."

"Okay." Sydney fidgeted as she awkwardly stood there, not knowing what else she should say or do.

"I'll see you tonight then." Ryan turned to walk away, and Sydney quickly spoke.

"Breakfast was great. I was starved. And thanks." She sounded ridiculous even to her own ears, but she couldn't stop talking.

"You're welcome. You needed to eat something other than donuts," he said and then turned and grinned before he jumped back over to his side of the deck.

Sydney watched as he walked up to his house and then he waved to her before he went inside and closed the door.

He obviously saw too much.

Chapter Six

RYAN SPENT HIS DAY running through tasks. He was laser focused for the first time in weeks, and he hadn't noticed it until the end of the day when he ran out of things to do. The wood for the flooring had to cure for a few weeks and the painted cabinets needed to dry for twenty-four hours before he sanded them down and added sealant. He double checked the tile work in the bathroom, and it was set, but the shower doors and fixtures wouldn't be in for a few more days.

He cleaned up his tools and placed things in the garage. It was four-thirty, and he was going to have some time to catch up on paperwork tomorrow. That wasn't his favorite part of the job, but his accountant would go berserk soon if he didn't send over his numbers. Actually, his sister would freak out because it was her accountant and he would call her and ask her to call Ryan. It was a vicious cycle, and he couldn't avoid it. Death and taxes and Reagan.

He pulled onto his street and caught Sydney walking up to her drive. She'd been running again, and he watched as she slowed down before she got to her driveway. She ran in the morning or the evening, but he hadn't seen her do both in one day. It was strange. He stared at her blue shorts and tiny white top before she removed her earphones and then turned to see him pulling into the driveway.

She gave him a short wave and then twisted around, stretching her limbs while he climbed out of his truck.

"Hi," she said.

"You ready to get that furniture moved around or do you need a few minutes to cool down?"

"You just got in from work? We can do it another day."

He looked at her, assessing whether she needed a few minutes or if she was just avoiding him helping her. He had no idea, but it had been bothering him for weeks, and he had to get it done. He wanted to get back to his normal life and regular schedule without thinking about his neighbor's problems.

"It'll take about ten minutes for me to put that frame together and get the mattress into place," he said, and then held up his drill. "Besides, I brought power tools."

Sydney nodded and then led him into the house.

Ryan was surprised how great the inside looked with her things in it. He could see her moving around at night, but he couldn't make out the details inside the house. He'd spent some extra time building the place with more emphasis on the moldings and finer points and was worried furniture would detract from it. She had pictures hung and lights placed where it showcased the minutiae in a classic way. She clearly had a knack for decorating.

They headed upstairs to her room, and he noticed the dresser drawers were out on the floor but filled with clothes. "You tried to move that on your own?"

Sydney nodded. "I thought I could move it with the drawers out." She shrugged like it wasn't a big deal. He couldn't explain why it irritated him so much, but it did. He was next door and could have done the heavy lifting for her if she'd simply asked.

Ryan set his tools down and asked her where she wanted things placed. She watched him effortlessly move the dresser, and by the time she had the drawers put back in, he had the wooden rails drilled onto the bed-frame.

She helped him pick up the mattress and box springs, then he quickly had the dresser mirror in his hands, asking her for directions on how high to hang it.

It took fifteen minutes, and she stared at him as he gathered his tools and headed for the door. He clearly was driven to get finished, and she realized that he must have wanted to get out of there as fast as possible.

She slipped off her tennis shoes and followed behind him when he abruptly stopped and turned around to survey the room. Sydney just about ran into him and was suddenly standing too close.

Ryan didn't appear bothered by it and smiled, looking down at her. "It looks good in here."

"Thanks. And thanks to your help; it does look a lot better," Sydney responded awkwardly.

"No. I was talking about the whole place. You did a good job with--" He waved his hand around in the air to motion everything.

Sydney smiled at the compliment. He was trying to be nice, and it was difficult for him. She'd spent so much time around phony people who were smooth and charming over the last few years. They were fake. There was nothing fake about Ryan Gentry.

She looked at him a little too long before she spoke. "Thanks. I enjoy it. Decorating and all. My mom died when I was young, and my dad raised me. He let me paint and do whatever I wanted to the whole house. I experimented a lot."

Ryan nodded his head, but he appeared to be thinking about what she'd told him. She knew it made people uncomfortable when they heard she grew up without a mother. She was careful not to give too many details, but it didn't make the conversation any easier. However, she hadn't expected Ryan to be so sensitive. She quietly walked him to the front door. He reached for the handle and then turned to look at her like he was going to say a lot more, but he simply said, "Good night."

"Night," she said and watched him walk slowly to his house.

Sydney's shoulders slumped as she turned to go back inside. She couldn't understand men. They had only two emotions, happy or mad. It was infuriating trying to figure them out.

Her father was the closest she'd ever gotten to understanding a man, and he didn't count because he loved her unconditionally. In the small town she grew up in, he was the sheriff, and tons of people loved him. He was big and burly with dark hair and eyes but had the warmest laugh of anyone she'd ever known. Jeffrey Bell was known equally for being tough and for having a big heart.

He was perfect.

She often thought about what he would have done to Drake when he cheated on her and then kicked her out of his house and life. Drake wouldn't have dared tell Jeffrey Bell that those boys weren't his grandsons anymore.

Sydney wiped her eyes. The loneliness consumed her.

Her father had died instantly of a heart attack three years ago. He'd spent the weekend with her and the boys, teaching the older three how to fish. They'd had a wonderful time catching dinner and cooking it over an open fire with their granddad. The following Monday at his office, he was pouring a cup of coffee when, without any warning, he dropped to the floor and was gone.

She was devastated but was comforted by her boys. They kept her going during the hardest time of her life. She couldn't give in to the sadness. They needed her whole; she was a mom.

Sydney looked around at her bedroom and how nice it was to have things in order. Still, it just felt cold. She went and stood under the scalding hot shower, wishing she could wash the past eighteen months away. She missed her boys desperately. The loneliness was her only excuse for her bad conduct. She wasn't prone to erratic behavior but a mother would do anything for her children. How could seeing them be against the law? She felt ashamed, but there were times the emptiness overshadowed her humiliation.

If Drake had let her have joint custody of the boys, she could have gotten through the separation and divorce just fine. He was such a selfish bastard. He wanted her gone, but not just gone; erased from everything. He didn't give her a moment to talk or discuss anything before he removed her and her things.

She'd never felt more alone, and she wouldn't let herself become that vulnerable again. She hadn't suspected a thing, but once he kicked her out, she saw the signs clearly, especially after he had her arrested.

No, she didn't understand the opposite sex, and she didn't want to try again.

Drake wasn't affectionate, but he had sworn he cared about her, even when he would sleep in the spare bedroom. After all, he was finishing up medical school when they married, and he needed to concentrate. He was ten years older than her and put her off about getting pregnant. He refused to discuss it and would shut her down with the fact that he had to work on building his medical practice first. When she was upset with his lack of attention, he would swear he appreciated her and the things she did for him and the boys. All the way until the day he didn't appreciate her at all.

That last week was on repeat in her head, and Sydney wished she could turn it off. It was March, and she and the kids had gone to the beach for spring break without Drake. He'd said he couldn't join them because he had to work and even explained he was sleeping at the hospital most nights.

When they returned home on Sunday afternoon, Drake acted differently. He skipped dinner making the excuse that he'd eaten a big lunch and wasn't hungry. He didn't sit with them at the dining table. Instead, he left the room to talk on his phone. At one point, he walked outside and paced the back patio as he focused on whatever the person on the other end of the line was saying. Later that evening, he took a break and went upstairs to tell each of the boys goodnight as they headed to bed. Then he walked past Sydney without a word, went into the den and closed the door.

It wasn't until early the next morning that Sydney realized he had slept on the couch instead of in their bed. She cooked breakfast and made the boys lunches as she planned the talk she would have with Drake after she took the boys to school. They didn't disagree often; he barely discussed anything with her. This time she wasn't going to be deterred. She would make him hear her. She was going to tell him that she and the kids needed him to spend more quality time with them. He was in the shower when she left to take the boys to school. She told him she would be back soon, and after dropping off the kids, she practiced her speech out loud in the car. She went over her words a couple of times and tried to keep herself calm over what would be an uncomfortable discussion when she returned home.

The conversation never happened. Thirty-five minutes after she had left the house with the boys, she pulled back into her driveway to see a large moving pod parked in her way. There were movers inside packing her things. Drake forced her to leave without saying goodbye to the boys. She'd been blindsided by him and his girlfriend and couldn't pull herself together enough to think clearly or defend herself. She had no one and nothing except a check he gave her so she could open a personal bank account and find a place to live. She spent that night in a dive motel because he'd canceled her credit cards. After seven and a half years together, she had certainly never figured him out.

Sydney wiped her eyes when she realized she was crying again. Would her tears ever stop? She wiped her eyes and swallowed the emotion as she sat on the edge of her bed, which was still unmade. But at least it was put together properly. She managed a faint smile because she did understand her young men.

The oldest, Darryl, started the tenth grade that year and would turn sixteen soon. He was strong, mentally and physically, but he was incredibly sweet, too. He helped keep his younger brothers in line and helped get them to bed. Afterward, he would sit up and talk with Sydney for an hour. They discussed his school and his friends, or he would talk about his future or girls he liked. Who sat up and talked with him now? He had to have more questions than ever, and Drake seldom had time for conversation.

What about her twins, Erik and Eli? They were so excited about playing football when they got to the eighth grade. Who was going to teach the game to them? Drake didn't know anything about sports.

Her baby, Little John, was now in the fifth grade but had played club soccer since he was five. Did Drake get him signed up in time? Tryouts were competitive at their local club, and she would set a reminder on her calendar so that they didn't miss tryouts or sign-ups. The information wasn't advertised clearly, and she assumed they did that on purpose to keep certain people out.

Sydney lived to take care of those boys, and they were her world. Did they miss her, too? After what happened, were they ashamed to tell anyone she was ever their mother?

Sydney gasped, needing more air in her lungs. Lately, the loneliness suffocated her.

She lay back, concentrating on breathing normally again, until she saw an outside light being turned off and then heard a chair scraping across wooden deck boards. No doubt, Ryan had taken a seat outside, and the sun was setting fast over the lake.

Curiosity forced Sydney to peek out her window at Ryan, and she saw him sitting with his feet propped up. He was eating a humongous sandwich and had a happy grin on his face.

Now that was a man she would never understand. At first glance, Ryan was beautiful and talented, an artist caught up in his building skills, and confident. But up close, he was modest, perceptive, and humble.

He was a complete contradiction.

Sydney was confused that morning after she met his sister. Ryan was close to Reagan and clearly cared about her. It didn't match the selfish, indignant, know it all first impression he'd given Sydney. Then there was the whole pancake breakfast that morning, and then the furniture assembly that evening.

He may be the most complicated man she'd ever met.

She spied on him a minute more as he watched the sunset and ate his messy sandwich. It made her smile, and her heart hurt a little. She couldn't remember when something so simple made her that happy.

The fall sky turned dark quickly, and Sydney hurried to turn out her bedroom light. She wouldn't forget Ryan explaining how easy he could see into her place at night. Did he see her walking around without any clothes? She closed her eyes. She'd seen him, and it was ridiculous that it hadn't occurred to her it worked both ways.

She was still watching when a leggy brunette walked out to surprise Ryan on his back deck. She was carrying several bottles of beer and swaying her hips as she circled the table before she had a seat next to him.

Sydney shook her head as she dropped her towel and dressed there in the dark. Perhaps Ryan wasn't that complicated after all.

Chapter Seven

THE NEXT MORNING, Sydney woke to a loud hammering noise. She'd fallen asleep on her couch again, eating a bag of pretzels. The salt still coated her mouth, and she stumbled into the kitchen, feeling like she had a hangover, when she heard banging noises coming from outside.

Her head was throbbing to the beat of that hammer. She squinted her eyes as the noise filled the room around her and she went to look out her back window. Ryan wasn't back there. She stepped out and looked over at his house but still nothing.

Finally, she went and yanked open her front door. There was Ryan on his hands and knees, nailing down floorboards to her porch. He'd already redone the steps, the railings, and the columns.

What time did he get up?

"Hey," he said and gave her a quick nod.

"Hey, yourself. What are you doing?"

He paused and stared at her for a second and without answering, started hammering again.

"What are you doing?" she yelled that time. She didn't like feeling ignored.

Ryan put his hammer down and stood up, wiping his brow. "I said I'd fix it, so, I'm fixing it."

Sydney nodded. "I didn't expect you to do it. It wasn't your fault. I hired the goon squad, and I was going to get it repaired." She didn't want to admit to him that she didn't have the money to repair it now. She didn't have money for anything extra.

He finished nailing in the last board and surveyed his work before he stood to his full height in front of her. It made her a little nervous being that close to him, but she didn't back up as he leaned down to speak to her face to face.

"I'm a man of my word, Ms. Bell," he said and then winked at her before he walked across the porch to pick up his sander and stain.

She wanted to say something, but the only thing that popped into her head was, *I'm surprised you have enough energy for any of this today, after entertaining company last night.* Thankfully, she kept her mouth shut for once.

"You may want to shut the front door," Ryan said. "This is going to make a lot of dust before I'm finished."

She watched him turn on the sander and get to work before it registered what he'd said. She quickly turned around and went back inside her house. Her head was hurting, and she didn't have the energy for him at that moment.

She needed to get dressed and make herself go out. She'd seen a help wanted sign at the diner downtown, and she needed to find a job. She was broke. She'd waitressed for the first few years of her marriage to help make ends meet, and now that she didn't have children at home, she could work late hours, too.

Sydney pulled out one of her dresses from what she now referred to as her previous life drawer and applied just the right amount of makeup, so she looked young and cheery. The complete opposite of how she felt.

When she headed out the front door, Ryan was gone. She felt a little guilty because she hadn't thanked him for doing the porch;

she'd only said that she didn't expect it from him. She didn't feel like apologizing and hurried to leave before he came back.

It didn't take but fifteen minutes for Sydney to meet the owner and get hired at Main Street Grocery, which was not on Main Street and wasn't a grocery. She and the owner, Miss Lynn, hit it off, and both decided she could start first thing tomorrow for the lunch shift.

Lucky for Sydney, Miss Lynn's cousin, Wesley, owned the only bar in town, and she called over to get her an interview with him.

By the end of the day, Sydney had secured two part-time jobs. They weren't fancy positions, but her life wasn't lavish before she met Drake. Honestly, it wasn't cushy afterward either. He may have been a medical student, but he had four kids to take care of and not much money to do it. She worked in a bakery and deli back then. It was how she helped put food on the table, but he refused to talk about their meager beginnings when they moved to their flashy new neighborhood and fancy lifestyle.

She was certain if Drake could see her now that he would be appalled. He was about keeping up appearances, and it made her happy to know that he would disapprove.

A small weight had been lifted, and Sydney felt more comfortable going to the grocery store since she didn't have to stretch her last fifty dollars much longer. She bought a few staple items and then headed toward home. She wanted to pick out her clothes for tomorrow and get a quick run in before it got too late. It may not have been a full list of things to do, especially compared to her old life, but it was as much as she could manage these days.

When she pulled up to her house, Sydney was surprised to see the caution tape wrapped around her porch. It scared her at first, thinking back to the way her father's office had been quartered off with the same type of tape the day he died. She took a deep breath, and when she stepped out of her car, she smelled the fresh paint.

She should have been gracious. The porch looked perfect, but she was irritated that she would have to walk around to the back with her bags, passing between her house and Ryan's. She bit her bottom lip to keep herself from grumbling. She didn't ask him to repair the house, but it was generous that he did it. Why couldn't she be thankful? The old Sydney would have gushed over selfless behavior. Usually because she rarely came across it. Still, she was irritated at the new perfect Ryan, his perfect repair work, and his perfect girlfriends.

She got her things into the house without running into him and then slipped out to run three miles. When she returned, there was still no sign of him or his truck.

She went out on her back deck to enjoy her donuts for dinner. She figured if she waited long enough that she would see Ryan, but he didn't return. It was nine when she gave up and went inside. She was changed and sitting on her couch when she heard a woman laughing. Sydney rolled her eyes and peeked out her side window.

There he was with a willowy tall blond with a bob cut. They were inside, but his lamp was on, and Sydney could see her flipping her head back and forth for attention.

"He's a sure thing, babe. No reason to put so much effort into it," Sydney said out loud to herself and then flopped back on her couch. She wasn't jealous. She just couldn't explain why she was mad; it didn't mean anything.

The next morning, Sydney went outside to do her yoga but again, Ryan never showed up. Had she gotten used to running into him? She felt ridiculous. She left him a note telling him thank you for her porch repairs.

As she headed out the front door, she could see that he'd removed the tape and the porch looked shiny and new. She looked down at her pressed dress and cute espadrilles and decided she kind of looked that way, too.

Ryan spent the next two weeks zooming through the house he was rebuilding and most of the single women in town. Rarely seeing the same woman two nights in a row, he was back to his routine. The routine before the redhead moved in next door and disrupted his schedule.

He watched her from inside his house now and made sure not to go outside when she was there. So it wasn't like his old routine exactly, but he decided it would do. He worked more hours, spent less time out on his deck and dated even more women than before Sydney came to town. So what if he made some minor changes. It was good to keep himself distracted from her and her problems.

He couldn't believe Wesley and Miss Lynn had both hired her. He could cook, but he liked Main Street Grocery. The locals called it Miss Lynn's, and he usually ate there a couple of times a week. Would he have to start cooking for himself more to avoid running into Sydney? He could get his dinner to go, but damn, Wesley had the only real bar in town. He needed to socialize once in a while, and he wanted an occasional glass of bourbon, and he didn't keep more than a little beer at his house.

He ended up avoiding both places, but after two weeks he decided he couldn't take it any longer. Maybe he wouldn't get Sydney's table at Miss Lynn's or perhaps it wasn't her night to work at The Pub. As he left his house, he noticed Sydney's car was gone and knew he would see her at one or both places.

Ryan stood outside Miss Lynn's restaurant and watched as Sydney buzzed around the room. She looked happier than he'd ever seen her, and the customers smiled at her when she stopped to pour water or check on them. He noticed a seat at the counter was open and that Olivia, who he saw last week, was waiting on those customers. He hurried in and slid into the open seat at the end.

"Hey, Sugar," Olivia said. "Want something in particular?"

Ryan knew what she was referring to and laughed at her forward behavior. He liked Olivia.

"Here for the meatloaf," he said, smiling her way.

"Alrighty. Mashed potatoes, too?"

"Yes, turnip greens and sweet tea," Ryan answered. He looked around to see if Sydney had noticed him here, but she was busy with another table.

"That's Sydney. She's new in town. Started two weeks ago, and boy, is she popular," Olivia whispered out of the corner of her mouth, "That table of highway workers has come in three days in a row, and they're working eight miles from here."

Miss Lynn walked over. "Aren't you a sight for sore eyes," she said and gave Ryan a big motherly hug. "Where have you been, Ryan Gentry?"

"You know I bought the old McHenry House. It's needed a lot of attention," Ryan said, not wanting to admit that he'd been hiding from his new neighbor.

"Well, you're going to love our beef stew that we added to the menu. I think you know your neighbor, Sydney. She is such a sweetheart and shared her recipe with me."

So she doesn't eat regular food, but she can cook it? Ryan half grinned but was irritated that Sydney was already a permanent fixture here.

"Thanks, Miss Lynn, but I've already ordered the meatloaf."

"I figured that was what you came for, so I'm going to give you a small cup of the stew to taste." She patted him on the shoulder affectionately. "I just know you're going to love it."

Olivia waited for Miss Lynn to move on. "So she's your neighbor, huh?"

Ryan looked at Olivia but didn't answer her. She wasn't the jealous type; she knew he dated others, and she did the same. He nodded, avoiding her eyes.

Olivia leaned in to whisper again. "So, is she seeing anyone? I mean, she must be seeing someone serious because she turns down all the single guys in town."

"I wouldn't know," he said, trying to make himself look disinterested.

Olivia wasn't buying it. "You? You wouldn't know?" She laughed. "Be real, Ryan. If there is a single lady within twenty miles, you know about it."

She giggled and then moved down the counter to help Reverend Carmichael, giving Ryan a moment to compose a good answer that sounded reasonable. When Olivia returned to refill his tea, Ryan gave her his most charming smile.

"She's going through a break-up. From what I can tell, a serious one, but I've been distracted. She could have started dating, but I haven't noticed. She's not exactly my type," Ryan said, sure that he sounded sincere.

"Uh-huh. If you're not interested in the gorgeous redhead, then you're the only single male in town who isn't." Olivia pointed to Chuck O'Malley and a couple of other men who came in and sat at one of Sydney's tables. He could see the way Chuck and the dark haired man with him were leaning over to check out Sydney as she delivered plates to another table. It made him furious, but he stayed in his seat.

Sydney walked over to talk to Chuck's table, being mindful to stay arm's length away from Chuck so he couldn't grab her. She swatted him with the menus once they ordered and then pointed a finger at Chuck, saying something that made the group laugh. So, she could take care of herself with those goons?

Ryan turned back around in his chair and drank the tea that Olivia had refilled for him. He thought about how helpless Sydney had been those first few weeks and how he'd helped her. He grumbled over her being so needy, but if he were honest, it made him feel necessary.

He shouldn't have avoided her the past couple of weeks, but she looked like she was handling things better now.

Olivia delivered his dinner and Ryan ate quickly so he could head down to The Pub, watch a game, and drink some liquor.

Ryan had his shot of bourbon and was now on his second beer when Sydney came in to work the late shift at the bar. He nodded her way when she saw him sitting there talking to Wesley, and she smiled back at him as she went to wait on a couple at the other end of the room.

He noticed some of the highway workers from Miss Lynn's

restaurant had also followed him down to the bar, but they didn't drink much until Sydney showed up.

    They kept calling her over to talk with them, and he saw her frowning after one abruptly put his arm around her and pulled her into him. Ryan jumped to his feet, but before he could do anything, Wesley put his arm out to stop him. Wesley shook his head at Ryan and then walked over to the man who had touched her. Wesley was in his mid-fifties, but he was six foot three and easily 280 pounds. He didn't let anyone upset the order in his bar. Without warning, Wesley reached over and picked up the chair with the man sitting in it, dumping him out on the floor.

    In a loud booming voice, he screamed, "Apologize to the young lady!"

    The man apologized and then ran out the door that Wesley had opened for him. "Stay out!" he yelled after him, and then the rest of the people in the bar went back to their drinks and conversations.

    Wesley sat back down. "Ain't nobody going to mess with little Sydney while I'm here. I won't put up with that nonsense."

    Ryan's face lit up and then he raised his beer to salute Wesley before he took a long drink.

    In fact, Sydney Bell did need looking after once in a while.

Chapter Eight

SYDNEY WALKED OUT onto her back deck in the early morning light with a muffin and a glass of milk. She still didn't do much grocery shopping, and although she had two jobs, she was mindful of spending too much money. She'd found the day old muffins on the sale rack and thought about how good they would be for a late night snack and breakfast.

She was surprised to see Ryan sitting outside. She hadn't seen him out there for a couple of weeks and figured he didn't want to have to talk with her anymore.

He nodded at her as she walked outside and down to the end of her pier. Then she heard his chair move across the wooden planks. She sat down and looked over as he sat down across from her on his side.

"Health food for breakfast, I see," he said, teasing her.

"If you're implying your two-pound bacon sandwich is healthy, then we are going to have to agree to disagree," she said and then took a bite of her blueberry muffin.

"I'll let it slide since you, at least, are drinking a glass of milk with it."

She watched as he attempted to tear his messy sandwich in

half and then held one side up for her. "I have plenty. Want some?"

Sydney didn't speak that time. She just shook her head and then looked out over the lake. Next thing she knew, Ryan jumped over to her side and sat down next to her. His knee bumped hers, and he leaned in as if he was going to tell her a secret.

"If we're going to be pals, Sydney Bell, you're going to have to meet me halfway."

Sydney looked into his sparkling gray-blue eyes, and she swallowed hard before she could speak. "We're going to be pals?"

"Sure. I mean, we're neighbors, and it would be nice if we could be friends, don't you think?" He took another bite of his sandwich and then looked out over the lake. He avoided looking at her and seemed a little nervous, like it would hurt him if she refused his offer.

She split her blueberry muffin and held up half of it. "I'll trade you," she said.

She was glad she was looking straight at him, or she would have missed the grin that flashed across his face for a split second. He covered up the smile quickly by shoving another large bite of sandwich into his mouth. He held out the half he had torn off for her and then accepted half of the blueberry muffin.

"Thank you," she said. "This smells delicious."

Ryan set his food down and watched her take a bite. "It's smoked Applewood bacon with fresh tomatoes and lettuce with extra mayo. It's my breakfast specialty."

Sydney wiped tomato from her mouth. "It's fantastic," she said, and he watched her finish the entire thing quickly. Then she drank the rest of her milk.

"It's my secret recipe. I add Sriracha and a couple of secret spices to the mayo. It's pretty special, and I wouldn't share it with just anyone."

Sydney smiled. "For your information, that blueberry muffin was made in a factory somewhere, likely three months ago, but has been preserved by the added sugar. I don't even think those are real blueberries, but still, it's pretty special to me."

Ryan cut his eyes at her and Sydney giggled.

"You think you're pretty funny, don't ya, Ms. Bell?"

"Sometimes," Sydney answered, staring into his eyes. She missed that confidence.

"How about you, with the whole 'it's special, and I don't share with just anyone' line?" she said, making her voice deeper so she would sound more like him when she mocked him.

"What? That was the truth."

"Sure it was, and I bet all the ladies love it when you talk to them like that."

Ryan stared at her. He wasn't sure if they were still kidding around, but he wasn't ashamed of his lifestyle. It was clear to him now though, that someone did a number on Sydney Bell, and she needed time to get over it.

Some time and possibly a friend?

It was the one thing he understood, needing time to heal. He was fortunate to have been born with a best friend, his sister.

Sydney didn't appear to have anyone.

"If you want to ask about my love life, Sydney, I'm an open book," he said and winked at her as he took a bite of the blueberry muffin she'd shared with him.

She watched as he chewed it for a second, made a face, and then spit it out into the lake. He then took a long drink of tea and stared at her.

"That is the absolute worst blueberry muffin I've ever had." He threw the rest of his into the lake and then reached over and took the rest of hers out of her hands, and threw it into the water, too. "You can't eat that; I swear it's poison."

Sydney stared at him with her mouth open, but before she could speak, he reached over and with a gentle hand, lifted her chin to make her close it. "Don't deny it. You can't eat that thing after enjoying an amazing homemade BLT."

He stood up and motioned her to follow him. "Come on, I've

got some pumpkin bread in my fridge that I can warm up, and I'll share it with you."

Sydney stood and followed him, but when they went into his house, she put her hands on her hips and was staring at him again. "First of all, I don't care about your love life. Second, those muffins are delicious, and if you didn't like them then you didn't have to eat them, but you could have left mine alone."

While she was scolding him, Ryan popped a slice of the bread into the microwave and poured her a cup of freshly brewed coffee. He didn't bother to respond to her comments. Instead, he held the cup of coffee out for her. He then broke off a piece of the pumpkin bread and fed it to her.

She was still glaring at him when she opened her mouth and ate the warm, sweet bread. She then closed her eyes as the buttery cinnamon taste coated her tongue.

"Didn't I tell you?" Ryan asked, grinning. He was a big fan of the noises she made when she ate something delicious. "That is the only proper ending for that amazing sandwich."

Sydney reached over and took the bread out of his hands so she could take another bite. "It is really good, and now I'm thinking you lure unsuspecting starving women over with food."

Ryan laughed so hard that his eyes watered. "You're a little obsessed with me, aren't you?"

"In your dreams, Ryan Gentry," Sydney said, and then she laughed, too.

They finished off the bread, and he offered her more coffee. They took their drinks out onto the deck and sat at his large handmade table together. They didn't talk for a while, but instead, drank and watched the sky. It was streaked with orange and gold as the sun rose up behind them.

"I want to set the record straight, Sydney," he said, making her focus on him. "You don't have to worry about me. I'm not trying to trick you or seduce you. I have all the dates that I could want, and I've never had to trick anyone into going out with me."

Sydney nodded.

"You're my first neighbor, and I'm just being friendly." Ryan had a serious look in his eyes.

"I'm sorry if I insulted you," she said, looking away to the lake again. "I haven't had a real friend in a while. You know, without ulterior motives."

"Ulterior motives?"

Sydney drank more of her coffee. "I don't want to talk about it."

Ryan nodded his head and kept his eyes on her.

"I mean, there isn't much to say," she added and then drank more coffee. "I grew up in a working-class family, and my ex-husband was a doctor who wiggled his way into a fancy neighborhood and fancy schools for his kids. My kids. I guess you could say I didn't fit in. At least not like I thought I did."

"You have kids?"

Sydney nodded, and he could see tears clouding her eyes, but she didn't look over at him. "They were technically my step children, but I was their only mother for seven and a half years. They were babies when Drake and I got married."

He looked at her. She had to have been a baby when she married him. What an asshole. "Drake?" he asked.

"My ex's name is Drake, Dr. Drake Winters."

Ryan rolled his eyes. "Sounds like a fake soap opera doctor."

"You watch soaps?" Sydney asked, and she couldn't stop her smirk.

"I was trying to be polite. It actually sounds like a porn star name."

Sydney nearly spit out her coffee as she laughed that time. It took her several minutes to compose herself as Ryan stared at her, straight-faced.

"Don't be polite on my account," she added, then smiled at him.

"He got custody of the friends and the kids?"

Sydney took a deep breath. She'd told him not to be polite but was second guessing that much honesty. She nodded but avoided talking as she drank the last of her coffee. Without a word, Ryan got up and went into the house to get her more.

"Thanks."

"No problem."

Sydney had drunk half the cup before she spoke again. She had to give it to Ryan, he was a patient man. "Drake refused to let me have joint custody of the boys, even though during our marriage he'd said that I could adopt them. The fake friends stayed with him, too."

"He kicked you out? What did you do?"

"I didn't do anything." Sydney slammed the cup down on the table, but before she could stand up, Ryan reached over and put his warm hand over hers.

"Sorry. I thought mothers usually got the house and the kids."

"The house and kids were his before we got married. It didn't matter that I had raised them from babies. Besides, his attorney was better than mine." Sydney pulled her hand away from his and picked up her coffee again. "He was sleeping with her. The attorney. She was motivated in a way that mine wasn't."

"You're going to be okay, Sydney Bell," Ryan said, staring at her until she felt it and then looked back at him.

"I'm not so sure," she said. "Some days, I miss them so much I can hardly breathe."

"But you do and then another day goes by, and you keep breathing."

"You know this from experience?" Sydney wiped her eyes. Was he the same neighbor who had yelled at her for being too loud just a few weeks ago? The same man who brought a different woman home every other evening and didn't invite them to spend the night? He had appeared so one dimensional. Could that arrogance actually be confidence? He was complicated and confusing. Her first conclusion was correct; she would never understand him.

He didn't answer her right away, but he watched her face. Her father had told her that her expressions gave her thoughts away to the careful observer. Did Ryan know what she was thinking?

"Different situation but a similar experience," he said and finished off his coffee. "Now I breathe easy and live at the lake."

Sydney smiled back at him. He did seem at peace in a way that she couldn't remember ever feeling. She stood and picked up his empty cup with hers. She was a little unsteady from the emotion, and Ryan watched her carefully.

When she struggled with her chair, he stepped around the table so he could help her.

"Thanks," she whispered to him and then handed the cups over.

He didn't say anything else, but he walked her to her back door and held it open for her as she walked in and then closed it behind her.

Sydney leaned against the door, thinking about the heavy conversation. She didn't mean to tell Ryan about Drake or her problems.

How did he get her to do that so easily? He could have spiked the coffee, or he might be the neighbor whisperer. She shook her head at the bad joke and then wondered if they could truly be friends?

Chapter Nine

RYAN COULDN'T GET Sydney out of his mind that morning. He knew she'd been through something terrible. He had a sixth sense about people in trouble ever since he found the help that he needed. He wondered if he had this new ability so he might pay it forward and help others. Then again, it could be a curse so that he wouldn't forget how badly he'd fallen. No matter why he knew these things, he was driven to help people. He certainly was going to help her. She was sweet, and her emotions ran deep. He could look into her brown eyes and see her soul. It was unnerving and exciting at the same time. He was thirty years old and hadn't thought about children, but he couldn't imagine what it would be like to have them and then lose them. Especially knowing they were so close and not being able to be with them. It was cruel.

What must the kids be going through?

He hurried to his early morning appointment, trying to get his mind off her. He'd attempted to refuse the buyers who wanted to take a look at his new project house but ended up giving in to their request to simply see it. He understood their fascination with it because he'd loved it his whole life. It was the largest house on this side of the lake and had an unmistakable charm. It was built in 1871 and had survived many a disaster, except neglect. He was going to save it, and it would be his most impressive work to date. The couple that he was meeting there were insistent about purchasing it, but he'd already explained to their realtor that it wasn't on the market yet. Still, he gave in and agreed to show it.

Ryan waited for twenty minutes and then went inside the house. It was a bit of a mess, even for a construction site. He'd had his crew shoring up the entire house; it had been sinking on one side. Now level, a few walls had been demoed, and he would have to limit their tour if they ever showed up. His crew would be here in a few hours so they could get to work on his new blueprints.

"Hello, anyone here?" He heard a woman's nasally voice near the front door.

"Coming," he answered, hurrying to stop them from coming too far inside.

He introduced himself to the realtor, Olga, and she turned and introduced him to Gina and Dr. Winters.

Ryan stared a little too long at Dr. Winters but covered it up with a strong handshake. What the hell was he doing here and with the other woman? "Welcome, Dr. Winters and..." He held his hand out for Gina. "And Mrs. Winters?"

Gina's eyes lit up, and she gave him a sly smile. "Not yet, but very soon." She held out her hand with a giant diamond on it, letting him and Olga both admire it.

Ryan gave her a half grin, but Olga gushed over it as expected.

"So what draws you to the property?" Ryan asked. "It's in a pretty bad state, and I can't even give you an estimate as to how long it will be until it's ready to go on the market."

Gina smiled that snobby smile that he was sure she thought looked sweet and then told him about their needs for a large house for their four boys and the children that they planned to have together. "Drake is a doctor and will need a nice place to entertain, and this is the only one with any size on this side of the lake. It's important with Drake's prominent station that we have the best house, and we want to be over here."

"Why?" Ryan asked, not caring how rude it sounded. There

was something so disingenuous about them that he couldn't put his finger on it.

Drake looked at him with a straight face. "I like your work, Mr. Gentry. It's impressive. There was an article written about you that said you were single-handedly revitalizing this township and I want in."

It sounded like he'd done his research, but Ryan wasn't buying it. "Oh, the *Parish Magazine*. What houses have you seen of mine?"

Again, with a serious air about him, Drake spoke. "A couple. There was a bungalow over here that had a large porch on the front and a giant back deck with detailed woodwork. I haven't seen anything like it in a house in the city. The back deck was this unusual oblong shape that led out to a pier. It was incredible."

For a man who didn't want anything to do with Sydney, he sure as hell could describe her house perfectly. And if he were able to move into that property, he would be less than a mile away from her, at least by boat. Ryan was sure it was about showing her up, and then again, possibly forcing her off the lake.

Ryan nodded his head, staring into Drake's eyes. There was a challenge in the doctor's stare, and Ryan grinned at the idea of beating the holy shit out of him right there, right then.

Their realtor, Olga, must have sensed the tension building as she gently interrupted. "I'm just so in love with the staircase and the molding details everywhere. Aren't they beautiful, Gina?"

Gina looked distracted, standing a few feet away, but she whipped around when she heard her name and began talking where Olga left off. "Yes. I do hope you can save some of those architectural features, Mr. Gentry. Of course, we would like it to look brand new. If you would knock out that wall from the great room into the dining room that would give us an open floor plan, which would be most useful." Gina ran away with her plans as if Ryan were working for her. She maniacally described the things they wanted in the house, and Ryan bit his tongue to keep from telling her there would be a blizzard in New Orleans before he ever sold property to them.

Instead, he let them dream of what it could be by teasing them with a vision. "This property will be exquisite. There are hidden architectural features that we will restore like the corbels covered in ivy right now that are in most of the large doorways and the hidden staircase in the study. The floors have beautiful inlays that we can salvage, except the formal dining room, which is marble."

He watched the smug looks on their faces as Gina winked at Drake and squeezed his hand. Ryan baited them with details of the kitchen remodel and then added how that property would be the most beautiful in town and unmatched by any other in size or detail.

"Name your price, Mr. Gentry," Gina said, stepping closer to him. It was hard to tell at first look, but she was in charge of the operation.

Ryan gave her his biggest smile as he walked them out the front door. He took his time to lock up before he finally turned around to answer them.

He cleared his throat, and he could feel their excitement growing. "The truth is there isn't a price you can put on the house."

Gina rolled her eyes and interrupted. "I'm an attorney and Drake is a physician; we can handle it. Tell us your price."

Ryan paused, looking at her. He couldn't explain exactly what it was, but there was something odd about Gina. It was more than just the way she overstepped normal boundaries, asserting herself where she shouldn't. He would have expected her, as an attorney, to read him or the situation better than others. She didn't.

Perhaps his irritation with her wasn't as obvious as he thought it was, but then when he looked past her at the realtor and Drake, he understood they both could see it.

Drake reached out and rubbed Gina's back to soothe her in anticipation for what he knew Ryan was about to say. "There isn't a price because the property isn't for sale."

The words were fire to Gina's internal anger. Her entire face was red with fury and Ryan watched as she unraveled. "You snake, you never planned to sell this house to us, did you?"

Ryan watched as he expected her hair to catch fire. Drake wrapped consoling arms around her and pulled her into his chest as if she were upset instead of raging.

"Mr. Gentry is a businessman, Gina. It's early into this project. Let him get to work, and we can revisit the idea in a couple of months."

Ryan was done with the charade.

"I'm afraid I won't change my mind," Ryan said, looking straight at Drake, who looked out of place consoling Gina.

Drake may be a doctor, but he wasn't a caregiver. He was awkward, petting Gina's hair and holding her. Ryan couldn't imagine him with Sydney, who was so full of life and passion. Even when she gave Ryan hell, he loved her intensity. Drake couldn't have known what to do with all of that.

Drake didn't say anything else but stood there staring angrily at Ryan.

Ryan stared back, wishing the doctor would give him a reason to punch him in his unremarkable face.

Olga rustled some leaves as she stepped forward to shake Ryan's hand. She looked ashamed of her client's behavior, and Ryan nodded his head in understanding. She managed a faint smile.

"Thank you for your time this morning, Mr. Gentry."

"Ryan," he said, correcting her.

"I appreciate you seeing us on such short notice, Ryan." She silently mouthed the words "I'm so sorry" before she turned to usher her clients to their eighty thousand dollar SUV and hurrying to her own more reasonably priced car.

Ryan shook his head as they sped off and went around back to meet his crew before he went to Miss Lynn's for lunch.

He was already hungry.

Sydney worked the lunch shift at Miss Lynn's and was

surprised when Ryan popped in for lunch and sat at one of her tables. He hadn't been in but one time since she started working here, and he had snuck in and sat at the counter.

Olivia had laughed telling Sydney he was cute sitting there and watching Sydney the whole time, pretending like he didn't know her very well. Olivia was honest like that, and although she was really pretty, she wasn't pretentious. She explained to Sydney that Ryan was a great guy and one day would fall hard for the right girl. She enjoyed going out with him once in a while, but Olivia was sure Ryan had a serious side he was waiting to share with someone else.

As Ryan stacked up sugar packets like little houses, she wasn't so sure that Olivia was right, but it made her curious just the same.

"What are you doing here?" Sydney asked.

"Call me crazy, but I thought you served lunch." Ryan laughed as he teased her.

"Crazy," she said, and she handed him a lunch menu. "Chicken and dumplings and pecan pie are the specials."

Before she could step away to another table, Ryan reached out to grab her hand. "I'm ready," he said, smiling at her. "I'll take the special."

She looked at his hand holding hers and then wiggled it free as he spoke again. "What's your hurry? Can't I talk to you for a second?"

Sydney cut her eyes at him. "I'm at work, Ryan Gentry. I have other customers."

He ran his hand across his slightly stubbled jaw. "I thought that you might like to go out on the lake with me this afternoon. What time do you get off?"

Sydney was curious but didn't think that was a good idea. Another customer waved to her, and she quickly excused herself so she didn't have to give him an answer right away.

When she returned with his iced tea and a hot plate of

dumplings, she stood there for an extra minute, thinking about what to say to him.

"I'm not interested in going out with you, Ryan."

"Hold up," he said, holding out an arm to keep her from walking away from him.

She looked at his arm blocking her and then back at his handsome face. "You forget that I live next door and have seen you *date* most the single women in Maisonville."

Ryan laughed at her comment. She didn't sugar coat things, and he found her honesty endearing. "I promise, I'm not trying to *date* you, Sydney."

He had that half grin that got to her, but she kept her eyes steady.

"I'm working the entire lunch shift today, and then I have to do some housekeeping and run some errands," she said, avoiding his direct stare.

"I need to show you something, and that isn't a good enough excuse. Don't you know, when you live on the lake that it's perfectly acceptable to post a gone fishing sign and push your chores off to another day?"

Sydney shook her head, but flashed him a smile before regaining her serious face. "Who would I post a 'gone fishing' sign for?"

"The universe, Ms. Bell. The universe."

"I'll think about it," she said and headed back to the kitchen. Ryan dated everyone. Why wouldn't he try to date her? What was wrong with her?

Ryan finished his lunch and paid his check at the register, leaving Sydney a note written in black felt marker: *I'll pick you up at your pier at 3:00.*

Sydney smiled at Miss Lynn, who was grinning at her, and was thankful she didn't ask any questions about Ryan.

The afternoon was busy, and Sydney didn't get home until 2:30. She peeked out her back door. No sign of Ryan outside. He could have changed his mind. She put on jeans and a flannel button down shirt. Drake hated that shirt and wasn't a big fan of her wearing jeans, either. She slipped on some short boots and smiled that Drake would hate the entire ensemble, and she wished he could see her now.

She made herself a cup of hot tea and walked outside just as Ryan was pulling up in a large boat and smiling at her. Damn that smile. What the hell was she doing? She was suddenly nervous and rethinking the outing with him.

"Hey," he said, waving her over.

He reached a hand out to help pull her on board; without hesitation, she reached back out for him. Instead of taking her hand, he put both of his hands on her waist and hoisted her over.

She blushed when he set her on her feet, but she still stared at him.

"I didn't want you to spill your drink."

"Thanks," Sydney said, looking into his eyes until he released her.

"Come have a seat," he said, and then directed her to a chair next to his.

He then steered the boat away from their houses and around the first curve of the lake. Sydney watched with interest, the view she'd only imagined until now. It was stunning.

Ryan watched her but didn't want to interrupt her thoughts by talking. After a few minutes, he handed her a thick blanket and she draped it across her legs as they pulled out into a more open area of the water.

Sydney drank her warm drink and sat back, watching the scenery. "It's beautiful."

Ryan nodded his head. "I know you go running down Lake Road, but I didn't think you'd ever seen it from the water side." He smiled at her. "It's something else, isn't it?"

Sydney nodded. "This is your boat?"

Ryan smiled proudly. "Yes," he said, and then he pointed up ahead to another pier that looked a little old and raggedy. "And this is what I've been working on lately. Want to see it?"

Sydney looked up at the dilapidated two-story clapboard house. It was nice, but it needed a lot of work on the outside.

"Sure," she answered him and watched as he expertly docked the boat and then jumped off to tie it to a post.

He reached out to help her onto the pier, and she saw that most of the wood planks on top were brand new.

She followed him up to the back deck, which also had wood replaced here and there, but wasn't painted, yet. Then he unlocked the double locks on the back door, and she followed him into the house. He had a saw and a few other tools in what would eventually be the living room, but the rest was spotless. There were built-in shelves underneath the kitchen bar and new kitchen cabinets that looked custom built. It had a similar layout to her house but had different moldings and details. The whole house looked brand new.

"You keep a lot of the original house design when you redo things?" she asked but didn't stop walking around, admiring his work.

"When I can, I do. It's important to the character of the property," Ryan said, but his voice trailed off as Sydney walked away toward the staircase and saw the beautiful spindles he had hand-turned.

Ryan followed her and watched as she ran her hands along the staircase and the moldings. He trailed her upstairs, silently, as she explored the bedrooms and then the bathroom that he had finished that day.

She turned around and saw the vulnerable look on his face. Was he waiting for her approval?

"It's incredible, Ryan. I haven't seen anything like it." She stared into his eyes and saw his vulnerability. He needed to hear what she thought, and she suddenly had to tell him.

"I mean, my house and your house are just as marvelous, but to see this place from the outside and know what you must have had to do to get it here... You have a gift."

Sydney didn't wait for him to respond but instead walked

down the hall to discover another room before she spun around to look at him. "This house is humongous!"

Ryan nodded his head. "Three thousand square feet."

"How long have you been working on this place?"

"I bought it five months ago, but I didn't get rolling on it for a couple of months. There were some structural issues that I had to take care of before I could demo things inside."

Sydney kept walking as Ryan talked. He explained how the house was practice for his next big project, but stopped talking as they stood together at the top of the staircase and stared out over the living room. She was awed by the hand sanded triple crown moldings and the built-in plantation shutters. When she turned around to look at Ryan, he was smiling bigger than she'd ever seen him.

"It would look nice if you did wainscoting in here." She held her hand up to show three-fourths of the wall. "Paint it white. You could then paint the top of the wall a deep blue so it would enhance the lake view."

He kept smiling and staring at her.

"What?" she asked.

He winked at her and then walked down the staircase, waiting for her to join him at the bottom. Sydney was winded by his staring, winking and smiling behavior and took a deep breath before she could move.

She didn't understand why she was nervous. Just because she couldn't remember Drake ever acting nice toward her didn't mean Ryan couldn't. She slowly descended the staircase, holding onto the rail to steady her nerve. Ryan wasn't Drake, and this wasn't a date. When she neared the bottom, he turned around so they were eye to eye.

"That could look good in here. What about the kitchen, though?" Ryan asked.

Sydney cut her eyes at him, attempting to look less affected by the handsome man, and then walked around the kitchen as ideas started firing off inside of her head.

"Obviously, you need a big island work space in here with some seating on the side. It would be great for a family space, but also for entertaining."

Ryan smiled at her and then added, "It would look nice with a thick stone top."

"Oh yes, and we could put wide shiplap planks on the bottom. Possibly replicate the corbels from the doorway under that extended counter top?"

Ryan stopped and looked at her.

Sydney realized she was getting carried away. "Not we. I mean you. You could do that."

Ryan shook his head. "I've seen your house, Sydney. I need your help with this project. You were right, it is humongous, and I've exhausted my creativity on the woodworking."

"You want my help?"

Ryan nodded his head. "Of course."

"Is that why you wanted to be friends with me?"

"Of course not." He looked irritated now. "It is one of the reasons I brought you here today, though. You have great taste, and I could pay you for your help. Preferably, after the house sells."

"You would pay me for my decorating ideas?" Sydney looked skeptical.

"Absolutely."

"I would do it for free. I mean, if you saw the chalk wall I did when I was a kid or the splatter paint bedroom, then you would rethink this plan."

Ryan laughed. "Splatter paint bedroom?"

"I was thirteen and having a hard time with the whole teenage girl thing. My dad thought he could cheer me up by letting me be creative. He said I could do anything I wanted, and so I had the bright idea to do splatter paint for our spare bedroom. It was awful."

"You mean, splatter paint isn't a good idea?"

Sydney bumped Ryan's arm. "I was a kid, and it seemed great at the time."

"When did it not seem great?"

"About half way through, I hated it. My dad came home, and I started crying. He changed his clothes and starting painting with me. He told me that I wasn't putting enough muscle into it. We were covered in paint, but I've never laughed so hard." Sydney jumped up to sit on the temporary plywood counter top. "He made me leave it that way for a few months and told everyone how great it looked. Finally, he paid a couple of guys to come repaint it white so I would have a blank canvas to paint something else."

"Sounds like you have a great dad."

"I did. He died a few years ago."

"No big brothers or sisters?"

Sydney shook her head. "Nope, it was Daddy and me after Mom died." She feigned a smile. "When he passed away, I had the boys, and it helped."

"Helped keep you busy?"

"Helped me not feel so alone in the world."

Ryan walked closer to her and then lowered his face, so they were an inch apart. "You're not alone, Red."

Sydney stared at him for a second and then squinted her eyes at him. "Did you just call me Red?"

Ryan nodded his head and kept staring into her eyes.

Sydney tried to keep a straight face, but her smile broke through.

"My dad used to call me that." Her eyes watered. "When I was little, he called me Strawberry Shortcake but shortened it to Red when I was a teenager."

Things were getting too cozy with them as Ryan stood ever so close. He felt the urge to hold her and stepped back to put some space between them. She looked up, and Ryan held his hand out for her and pulled her off the counter. "Come on, Red, I want to show you another house."

Sydney followed Ryan outside. What was she doing, sharing intimate stories about herself with him? She didn't want to be another member of his harem. He had said he didn't think of her that way, and he had the good sense to interrupt the moment before she got carried away. How freaking awkward.

Could she have a male friend as an adult? She was a tomboy when she was younger and was friends with a couple of boys on her street. She would tease and tell them that she was her father's first born son or the son he never had when she caught the most fish. She had more in common with the boys back then, but when her mother died, her father became over protective and disapproved of Sydney being alone with boys. In fact, he took her to work with him after school most days, and she did her homework there. During the summer she went to summer camp until she was old enough to work, and then he paid her to do odd jobs around the police station. She memorized most of the police codes and would rattle off the various meanings of each one, impressing the deputies along with her father. It was a great party trick during her first and only semester in college.

Being that close to Ryan was trouble, *or a 10-24*, she thought as she wrapped up in the blanket while they pulled away from the dock. Sydney felt comfortable with him, and that couldn't be good. She needed to stop talking so much. She distracted herself by recalling more of the police codes she used to know so well. It worked for a while, and she and Ryan didn't speak as they headed a half mile down the lake.

Ryan steered the boat toward a large three story house with a two story screened in back porch and multi-level deck. The closer they got, the more she could see the state of disrepair. It looked more like it should be torn down than restored.

She didn't say anything as Ryan pulled the boat around and then tied it to a large pole. As Sydney stepped forward to get off the boat, he stopped her.

"Hold on, Sydney. This one's pretty bad, and I don't want you to get hurt."

Ryan had surveyed the landing before he made a move, and Sydney watched the serious look on his face as he stood up there on the pier.

He'd been solemn since they left the other house, and she wished she hadn't made things uncomfortable. She liked his humor and could have used a lighthearted day instead of being reminded of what she no longer had. Ryan seemed distant since she brought up her family, and she blamed herself.

He stood up there, and for the first time since they had left the other house, he looked over at her and shook his head. "I'm not so sure I want you up here. It's in pretty terrible shape."

Had he changed his mind? She had to fix things.

"Well it's too late now," Sydney said, rolling her eyes. "I'm tougher than I look. Let me see it."

Ryan grimaced but reached over to help her up anyway. Sydney jumped to his side, but as her second foot came down on the decking, a board gave way. Sydney gasped, but before she tumbled into the lake, Ryan grabbed her and pulled her into him.

His face had lost most of its color, and Sydney reached up to put a hand on his cheek. He looked into her eyes, and she winked at him.

"I can swim, Ryan," she said and then bit her bottom lip.

Ryan stared at her mouth and then, finally, smiled at her. "Glad to hear it, but it's best if you don't go into the lake with the pier falling on top of you."

Sydney was relieved that he was acting normal again and listened as he pointed to the property. "So what do you think of the place?"

"It looks haunted."

"Seriously, Sydney?"

"No, I am being serious. I hope you didn't buy it already. It should be condemned or used for one of those reality shows where they try and communicate with ghosts."

Ryan smirked and then shook his head. "Actually, Sydney, I did buy it. It's my next project. It's going to be a lot of work, but it's a huge house and will have a lot of awesome features when I'm done. There are already some cool things like a hidden staircase, and a dumbwaiter..."

"Oh my gosh, I told you that it was haunted. Why else would anyone put in hidden passageways?"

Ryan guided her back onto the boat, following her. Once she sat down, he pulled the boat back so that they had a great view of the expansive yard and house. "Well, I hope you're wrong because this house is going to be incredible, and I don't want your decorating to go off the rails because of some pesky ghosts."

Sydney stared at Ryan. "My decorating?"

"I told you that I think you have a knack for design. You can get your feet wet on the other house, but I would like to see what you can come up with for a place like this."

Sydney was biting her bottom lip again and looked back up at the large house. She'd thought he was pushing her away after she got too personal and yet, he was offering her a dream job.

"Are you sure about this? I mean, each house you work on is bigger than the last. You should hire a professional."

Ryan started the boat and turned it around so they could head back home. He didn't look at her as he spoke. "If you don't want the job, Sydney, then just tell me."

"You don't have to always get so mad at me."

"I don't get mad."

Sydney smirked. "Really? You could have fooled me."

Ryan slowed the boat down so he could stare at her and raised a critical eyebrow her way.

She wished she didn't always say what was on her mind. "The moment I drove into town, you got mad at me, first, when I had that flat tire, then when I got into a fight with the movers. I couldn't seem to do anything right."

Ryan squinted his eyes at her, but he didn't deny it. It was true. She'd irritated him, and he couldn't explain why. It wasn't like she did any of those things on purpose. It didn't make sense. Even when she slept on her couch, it aggravated him. His sister was the one who had figured it out. It just wasn't the way Reagan had hoped. He wasn't attracted to Sydney. Actually, he was a little, but not like Reagan wanted. Sydney was simply in need of a friend. He knew what it was like to feel alone; even though he'd had Reagan, he felt hollow for a while. He needed someone to show him how to get back on the path and live life. He could do that for Sydney. He could help her by showing her how to live a little each day until those minutes added up to hours, hours added up to days, and then before she knew it, she would be fine.

"I'm not mad now," he said, over the sound of the boat and wind.

"You sure about that?" She kept poking at him, but he understood when a person needed help, they usually didn't make it easy. "You don't want to hire me, Ryan. I don't have a lot of free time. I have to work, and I have two jobs, you know. The bar doesn't give me many hours, but together I get fifty hours a week."

"No problem," Ryan said, and this time his face was expressionless. It was a sign to Sydney that he had given up on the whole idea.

He must have realized that he didn't want her around that much and these jobs would've put them together for hours at a time. The women in his life didn't stick around for long. The women that came over at night left as soon as the date was over. Sydney didn't see him with anyone during the daylight hours. Even his sister came for dinner and left early the next morning. He appeared to enjoy his alone time, and he didn't need Sydney to screw that up.

He pulled his boat into his boathouse, and she watched as he tied it off and then jumped to the side. When he reached over to help her out, she ignored his hand and jumped out on her own.

He didn't say anything but watched her as she stammered to leave, looking like she was ready to run. He knew that feeling. Ryan walked over with his key to unlock the door for them to walk out onto the pier and saw her looking around the boat house at his water toys. She kept quiet, but he could feel the energy rolling off her. She was ready to crawl out of her own skin.

Before he set her free, Ryan turned and looked at her. "It's fine, Sydney."

She nodded and watched as he turned to lock the door behind them. It was an extraordinary boathouse, and she hadn't realized it was large enough to hold two boats and tons of water accessories. The lake and those lake houses were Ryan's life. She didn't belong there. His offer was clearly rescinded. It was done. That was the same way Drake would dismiss her when he didn't want to have a discussion. She should have been relieved because she didn't want to be around Ryan that much, either.

So why did it hurt so much? She avoided his eyes and quickly turned so she could hurry down the pier and jump over to her side. She caught her foot on the edge and barely made it without falling, but she didn't stop and catch her breath before running inside her house to hide.

Chapter Ten

Sydney worked two double shifts back to back and was finally home for the night and off the next day. Her feet were throbbing, and she promised herself that she would go online and order some new comfortable shoes when she got paid again.

It was late, and she hadn't eaten anything since eleven that morning. She was happy to have donuts again, and she grabbed the whole box to take outside with her. She needed to unwind, and if there was anything her neighbor had said that was true, it was the fact that life slowed down so you could breathe here, even if it didn't work like that anywhere else.

She quietly opened her back door so Ryan wouldn't hear her if he had his back door opened. She hadn't seen him since that day he took her to look at his houses. If she were honest, she was avoiding him. He was probably still mad. More likely, he had a lot of female company and was preoccupied, but when he wasn't distracted, he was undoubtedly mad.

She carefully walked down the steps of her back deck and onto her pier. Halfway across, she peeked back to see if she could get a glimpse of Ryan, but his house was dark. Thank goodness. She could stuff her face in peace.

He liked to tease her about her diet, and she didn't want to hear it.

Her ex-husband had insisted no sugar in the house. He didn't want the boys eating sugary snacks and in no way approved of his wife doing it either. She had to keep up her perfect appearance.

She grinned as she sat down. She could eat as many donuts as she wanted while she was out here all by herself, and she had six giant specialty donuts and six glazed donuts to choose from.

Just as she had a mouth full of a croissant donut, Ryan walked out of the shadow of his dark boathouse. Sydney screamed, but it was muffled by the sugary bread.

"Whoa, Sydney. It's me," Ryan said, staring at her.

She swallowed the half chewed donut and wiped her mouth with the back of her hand. "You scared me to death. What are you doing lurking out here in the dark?"

Ryan smiled and jumped across from his pier to hers to sit down beside her.

"I wasn't lurking, Red. I just got in from work."

So he wasn't mad? At least, with that smiling he didn't look mad.

He was giving her whiplash with his many mood swings.

She didn't want to be nice to him. Dang it; she wanted to eat donuts in peace. But she couldn't help herself.

"What happened? Why are you so late?"

The supreme smile on Ryan's face made her wish she hadn't asked, but she wanted to know. Just because she hadn't accepted his offer of a job didn't mean that she didn't want it. She just didn't think working for her next door neighbor would be a good idea. Once it went bad, there would be no going back. He'd already gotten mad at her countless times, and that was when she'd been avoiding him.

"I hired a professional decorator and then had to spend the afternoon repainting and reordering most things for the Clap House."

"Wait. You call it the Clap House? That's funny."

"What's funny about that? It's short for clapboard."

Sydney rolled her eyes. "Never mind."

Ryan stared at her for a minute and then looked down at the whole box of donuts she was holding. "Are ya going to eat all of those donuts?"

The question aggravated her; she could eat as many as she wanted.

"Do you mind if I have just one?" he asked.

Sydney took a deep breath because she'd been sitting there judging him like he was making fun of her weight when he'd simply been hungry. She opened the box and held it out to him.

He had a boyish smile as he looked each one over carefully. Then he chose a strawberry filled glazed donut. When he looked over at Sydney, she finally smiled, too.

They ate in silence for a few minutes, and then Ryan leaned into her. "No milk?"

"Too tired to get milk."

"Me, too," he said, and she saw the exhausted look in his eyes.

Could she have been wrong? Maybe he wasn't mad at her most of the time. Just because Drake was a jackass didn't mean Ryan was too. She hadn't considered the reason she hadn't seen him was that he was working.

"So, are you going to tell me what the decorator picked out?"

Ryan shook his head and ate the rest of his donut in two bites.

"I'll give you another donut if you tell me," Sydney said, making her brown eyes look bigger and then batting her eyelashes at him.

Ryan laughed at her. "Alright, but only because I'm starving."

Sydney snatched the box and held it away from him, "And because these donuts are divine, right? Say it."

Ryan's eyes sparkled in the moonlight. "Of course, they're divine."

Sydney handed the box over and watched him look each one over again as if he hadn't just seen them. He chose one with sprinkles and took a large, slow bite. She was losing her patience.

"Alright, already. Was it paint? Wallpaper? What happened?"

Ryan gave her a serious look and then leaned in like he was going to tell her a secret. "Paint. She spent the entire afternoon painting the living room with this ridiculous old technique called splatter paint."

Sydney stood up with her hands on her hips. "That wasn't funny, Ryan Gentry."

Ryan nodded his head and acted as if she was still sitting there calmly. She stomped her foot, and he slowly glanced up at her and then back down at his donut that he continued to eat as slowly and dramatically as possible.

Sydney sat back down. "Fine. I don't care. She can paint the entire kitchen in polka dots."

"Well, if you hadn't left me in a lurch then I wouldn't have had to deal with the orange living room and the bright yellow kitchen with white quartz countertops."

Sydney sat down in front of him. "Oh, please tell me you're kidding."

"I wish I was kidding. The worst part is that the decorator ordered the majority of it yesterday without telling me, and I found out today when the store called to verify the delivery for the credit card."

"So you were able to change it?"

"Sure, for the low price of a thousand dollars. Restocking fee."

"Ouch."

"Ouch is right. I've spent most of the afternoon calling her office in the city and had to leave multiple messages, but she hasn't called me back. I want to fire her, but other than painting the house white or beige, I don't have time to pick out finishes. I've got people at the new house that I need to manage and plans to draw up so they're not on the clock with nothing to do."

He looked out over the lake, but Sydney could feel the pressure of the words left unsaid. She stood up and walked to the edge of the pier and then turned around to look at him. He was good at that game and didn't glance her way.

Sydney sighed loudly, but he still sat there, avoiding her stare.

"Alright. I can help you out tomorrow."

He tilted his head up casually. "You sure?"

"Don't press your luck, Gentry. I'm off tomorrow. I can get some things picked out, possibly put together a palette board so you can give the okay on colors and textures."

Ryan stood up and smiled at Sydney. "You want to ride in with me at eight?"

"No. I'll need my car to run to the store. Besides, you need to get to the Haunted Mansion and oversee the crew there, right?"

Ryan nodded his head and then leaned over closer to her. "It's not haunted, Sydney. You'll see."

"No, sir. I'll help with the Clapboard House, but after that, you are on your own."

Ryan looked into her eyes, and she could see there was more he wanted to say, but he kept quiet. Sydney wished she could keep her thoughts to herself like that at times, but it seemed strange to keep so much locked inside of yourself.

Ryan reached down and picked up the donut box and then walked Sydney up to her back door. "I'll meet you at The Clap House at eight?"

Sydney laughed. "You know, Ryan Gentry, for a promiscuous guy, you really should know what the clap is."

His eyes widened, and she could see the corners of his mouth turn up, slightly, but he didn't give her a full on grin. Oh, how she envied that control.

She shook her head and then headed inside for the night, unsure of how he had talked her into working with him.

Ryan waited until he was inside his house before he laughed. Sydney was one of the most difficult women he'd ever come across, and he couldn't believe he'd finally gotten her to accept the design job. He was smiling so hard his face hurt until he remembered that she could see into his living room with the light on behind him. He stopped gloating. That redhead next door was more hard headed than anyone he'd ever met. He hadn't had to work that hard in a long time. He knew what she needed, and he was going to find a way to help her heal her heart. Rehabbing these lake houses had saved his life. It could be that decorating them would do the same for her. At least, she was moving in the right direction.

The next morning, Sydney walked in at eight-twenty with a large travel mug of coffee and sunglasses on. "Sorry I'm late."

"Didn't sleep?"

"I seldom sleep."

Ryan stared at her, and for a second he thought she wasn't going to say anything else. But that wouldn't be Sydney.

"I've never lived alone. I haven't slept alone in eight years."

"You don't have to..."

Sydney held her hand up to stop him from talking. "If you know what's good for you, then you won't finish that sentence."

"What?" Ryan gave her an innocent look. "I was just going to say that there are plenty of single men in our little town."

"Whatever," Sydney whispered, rolling her eyes.

"Don't tell me that you thought I was offering to sleep with you?"

"Of course not," Sydney shifted her stare out the back double window. "Where would you fit me into your schedule?"

"Good one, Red."

"Don't push me," she warned. "I have to work another double tomorrow, and then the breakfast shift the day after. You've got me today, and then I'll have to see when I can come back."

"Thanks, Sydney. Honestly, I'm grateful for the help, and if you can't get back over here for a few days, then I can let it ride."

Sydney smiled at his words. It had been a long time since she felt needed, and even longer since she felt appreciated. She walked around the kitchen and made some notes, then she walked into the living room and made a few more.

"Alright, I've got what I need. I'm off to put some ideas together, and I'll call you when I'm done."

They exchanged cell phone numbers, Ryan gave her a key to the house, and Sydney headed to the closest hardware store for paint, stone, and hardwood samples.

Late that afternoon, Ryan received his fourth text from Sydney. She'd asked him several questions on styles and ideas, and he was interested to see what she'd put together. When he met her at the house, it was almost dark, and she again showed up wearing sunglasses and had a large cup of coffee.

"You okay, Sydney?"

She gave him a subdued smile. "I will be once you take a look at the two idea boards I put together for you."

He watched her as she spoke. She was fidgeting and kept nervously clicking a pen she had in her hand. He reached over and gently took the pen from her.

She licked her lips and then took a deep breath before she began talking again. "I hope you like them, but if you don't then just remember that I haven't done anything like this before. At least, not for anyone other than my dad, and that was a long time ago."

"Stop talking, Sydney, and show them to me."

She was about to argue with him for telling her to stop talking but realized that he had a huge smile on his face. He was just as excited to see what she had done as she was nervous about showing him.

She held up the samples that she'd put together, and he studied them closely. Then he walked over to the window and looked at them in the little bit of natural light that was left outside. He didn't say anything but walked back to the center of the house so he could see the changes with just the inside lighting again.

When he looked over at her, Sydney was about to explode with questions.

He slowly grinned her way. "The only problem I see is they're both incredible, and I can't choose."

Sydney launched herself at him and hugged him fiercely. She was so worried that he wouldn't like them that she hadn't considered he might like them both.

She had the biggest smile he'd ever seen, and he was proud that he was the person who had made that happen. She stepped back and straightened out her clothes, pretending that she hadn't just attacked him.

"Okay, so you might want to consider costs," she said, aiming to sound professional. "Honestly, the paint and trim cost more on the gray-blue one, but the granite and flooring cost more for the mossy green one. They're close in overall price, with the green being a couple of hundred dollars more."

Ryan was instantly happy. Decorating was definitely her thing. He remembered what it was like when he had found his place here and he stood there watching her for an awkward moment until she put her hands on her hips in that bossy way that she had.

He recovered his disposition. "I like them both. You choose. Surprise me," he said, and then he turned around and headed for the door.

Sydney was stunned for a moment and then ran after him. "No, wait."

He stopped and turned to look at her. "What?"

"This is a big decision. I'm not sure that I'm the one who should make this call."

"You're the exact person. Order the items and charge them to my account. I've got to get back to the other house, but I'll send a couple of guys over here tomorrow to paint or do whatever you tell them."

"I can't be here tomorrow. I've already told you I have to work." He watched her as she opened up her phone calendar and looked at her week. "I could meet them here Thursday morning at nine. I don't have to go into the diner until 10:30 for the lunch shift and then I could come back later that day to check on them."

Ryan nodded. He'd hoped she would love it so much that she would rearrange her schedule to be there. That's what he did during his recovery and still did today. "Sounds like a plan to me."

He turned and quickly left before she figured him out.

***

SYDNEY COULDN'T STOP THINKING about the Clapboard House. She had worked into the night on measurements and double checking the order she'd made earlier for supplies. That job was hands down the most exciting thing that had happened to her since Drake pulled the floor out from under her life.

When she walked into the diner the next morning, she was beaming over the opportunity that Ryan had given her. Maybe they were going to be friends.

"Better be careful, sugar, your face is going to crack from smiling so much," Miss Lynn said. "Wanna spill the beans on what's got you so happy today?"

Olivia put her arm around Sydney. "I think a man put that smile on her face."

Sydney laughed at them both. "I have no idea what you two are talking about. I'm just happy to be at work."

Miss Lynn and Olivia laughed and then cornered her by the coffee pot.

"I need gossip, Sydney. I'm an old woman; it's all I've got anymore," Miss Lynn said, pleading.

"Let me guess, Ryan Gentry?" Olivia asked.

"Okay, don't make a bigger deal out of it than it is. It's not going anywhere, but I'm excited."

"It is Ryan Gentry!" Olivia squealed. "I knew it. I could tell he had a thing for you."

Sydney smiled. "It is Ryan, but not the way you think. He gave me a job. At least a small one to help decorate one of his new houses. It's silly, I know, but it's the best thing that has happened to me in years."

Olivia rolled her eyes. "Work? You're this happy over work?"

Miss Lynn leaned against the counter, pondering what Sydney had said. Sydney and Olivia realized that she was suddenly quiet and both looked her way.

"You used to be a decorator, honey?" Miss Lynn asked.

"I've never been a decorator; it's just more of a hobby."

Miss Lynn nodded. "Don't you think it's odd that Ryan Gentry asked you to do it when you're not a decorator and never have been? It's even stranger because he hasn't used one before. He actually dated a girl from the city who was a designer for some big fancy group and wouldn't let her into one of his houses."

Olivia laughed. "You mean Sylvia, darling?" She made a gagging face and then laughed again.

"So you liked her?" Sydney asked, shaking her head at the two gossipy women.

The coffee pot finished brewing, and Sydney reached over to pick it up to go and refill cups around the room.

"It may seem odd, but Ryan Gentry is odd. There. Is. Nothing. Going. On. Between us," she said and then scooted out from behind the counter to work the room.

She thought about what Miss Lynn had said. Why would Ryan go out of his way to coax her to work with him? She didn't want to think too hard about it. She was happy for the first time in a long time, and it was just one house.

Thankfully, it was an incredibly busy day, and the crowd didn't slow down until long after lunch.

"What is going on today? Where are these people coming from?" Sydney asked, wiping her hands on her apron.

"It's fall break for the area schools," Olivia said. "Most people don't come into town until Friday, but with the warm front sneaking in, I bet we have record numbers this weekend."

"Yippee," Miss Lynn added as she walked by, but Olivia shook her head.

"It's going to be a pain in the rear. Thanks for grabbing my shifts last week. I'll be thinking of you when the crowd is lined up out the door tomorrow."

Sydney made a funny face at her friend. It might have seemed like Sydney had it easy with fewer hours at the diner, but she would be working for Ryan before and after her shifts. She was ready to fire off her retort to Olivia when her mouth went dry because Drake walked through the diner door.

"Sydney? Are you okay?" Olivia put her hand out to touch Sydney's arm. "You're shaking, hon."

"I-I have to leave," Sydney whispered and quickly turned to run into the small kitchen.

She shucked her apron and ran out the back door before she realized her purse and keys were still inside. She didn't know what she was going to do; she couldn't go back in there. She absolutely couldn't.

As she stood there wringing her hands, Olivia came out carrying Sydney's things. "Was it that snobby looking dude with the stick up his ass?"

Sydney's eyes watered. She had only ever referred to him as her ex. She didn't explain whether that meant ex-boyfriend or ex-husband. She hadn't shared any of the details, certainly not about the boys or that she was a full-time mom for seven and a half years.

"Was he alone?" Sydney asked, but she already knew the answer before Olivia shook her head.

"He had three boys with him and a skinny brunette with an equally large stick up her ass."

Tears flowed down Sydney's face, but she didn't bother to wipe them. She had known they would eventually come here; it was the main reason she chose a house at the lake. They'd loved coming here for Fourth of July, and she was thrilled at the prospect of seeing the boys then, but it was too soon. Drake would call the police.

Olivia told Sydney to go and that she would cover the last two hours of her shift, but before she could turn to leave, the back door opened and Drake came marching outside.

"You should listen to her, Sydney, and get the hell out of here. Now."

"You should mind your own damn business!" Olivia shot back.

"I wasn't speaking to you. Please leave," Drake said, not taking his glaring eyes off Sydney.

Olivia stood up straighter, but before she gave him a real cussing, Sydney grabbed her hand and nudged her toward the restaurant, so she would leave them alone.

"You sure?" Olivia asked, clearly worried about Sydney.

Sydney could hardly look her new friend in the face as she nodded.

Olivia didn't like being told what to do and especially by a rude and arrogant asshole like Drake. She purposely bumped her shoulder into him and called him an asshole before she walked back inside.

"Classy. Friend of yours, Sydney?" he asked and then took two menacing steps toward her. "What are you doing here? Do you work here? Are you living near here? No contact! That's what you were told. Are you going to force me to call the police? I can make sure you're arrested. Do you want that? Do you think you can pass another mental evaluation? Do you want to be locked up?"

Sydney kept walking backward, but as Drake berated her with questions, he kept physically crowding around her. It was like they'd never shared anything but hate toward each other. She couldn't see clearly from her tears, and she began hyperventilating the moment Olivia went back inside.

She was shaking and accidentally dropped her purse. Instead of picking it up, she defensively covered her face with her hands as Drake continued to yell. She had to think. Her car was in the front lot. She couldn't breathe with him all around her. She had to do something. Finally, she did the only thing that she could;

she ran. She was half a mile down the road before she turned around to make sure he wasn't following her, but she didn't stop until she reached her house. It was seven miles from the diner.

When she reached her road and could see her home, she slowed down. She didn't have her keys. She wouldn't be able to get inside without breaking a window, and she certainly couldn't afford to have one of those huge things replaced. She needed to stop and think, but she couldn't catch her breath, and she was sure she would pass out any second. She stumbled around to her back deck and then sat down as she sobbed uncontrollably.

Chapter Eleven

It was seven before Ryan got home, and he went straight into his kitchen for a glass of iced tea. Sydney's car wasn't there, and he remembered she was working late. He shut his back door and was startled. There she was, asleep on the wooden deck.

She was curled up in a ball with her hands around her chest, and he couldn't remember the last time anything had shaken him that badly. He ran across to her and knelt down to see if she was alright. She jumped as soon as he touched her and blinked her swollen red eyes at him.

She was disoriented and shaking as he spoke calmly. "Sydney, it's me, Ryan, your neighbor. Are you okay?"

She was nodding but didn't appear to understand what he was asking. "Sydney? Where's your car? What are you doing out here?"

"Locked out," she said, not explaining anything.

Ryan wanted to ask her more questions but thought it was better to get her inside. "I think I can shimmy your back door open with some tools. I'll be right back."

He ran to his house, and within a few minutes, he had her door opened. She was still in the same spot, and without asking, he scooped her up and carried her inside, laying her on her couch.

She didn't move or speak; she just lay there while he covered her up.

He went into her kitchen, but as usual, she didn't have anything in her fridge. He poured her a glass of water and went to sit in the living room chair. She took a small drink from the water and then closed her eyes again.

Ryan slept in the chair all night.

Somewhere around sunrise, Ryan woke up to find Sydney gone. He was shocked that he hadn't heard her, but he calmed down when he heard the shower upstairs turn on.

He went next door to grab some orange juice and make a pot of coffee and had it on the table by the time she came down. She was wearing fresh clothes, but her hair was still wet and her eyes slightly swollen. She avoided looking at him.

"Thanks," she said as she had a seat.

She went for the coffee, but at the same time he poured her the juice and handed it to her. She nodded and drank the juice first.

He sat there for what felt like a lifetime. He was a patient man, but he couldn't wait another minute to speak. "Are you going to tell me what happened last night?"

"I don't want to talk about it."

Ryan sat there watching her face carefully. Sydney talked more than most, and he was caught off guard the first time she remained silent.

"Where is your car? Why don't you have your house keys?" he asked.

She shrugged her shoulders.

"Fine. I have to go meet the crew at the new house at seven this morning," he said and stood to walk to the door.

When she didn't respond, he stopped. "What time will you be at the Clapboard House today?"

Sydney set her glass down. "I have to work at the diner today."

"I know, but you told me to schedule the crew this morning

and that you would be there. You also said you would follow up with the workers after your lunch shift was over, remember?"

She was angry that he remembered her words exactly. "I don't want to do this," she said.

He didn't give her any slack. "You said you would do one house. You already picked out the finishes, and things were ordered and will be delivered today. You gave me your word, Sydney."

Damn him for knowing exactly what to say to make her do what he wanted.

"Fine. I'll get the work started, but I can't go back this afternoon. I told Miss Lynn that I could pick up another shift."

When he stared at her, she elaborated her lie. "I didn't realize it was fall break and that Miss Lynn's was going to get busy with the surprise warm weather weekend. A lot of people from the city are attempting to get one last vacation in before the weather turns cold. I can't help it."

"Alright," Ryan said. He wasn't sure if she was being honest, but after seeing her so fragile last night, he didn't think it was wise to push her too hard.

"Do you need a ride?"

Sydney shook her head, not knowing how she was going to get around without her car, but it was closer to the Clapboard House than Main Street Grocery, and she'd certainly been able to run that distance yesterday.

She stood up to walk Ryan to the door, and as he turned to walk out, he heard her faintly whisper, "Thank you."

He gave her the slightest nod, acknowledging volumes of information she had expressed in those two little words.

It was later in the afternoon than he'd wanted before he was able to check on the Clapboard House. When he walked in, he was relieved the painting was finished, and the counter tops were ready to be installed. The tiled floor was going down, and the wood flooring was sitting in the corner acclimating to the area before it could be installed. The workers had precise lists of what to do and where, but there was no sign of Sydney.

He had to finish up his day at the new house and then went to the diner for supper. When he pulled up, he saw Sydney's car in the parking lot, but it didn't take more than a few seconds to tell that she wasn't working. The place was a zoo.

He sat at the counter, and Miss Lynn ran by with a glass of water and handed him a menu. "Out of the special, Ryan. Sorry," she said but didn't stop for him as she headed to a table of six to get their order.

Finally, Olivia came by and took his order. She turned it into the kitchen and then asked, "How is Sydney doing?"

"I thought she was working, that's how she's doing," he said.

"She called in sick. I figured she would since her ex showed up here yesterday." Olivia gritted her teeth. "What a piece of work he is."

Before she could move on, Ryan stopped her. "Wait. He was here? In town or the diner?"

"Here in the flesh," she said, rolling her eyes. "She bolted, and the jerk followed her outside. I stood at the door, but I couldn't hear because of the damned ice machine. It sounded like the bastard threatened her if she came near him or the kids."

Ryan clenched his jaw as Olivia spoke. "The funny thing is, instead of telling him to go to hell, Sydney just stood there and took his bullshit."

"She left her car overnight?" he asked.

"Yes, it wasn't until late last night when my shift was over that I realized her car was still here. I wonder how she got home? Miss Lynn was worried sick because the dishwasher came in and said he found her purse and keys on the ground out back. She must have dropped them."

Ryan knew how she'd gotten home. He saw what a wreck she was last night, and she'd obviously walked or run home. He almost lost his appetite, but he figured Sydney hadn't eaten, and so he picked up her belongings along with two plates of spaghetti and meatballs before he headed home to find her.

There were no lights on in her house, but she wasn't fooling him. He knew she was in there and that she was attempting to make it look like she wasn't home. She must have thought with her car gone, too, that he wouldn't suspect a thing. Little did she know he had been a hermit when he moved back to Maisonville. In fact, other than the car he let take him into the city, he hid away for a month. He wasn't going to let her off that easily, and he had the keys to her house in his hands.

He knocked one last time and then unlocked her front door and let himself in.

"I know you're here, Sydney," he said, looking around for her. She didn't respond, and he started turning on lights until he saw her sitting on the floor in front of her couch. "I brought you some spaghetti."

"I'm not hungry," she said, staring out the back doors.

"I didn't ask if you were hungry. I simply said that I brought you something to eat. You need to eat."

"Give me back my keys, Ryan. I didn't invite you in here."

"Want me to leave?"

He watched her hands go from her hips to her sides. He didn't like seeing her defeated.

"I'll leave if you want me to, Red."

She shook her head no.

He was relieved that she didn't kick him out. He wasn't so nice to his own sister when she attempted to help him.

"I have meatballs and bread, too. Come eat with me?"

She nodded, and they walked outside to sit on his patio set. Ryan went back inside his house and brought back two cold beers and handed her one.

"You went to the diner?"

He nodded as he took a bite of his dinner.

"How did you know I was here?"

"It's what I would have done."

Sydney watched him for a couple of seconds, and then he picked up her fork and handed it to her. She hoped if she ate, then she wouldn't talk.

"Drake came to see you at Miss Lynn's yesterday?"

Sydney put her fork down and drank half the beer. "No. I'm pretty sure he was just as shocked to see me as I was to see him."

"And you could tell that because of the way he threatened you?"

"We don't get along, Ryan."

"Were you scared of him? Is that why you ran home and were hiding in the back?"

"You don't understand."

"I don't agree with threatening women, Sydney. There are laws against that, you know."

Sydney wiped her mouth purposefully and then sat back in her chair. "It's not like that. I've done some things. Some things I'm not proud of." She closed the Styrofoam box that her food was in and then placed the fork on top before she stood up and pushed her chair under the table.

"We've all done things we wish we could take back. Life is hard, and it's harder for some of us than it is for others," he said quietly.

Sydney nodded, and a sad look crossed her face, making him wish he could take back his last comment.

"And sometimes it's harder because we make stupid choices and bring it on ourselves," she said. She began walking away but stopped long enough to make sure Ryan understood. "You don't want to get mixed up in this, Ryan. I'm not the person you think I am. I'm here under false pretenses, and you need to steer clear of me."

Ryan stood but didn't move. He was afraid she would run. "I know you're hiding something, Sydney, but I just can't see you as trouble."

"I've been to jail," she said, leveling her eyes at him and watching to see that she had his full attention. "I don't know how things got so complicated, but trust me when I tell you, you don't want to be caught up in the mess around me."

She turned and ran to her back door, but before she went inside, she said, "I'll return your keys to the Clapboard House in the morning."

Ryan just stood there struggling to comprehend what she could have done.

Chapter Twelve

The next morning, Ryan found the key for the Clapboard House in an envelope taped to his truck window. Sydney was nowhere around, and he wondered when she planned to get her car. He could give her a ride, but she had made it clear that she didn't want him around.

He understood that because he didn't like Reagan hanging around when he got out of the Marine Corps, and she wasn't just his friend, she was his family. He didn't want her asking questions, and he certainly couldn't explain what was wrong with his head back then.

He had to find a way to help Sydney like his sister had helped him.

He checked his watch because the crews were showing up early at both houses, and he needed to inspect one and direct the other. He would come back to see Sydney in a few hours. He could possibly bring her some lunch and then drive her to her car. She might even feel like seeing the Clapboard House and the progress they were making with her design elements. He was calmer as he headed to work and came up with a complete plan to get Sydney out of the house.

What he didn't know was that she had run to the diner to pick up her car at five that morning.

It was daylight by the time she got there. The whole way over, she couldn't stop thinking about her family being there in town. She knew the SUV that Drake drove, and she planned to find out where he was staying with her children. She could be careful.

Within forty-five minutes she found the house they were staying at for the weekend. The boys would've wanted to be on the water, but Drake wanted nice amenities when he roughed it for a few days. Rentals weren't open this time of year, but one of the other doctors who Drake worked with owned a place on the east side of town. It was a nice neighborhood with large waterfront homes. She remembered the street, but most of the houses looked just alike there. Thankfully, the garage door had been left open, or she would have driven right by the place.

Instead, she rolled by slowly, straining to get a good look. She then turned around and did it again from the other direction. No sign of anyone, so she drove around that side of the lake, familiarizing herself with the area. There were more new homes in the east, and it looked a little more modern than the downtown area or west side of town. She could see a small cafe and a snowball stand, and there was a new steakhouse that only opened for dinner on the weekends. It helped her to know where her babies would eat that weekend. She knew Drake's girlfriend, Gina, wouldn't cook and they both liked to get dressed up and go out so they could be seen.

Sydney chewed her bottom lip, thinking about the first time she ran into them at the fancy Italian restaurant in the city. It was three weeks after Drake had kicked her out of the house. She'd followed them and then waited by the restrooms so she could talk to the boys. It would have been fine if Gina hadn't been drinking so much wine and then had to pee so often. Her fancy dress was tucked into the back of her panties when she walked out, and Little John started giggling, and that was when she turned around and saw Sydney.

It was the first of several times, and then they called the police. It shouldn't have gone that way, and she could have handled it better, but her emotions had been raw. She felt so alone, and if she could've just had time with her boys then she would've left Drake and his true love or, as he called her, his soul mate, alone.

Sydney didn't consider the consequences as she drove back by the house. She eased the car down the street and then turned around once more. That time she saw the twins, Erik and Eli, walking down the pier of the large house. She stopped completely in the middle of the road with tears in her eyes. Was the dog with them, too? Beezus loved the water.

She willed them to turn around, but they kept going. She could see they both had neat haircuts, and it hit her in the gut that someone else was taking them to get it done. Their private academy had strict policies on short haircuts for the boys and she had usually been the one to take them.

Tears slipped down Sydney's face, and she suddenly realized what she was doing. No matter how awfully she was treated, she wouldn't knowingly break the law. It was wrong. The other times before, she had a right to see her boys. She didn't have any right at the moment. There was a court order against her and until she had the money for another attorney that could help her get the restraining order changed, she had to follow the rules.

She could still hear Drake's threats from the day before. Suddenly, as she felt sheer panic over her foolish decision to look for them, her oldest son, Darryl, walked into the garage. He froze and stared at her for a minute before he raised his hand to wave. He then leaned back against the door to the house and motioned for her to hurry and go.

She wiped at her eyes as she sped down the street until she came to a stop sign. She loved that her son held the door closed because he wanted to protect her almost as much as she hated that she put him in that position. She was a better mother than that.

She wiped her face and blew her nose. She would do anything for those boys, including keeping her broken heart to herself so they didn't worry about her. She looked up in her review mirror in time to see Drake's SUV barreling her way.

She stepped on the gas and launched her car into the intersection without looking, narrowly being missed by Ryan, who was coming from the other direction. She didn't stop; she didn't see him because she was too busy looking for a place to hide. She pulled into a gas station and threw some change into the car wash to let the blue foam camouflage her car so that Drake wouldn't see her.

She calmed her racing heart by talking to herself. "They didn't see you, Sydney. Drake would have laid on the horn and Gina would have already called the police." There weren't any sirens, and there definitely would have been sirens by now.

Sydney took a deep breath as the rinse cycle started drizzling down on her car and the green light told her to pull forward. She had to slam on her brakes when Ryan pulled in front of her and blocked her exit.

He jumped out and was standing beside her door in seconds. She watched him, standing there tapping his foot. What was his problem?

"Get out of the car, Sydney," he said.

"I don't want to get out of the car," she replied, staring back at him.

He didn't budge. He just stood there expectantly.

"Fine," she said, and slowly opened the door, looking around to verify that Drake's car was nowhere around.

As soon as she stood up, Ryan closed her car door and crowded her against it. "Do you have a death wish? What the hell were you thinking, blowing past that stop sign? I nearly hit you!"

"What? When? I didn't go through a stop sign."

He put both arms on her car, caging her in. "Where have you been?"

Sydney rolled her eyes but didn't say anything. He was standing too close, and she put her hands on his chest to shove r personal space, but when she did, she could feel his

...oked up and noticed the concern in his eyes. She felt ...and dropped her hands to her sides. She couldn't admit w... she had been or what she'd been doing. He wouldn't understand. She didn't understand it, either.

"I went to get my car is all."

Ryan shook his head. "The diner is in the opposite direction."

"I drove around. I haven't done much exploring, and I wanted to see what was on this side of the lake."

Ryan shook his head as he stared at her. He knew Drake, Gina and the kids were spending the weekend at Dr. Marshall's house. It was a small town. He'd asked around until he found out what he wanted to know. They were less than a mile from the car wash.

Ryan reached over and moved Sydney's hair out of her eyes. Then he lowered his head, so they were practically nose to nose.

"You know I know better, right?"

Sydney shrugged and diverted her eyes.

Ryan reached down and gently turned her face so she would look at him. "Talk to me."

Tears filled her eyes as she shook her head. Ryan pulled her into him and hugged her. He didn't say anything else, just held her for a few minutes.

No one had hugged her in so long. She let herself lean into Ryan and closed her eyes. He held her a little tighter and it soothed her in ways she didn't want to acknowledge.

Ryan closed his eyes as he held her tightly. Something was happening between them. They were in sync, or had an understanding, it was difficult for him to put into words, but they were connected in a new way.

"Come on. We have work to do. We'll drop your car at your house, and then you can ride with me," he whispered.

Sydney nodded.

He kept his arm around her and gently guided her back into the car, and she followed him to their street. Once there, he gave her an encouraging smile as she climbed into his truck, and then patted her hand as he drove them toward the Clapboard House.

Sydney waited for Ryan to question her again about trying to see her boys, but he didn't. He just smiled and drove the truck in silence. He didn't bring it up or scold her for it. It was comforting to be around someone who'd seen her at her worst and still wanted to be around her. She didn't have to hide anything or pretend to be something that she wasn't. It made her feel stronger than she'd felt in years and for the first time since her father passed away, she felt like she had another person in her corner.

At the house, Ryan stepped back and nudged her to go into the house first. He couldn't wait to see her reaction.

It was everything he'd hoped.

Sydney's hands went to her mouth as she walked in and saw the house. She looked at him and then looked back at the modifications. The changes she'd designed had come to life. She had tears in her eyes.

"Oh, my-my-my," she said. She slowly twirled around, looking at everything.

"Are you part ballerina or what?" he teased, but Sydney just cut her eyes at him and then glided into the kitchen running her hands over the counter tops.

"It's incredible, right?" she asked, and then walked over to him and put her arms around him. "This is the coolest thing I've been a part of since—" She looked up at him but couldn't finish her sentence.

"In a long time?" he said, helping her out.

She nodded, and he gave her a smile that made her stomach tighten. She quickly let him go and stepped back.

She took a deep breath and composed herself before she spoke again. "This place is going to be stunning when it's finished. You're going to sell it the first week."

"A couple already came in yesterday. They loved the finishes you chose and sent in an offer this morning. It's a rush job now. They sold their house in the city and are retiring here."

"Really?"

"Yup." Ryan's face was brighter, and she couldn't look at him smiling like that without getting butterflies in her stomach. She knew she was being ridiculous, but her emotions were on a hairline trigger ever since Drake had come to town.

She walked across the room to stand by the large picture window. "The floors are the last thing?"

Ryan nodded. "They're going down tomorrow, and then the trim will go up. I have a professional cleaner who will come in to give it a spit and polish, and I'll sign papers on it in a couple of weeks."

Sydney imagined how it would look with the hardwood floors finished and furniture warming it up. She didn't pay attention to Ryan walking over to stand beside her.

"I need to talk to you about the other house, Sydney."

He watched her right eyebrow raise and then continued talking. "You did a great job here. We work well together. I wouldn't have had it ready for that couple to come and take a look at it, and I would've potentially missed the sale. I need your help with the White House."

"The haunted house? No thanks! I'm good."

"You know that place isn't really haunted. It's going to be the most beautiful house in town and will be a great family home. Don't you want to be a part of it?"

Sydney shrugged her shoulders. She loved working on this house, and no matter how much she tried not to, she liked Ryan. But none of that would matter when he found out her past, and what had driven her to Maisonville.

She had to maintain her distance. She didn't need to drag anyone else down with her, and for once she would need to conjure up some self-control. She glanced at Ryan's blue eyes and bit her bottom lip, forcing herself to concentrate.

"I've already told you that I'm working two jobs that keep me way too busy for the decorating thing."

Ryan lowered his eyes at her. "I know you called in sick to

Miss Lynn's yesterday and today. I also heard that Will was cutting the wait staff's hours because his new girlfriend was picking up extra shifts until January."

"You don't get it, Ryan. I can't just play around. I have to have the money."

"This gig pays well."

Sydney shook her head. "I don't have money saved up. I pretty much live off tips, and they're paid in cash, daily. I couldn't wait months for a house to sell."

Ryan pulled out his wallet. "I'll pay you up front. How much?"

Sydney stepped back with her hands up. "No."

Things were getting too personal, and she wasn't going to depend on anyone else again.

"I told you that I was going to pay you for the work, Sydney. We didn't discuss rates, and I know that some designers get paid by the hour and some by the job. It would work best for me to pay by the job so I can budget properly. I figured $5,000 for this house would be appropriate. That's more than you're making as a waitress, right?"

"$5,000?" Sydney shook her head and said it again. "Five thousand American dollars?"

"Yes."

"Why are you doing this?"

"I need a talented decorator on my team. You have talent."

Sydney leaned against the granite counter top and crossed her arms in front of her. She wanted that job. If she talked to her seventeen-year-old self, it was what she dreamed about doing. When she had told her father that she was going to go to college for interior design, he hugged her and told her she would be great at it. If she hadn't met Drake her freshman year, design would have been her life.

No matter, she would still give it up for those boys. She bit her lip harder, reigning in her emotions. For now, she didn't have them and couldn't be with them, but she could work with Ryan.

"You don't have any ulterior motives, right?"

"Nope."

"This next job is going to be a lot bigger and take a lot longer?"

"Yup." He grinned at her. "I'll pay you twice as much for it and pay you half up front."

"Ten thousand dollars?"

Ryan just smiled and nodded his head. Sydney couldn't believe it. She had never made that much money at one time, and she'd worked like crazy while Drake was finishing medical school.

"Say yes, Sydney."

"Yes, Sydney," Sydney said, and then she grinned up at him.

Ryan's eyes twinkled as he looked at her. He grabbed her hand and pulled her to the door. "Let's pick up some fast food and head over to the new house. I want you to take a look at how much progress we've made so far."

"Okay," Sydney said, and she couldn't stop the nerves in her stomach as he held her hand all the way outside.

Chapter Thirteen

Ryan finished his hamburger as they pulled into the driveway of the White House. Sydney had just finished her fries but was only halfway through her chicken nuggets.

"There were only six of them, Red. Hustle up."

She shook her head and took a drink of her soda. "I'm stuffed. I drank too much Coke."

"I don't know, I've seen you eat donuts," he said and started laughing.

"My donut habit is not open for discussion."

He held his hands up for surrender, and Sydney kept staring at him.

"You don't want to pick a fight with me, Mr. Gentry."

"You talk tough for a little thing," he said before he opened his door and stepped out.

Sydney huffed at him as she jumped down out of the truck. He was standing there watching her and grinning that smug grin that he'd been giving her for most of the day.

"Alright, show me what you've got," she said, walking toward the front door.

Ryan smirked again and walked ahead to unlock the door for her.

She gave him a challenging look, but he didn't say anything. It would have been too easy, and he was sure she was setting him up for another smart comment. She was full of them. That cute woman drove him crazy.

He held the door for her. "The workers take a lunch hour from twelve to one, but watch your step for nails and loose tools."

She stepped inside, and her whole body shivered. "Oh, this place is huge!" Sydney's brown eyes were shining as she walked through the first floor rooms. "It has a formal den, a butler's pantry, and a large office, too. Wow!"

Ryan was happy that she was impressed. "I was thinking of built-in wall-to-wall shelves so that it could be a library. It also has two master bedrooms, one upstairs and one down. There is also another smaller bedroom downstairs that we are going to turn into the media room."

"I think I'll need to focus on the bedrooms and bathrooms first. Is that okay? Or would you rather I do the kitchen and living spaces?"

"Whatever you want to do first is fine with me. We fixed the subfloors, and there was some water damage that we have to take care of now that the plumbers replaced the pipes."

They walked around with Sydney taking some notes but mostly letting him tell her about the work that had already been done. She was impressed with the multi-level back porch, but she loved the wide-paned windows that must have been original to the house. They had that wavy look that new windows didn't have anymore.

They spent the rest of the afternoon there, with Ryan working with his construction crew and Sydney taking measurements and making notes for each room, including square footage and window sizes. The day flew by, and she'd remained distracted for most of it with the new project. Ryan checked on her from time to time but didn't chat more than a few minutes until he finished for the day. He found Sydney out in the front of the house where she was watching the giant wooden doors being installed along with heavy iron door handles and a knocker.

She was grinning that quirky cute grin of hers when he sat down next to her.

"Ready to go?" he asked.

She nodded but didn't offer up what was amusing her. It killed him not knowing, and when they got to the truck, he had to ask. "Alright, what's so funny?"

"Nothing. I just like the doors and accessories that you chose."

"You would have picked something different?"

"Nah. As usual, you kept it in the style of the original house."

"I did."

Sydney handed her phone over with a straight face. There on the screen was a picture of a scary looking house with similar doors as were being installed. Underneath the picture was the caption, "The Haunted Mansion."

When she saw the recognition in his face, she cracked up laughing.

"Get in the damn truck, Red," he said, and she could see he was stifling a smile.

It started sprinkling when they pulled up in Ryan's driveway, and Sydney told him she was going to go run a few miles before the weather got much worse. She'd ran that morning, but he didn't question her. It seemed like she worked out a lot of her stress by exercise, and he understood that worked well for some people.

Sydney looked toward the western sky at the storm clouds rolling in. The warm snap of weather was hitting a cool front, and the beautiful weekend was now going to be full of stormy days. She was sad for her boys and knew they would be unhappy if they couldn't go fishing or swimming that weekend.

It didn't take her long to change clothes and head out for her favorite path around Lake Road. The sprinkling of rain stopped for the first mile, and she could imagine her boys in the lake, swimming. However, the last half mile back to her house, the rain came down in sheets. Sydney was soaked and sat on her porch to take off her shoes and pour water out of them.

She took the hottest shower possible and was dressed in sweats as she was towel drying her hair, when she heard a faint knock at her front door. She figured it was Ryan, but she just about fell to her knees when she opened her door and saw her oldest son, Darryl, standing there.

She hugged him fiercely and pulled him into her house. "Are you okay, baby? How did you get here? Gosh, you've grown so much." She had happy tears in her eyes and Darryl did, too.

He held up a set of keys. "I drove."

"What? You drove?" Sydney stared at him. "Your birthday isn't until next week. Your father is going to flip out."

Darryl shook his head. "I've already taken drivers ed, and he lets me drive all the time."

The man Sydney had been married to wouldn't have done that. She had a confused look on her face, and Darryl gave her that sweet smile that she'd fallen in love with the first time she'd met him as a seven-year-old.

"He and Gina are too busy, and someone has to take the twins to football practice and John to soccer practice. So, I offered to do it. I help him, and he lets me go drive around."

Sydney wanted her sons to have the best kid years possible. They'd already had to deal with the untimely death of their biological mother, and Sydney did everything in her power to take any other burdens off them. However, she still had rules and taught the boys that a rule was only a suggestion if it wasn't enforced. The boys repeated her little sayings back to her whenever given a chance, especially once they found out they came from her dad, their grandfather.

"I'm so glad to see you, but I don't want you riding around until you're legal, especially in the rain," she said and hugged him again.

"I had to come see you, Mom." His voice cracked when he

called her "Mom", and she almost started crying. She hadn't heard those words from any of her sons in such a long time.

Her heart ached.

"I couldn't believe it when I saw you this morning, and this is such a small town, it took only one stop to find out where you lived." He shrugged his shoulders. "Actually, one stop and GPS." He grinned. "You live here at the lake permanently?"

Sydney nodded. She didn't want to take up any of the time they had to visit with her own voice. She just wanted to hear him talk.

"I wish I lived at the lake with you," he said, and her heart broke over the sad face he made.

"One day, okay, Darryl?"

Darryl shook his head. "I don't think so. Gina pretty much lives with us now. She made Dad buy new furniture because she didn't want anything that you picked out left in the house. They had a huge fight about you, and she's insisting that he make the restraining order permanent."

"No." Sydney let the words slip out before she thought about it. "I mean, no, I'm sure your father won't do that. Baby, don't worry about adult problems. We'll work it out, I promise."

"She's not going to let you, Mom." He took her hands in his. "You have to be careful sneaking around us. She's mental about you. There are cameras everywhere, and if she catches you, she'll show the judge and stop us from ever seeing you. She's sworn to it and made Dad agree. You know he's hardly around."

"Darryl, please. I don't want you to fight with your dad. This is just grown up stuff, and we'll get it worked out. I promise." She gave him a confident smile, a fake one, but he didn't need to know that. She had to keep things positive. "Tell me about school and your brothers."

He talked for fifteen minutes, and Sydney laughed and listened to his storytelling. She made him a drink and gave him a towel to dry off as they stood in the kitchen and pulled out a few snacks.

Suddenly, there was pounding on the door, and she felt her stomach drop.

Her heart was hammering in her chest until she realized it was coming from her back door and that it must be Ryan.

She quickly answered it, only opening it enough to stick her head out. "I've got company, Ryan; can I call you later?"

Ryan opened the door more and shook his head. "Are you certain this is a good idea?"

Sydney glared at him. "For your information, seeing my son is always a good idea."

Darryl walked over, looked Ryan in the eye and reached out to shake his hand. Sydney's father had taught him that, but when did he turn into such a young man? She swiped at her eyes and smiled.

"Darryl, this is my neighbor, Ryan Gentry. Ryan, this is my oldest son, Darryl."

Ryan and Darryl were cordial to each other. As Darryl explained what his brothers had been doing and how school was going for him, Ryan went into the kitchen. He poured himself a cup of day old coffee and had a seat in the living room.

Sydney couldn't believe he was staying but didn't want to make her son uncomfortable. Instead, she laughed and listened to Darryl like the champion listener she used to be.

Darryl stayed for half an hour, but it felt like five minutes. Sydney kissed him at least ten times as she walked him out to his father's SUV and told him to be careful going back home in the storm.

She didn't go back inside until he pulled off her street, and then tears filled her eyes. Slowly, she walked back into her house where Ryan was waiting at the front door. She expected him to scold her, but instead, he wrapped his arms around her, and she cried for ten minutes. As she sobbed, he carried her to the couch and watched the sadness fill her up.

He pulled a blanket over her and held her close. It wasn't

exactly what friends did, but it felt right. Sydney leaned into him and eventually started talking.

"I lost my mother when I was a little girl, and my dad became my whole world. I lost him three years ago." She wiped her eyes and exhaled. "But nothing has ever hurt as much as losing my boys."

Ryan hugged her a little tighter. He inhaled the scent of her coconut shampoo she used and realized he needed to put some space between them. Things were definitely getting too friendly. He reached over and picked up his coffee cup and took a drink. It was awful.

Sydney watched him grimace as he swallowed the cold, bitter coffee. "You don't have to drink that gross coffee. I can make a fresh pot."

"Your fresh coffee isn't much better, Red," he said with a straight face.

"It's not me. It's the coffee pot. It was the only one I could afford at the time. It needs a water filter, and I should grind the beans fresh."

He winked at her, and she automatically smiled at him for teasing her.

"You're not supposed to see the boys at all, are you?"

Sydney shook her head. "It's complicated."

"Most divorces are that way."

Sydney stared at him like he had some experience with divorce.

"Not me," he said. "My parents."

"Oh, sorry. How old were you?"

"Twelve."

"That's so tough; my twins were twelve."

"Reagan and I went back and forth between our mom's and dad's houses. It was better than listening to the fighting."

"Drake and I didn't fight. We rarely talked. He was gone most of the time. I guess I should have realized that something was wrong, but I was busy with the boys, and I was happy."

Ryan watched the emotion washing over Sydney's face.

"You loved him?"

"In the beginning. Later, I was comfortable with him. I loved the boys. I still love them, so much it hurts."

Sydney leaned back on her couch.

"Drake had planned the whole thing while I was gone on vacation for spring break with the boys. I dropped the boys off at school the next morning, and when I returned home, he told me I would have to move out. The news blindsided me, and then Gina showed up. She sat down beside him to tell me that I would have to leave the house right then. They didn't want a scene to play out in front of the boys, so while he told me how it was going to go, she went and packed me a bag."

"You left that night?"

"I didn't have a choice. Drake knew that I wouldn't want the boys upset and convinced me that leaving peacefully would be the best for them. I thought he would miss me and change his mind, but he wouldn't let me come back. I didn't realize that he'd already canceled my credit cards and our joint bank account.

"I didn't have anything except a check that he gave me, and I had to stay at a roach motel that night. The next day I tried to go home, but Gina had a locksmith there at 6:45 in the morning while Drake took the boys to school."

Ryan stared at Sydney. She'd abruptly stopped telling her story, and he watched as she warred with herself over telling him the rest.

The thunderstorm outside was raging, and the lights flickered a couple of times. It matched Sydney's mood right now, but Ryan didn't make the comparison out loud.

Sydney got up to check the back door and pulled her drapes in as far as they would go. They weren't wide enough to close the entire opening but helped hide the lightening a bit. She sat back down, but she sat in the chair instead of beside Ryan on the couch.

"You sure you don't want me to make a fresh pot of coffee?" she asked.

"Not unless you want some. It'll keep me up, and I need to go early in the morning to check on the White House because of the rain."

"You mean the haunted mansion?" Sydney said, easing the tension.

Ryan understood she needed to change the subject about Drake and her past, and since the drama of the evening had ended, he figured he should go.

"It's not haunted, Sydney," he said, shaking his head and standing to walk toward the front door. "You want to take a ride with me in the morning to check the roof over there?"

Sydney looked at the water rolling down the driveway as he opened the door. She hadn't seen a rainstorm like that before, and she was worried about Darryl.

Ryan stepped to her and squeezed her hand. "I'm sure he's back home by now. It wouldn't have taken him more than ten minutes, and it just picked up like this."

Sydney nodded.

"We'll leave around 7:30 in the morning," he said but could see she was still thinking about Darryl and not about going with him. He couldn't give her any wiggle room or she would get herself into trouble. He had been down the road she was on. He repeated himself, "We're going to leave at 7:30, okay?"

Her eyes focused on him, and she agreed. Ryan stepped out on the porch and pulled his jacket tightly around his body, but before he threw his hood over his head, he turned to look at her. "I don't want you to worry about anything, okay, Sydney?"

She shook her head but looked past him at the weather. He reached out and touched her cheek, making her look at him. He could see the concern in her eyes.

"The storm may get a little rough, but you're protected. You have hurricane windows in the house, and I have a generator if the power goes out."

Sydney knew he was reassuring her over more than just the storm. Had she been wrong about him? Was he looking out for her? She closed the door and leaned against it for a minute. She was going to have a hard time not thinking about her boys tonight, but she also couldn't stop thinking about Ryan.

Ryan stood on her porch until he heard her lock the front door. He then ran to his house and stripped out of his wet jacket and shoes inside the doorway. He ran his hands over his face and through his damp hair, frustrated over what had happened tonight. He should have known she was getting over more than just a breakup. How could a man take her children away from her? Wouldn't giving her visitation be more sensible? He took a deep breath and walked through his house to the living room, attempting to calm down. He stood at his back door, looking out over the lake at the lighting show performing in front of him. He felt the same energy inside as he became more aggravated thinking about her ex-husband cheating on her and kicking her out. Who could tear a mother, even a step-mother, away from her children? Especially a woman as loving and kind as she was with her kids? He had watched her for an hour with her son, and he fell even more for her.

He looked over and could see her standing at her back door, too. She must have sensed he was there as she looked up at the same time and waved to him. She was beautiful and deserved so much more than what had happened to her. He thought about how much he wanted to help her, and he knew it wasn't just about paying kindness forward. He smiled at her and then stepped back to sit on his sofa. Watching over Sydney was going to get a lot more difficult, particularly now that he couldn't understand how anyone could leave a woman like her.

Chapter Fourteen

The rain was constant the next morning, and as Ryan knocked on Sydney's door, he remembered how sad she had looked last night when he left. He knocked a little louder.

"I'm coming," Sydney said as she wrapped the blanket from the couch around her body.

Ryan took a deep breath looking at her mussed up red hair and sleepy brown eyes. "I'm guessing that I woke you up?"

Sydney poked out her bottom lip. "Sorry, Ryan. I set the alarm on my phone, but I forgot to put it on the charger, and it died last night."

"I can wait for you," he offered. He knew better than to leave her there. What if she went to see the boys again?

"Are you sure? I don't want to make you late, but I can throw some clothes on and be ready in five minutes." She looked sincere, and he felt guilty not trusting her to be alone.

"I'll wait," he said and went to have a seat on her couch.

While Sydney rushed upstairs, he looked around. Why in the hell did she insist on sleeping on that couch? She had a nice bedroom and a decent looking bed. The couch was small, and surely she wasn't as comfortable as she would be upstairs. He shook his head and patted her pillow that was indented from where she had laid her head that night. He thought about how small the couch would be for two people and then thought about her lying there without any clothes on.

He immediately stood up, ran his hands over his face and then walked to the back door, opening it to get some fresh air. The rain hit his face, and he calmed down. What was he doing thinking about getting her naked? She was his friend, his neighbor, and she was going through a terrible breakup. Those things added up to "Run the other way, idiot."

"Everything okay?" he heard Sydney ask as she came down the stairs. He quickly shut the door and wiped the water off his face. "Sure. I just wanted to take a quick look out at the lake.

"I heard some workers yesterday saying that the lake would rise by tonight. Do you think that's true?"

She sounded worried.

"We'll be fine, Sydney. Our houses are raised well above flood stage, and the lake drains into a spillway that keeps us safe during storms."

Sydney relaxed a little after hearing his explanation and was soon ready to go.

Before he backed out of her driveway, Ryan caught a glimpse of her car as she was closing her garage. It was parked several feet from where it had been last night. When did she go out? He didn't leave her house until midnight, and he'd been up since five that morning. He didn't want to argue and held his temper as he carefully worded his next question.

"Where in the Sam Hill did you go last night, Sydney?" was the nicest he could manage at the moment.

"Who said I went anywhere?"

"I know you did; just tell me." He couldn't hide his disappointment. He'd believed she was making progress with him and by working on the houses.

"Look, I had to make sure Darryl made it home yesterday. I lay down, but all I could think about was how he could have had an accident, and his father could have gone to bed early, and he wouldn't miss Darryl until the morning. I couldn't take it any longer and decided I had to be sure, so I checked on him myself. I drove there and right back, okay? No one saw me."

Ryan took a deep breath, struggling to calm his blood pressure. He had a bad feeling that things were going to get a lot worse before Sydney would listen. At least that was what had happened to him.

Ryan shook his head and avoided discussing it with her anymore. They drove to the house in silence, and Sydney watched the rain steadily fall, filling up the street drains and slowly creeping over the roadways.

At the house, Ryan checked the new gutters were working properly and that there were no leaks around the newly framed windows or with the new roof. It didn't take but forty minutes, and after he came down out of the attic, he was ready to go.

He locked up the house and watched as Sydney held her head low and quietly followed him out. He held up his large umbrella and pulled her in close so he could walk her to the truck door. The rain was coming down harder, and now the wind had picked up, so they ran attempting to keep dry. As she started climbing into the truck, they heard a loud cracking sound and turned to see a large pine tree falling their way. Ryan dropped the umbrella, wrapped both arms around Sydney and hauled her into the cab of the truck, tumbling in on top of her. Sydney buried her face into his chest as they heard the crashing noise and felt the ground shake.

"You alright?" Ryan asked, worriedly looking at her.

"Shaky, but I'm good," she said, forcing her voice to sound normal.

Ryan tucked a lock of her wayward red hair behind her ear and then peeled himself up to look out at the damage. The tree crushed his umbrella but fell between his truck and the house, missing both by just a couple of feet.

"Wow, you're the luckiest person I've ever met, Ryan Gentry."

Ryan's stomach felt hollow. He'd thought that tree was going to kill them, but he didn't want her to know. He nodded and hurried around the truck so they could get back home, where he'd personally had the pine trees removed and the large oak trees pruned regularly, so there would be less of a chance for that sort of danger during a storm.

A couple of minutes into the drive, he still hadn't spoken to Sydney. She reached over and touched his forearm. "Would you mind driving through somewhere so I could order a cup of coffee?"

Ryan found a place quickly and ordered them both a cup, putting them in the drink holders and handing her sugar and cream before they drove off. She prepared her coffee in silence and put a couple of sugar packets into his before handing it over to him.

Sydney worriedly looked out the window at the water that was now covering a lot of the small secondary roads. She was relieved to be inside Ryan's large truck.

He watched her but didn't have anything to say. He was still mad at her for putting herself in danger last night by going out.

He thought about when he'd started caring for her and figured his sister was right that it happened from the very beginning. It didn't matter anymore because there was no denying how he felt, but he wasn't sure he would be the one who could help her.

He pulled into his driveway and handed her his rain jacket since the umbrella was gone. She quickly put it on, and before he was out of his truck, she had climbed down and was already walking past him toward her own house.

"Sydney."

She turned toward him but didn't speak. She looked small wearing his jacket, and he wanted to lock her in his house and protect her.

"You don't need to go out in this weather. You'll be safe at home, but the roads are going to flood over, and I don't want you to take a chance in your car."

"O-okay," she said.

"If you need anything, let me know. I'll be home."

He watched as she gave him a quick nod and then hurried into her house. The afternoon brought heavier rain, and the lake rose higher until it was even with the end of Ryan's pier. It had been dark most the day, but now in the early evening, it looked like the middle of the night. Ryan walked outside to check the water level. He'd raised both of his boats in his boathouse but still went to double check that things were fine.

He'd thought about Sydney most of the afternoon, and when Reagan called to check on him, she asked about her, too.

From his back deck, he could see the small lamp beside her couch was on and that she was curled up asleep. He remembered sleeping most of the days and being up a lot of the nights when he got out of the Marines. His internal clock had worked against him having a normal schedule or life, and until he had counseling he didn't understand how to turn it around.

He ran back inside and started cooking dinner. The bad weather made him crave comfort food, and he whipped up some chicken Alfredo in less than twenty minutes. It was Reagan's recipe, and he laughed that it was most likely the only thing she could cook. He pulled hot garlic bread out of the oven just before the lights dimmed three times and then went out for good. He heard the loud crashing sound of a transformer going out nearby. He sat the bread down, and then his generator popped on. It wasn't a huge generator that would handle the entire house, but it did keep the refrigerator, microwave, and a few lights on so that he could make it through during a bad storm.

He thought about Sydney, and when he looked out back to see how far the lights were out around the lake, he could see her using her cell phone light and standing by the back door.

He waved to her, and she gave him a wave back. She motioned

for him to meet her at the front and he hurried to his front porch to see her.

"Did you hear that?" she asked, and he could see by the look on her face that she was spooked.

"It was just a transformer. The electric company will send a crew out as soon as the storm passes."

Sydney nodded and, although she was pretending to be fine, he could see she was shaken.

"Sydney, I just finished cooking some dinner. Are you hungry?"

She shook her head but didn't answer. He wasn't used to her not talking much, and he didn't like it.

"Come over and eat with me, Sydney. I haven't cooked chicken Alfredo before, and you can tell me if it's any good."

Sydney gave him a half smile and accepted his offer. He watched her pull his raincoat on and then she ran over to him.

Once inside she hung his coat on the rack and walked over to his oven and stood in front of the door to warm up.

"I can light a fire for you," he offered, and she followed him into the living room and watched as he lit some huge logs in his fireplace.

He made them both plates, and they sat on the floor, using the coffee table for their food. Again, Sydney didn't say much, and he worked at engaging her in small talk.

"So what do you think about Reagan's pasta recipe?"

Sydney took a deep breath before answering him. "It's really good. Thank you for inviting me."

She seemed to like the food, but her eyes told him that she was feigning interest because her heart was somewhere else.

He still kept trying to get her to relax. "Reagan gave me the recipe, but I'm not actually sure she's ever made it. My sister can't make toast. She usually burns it and swears it's because she likes it that way."

Sydney laughed at his comment. "Reagan looks pretty competent with everything. I'm sure if she wanted to cook well, then she would."

Ryan ate another piece of bread. "She's amazing at most things, but she has some sort of mental block when it comes to domestic work."

Sydney smiled at him and drank some of her water. They finished eating, and she picked up both plates and took them into the kitchen. As she washed the dishes, Ryan put the remainder of the food away.

They worked well together in the kitchen. Sydney was surprised how easy it was to just be around Ryan that way, especially since she felt like she didn't belong anywhere anymore.

She'd told Ryan a lie about checking on Darryl. She did go to the east side house to make sure he made it there okay. But when she slowly drove by, she could see into the dining room of the house, and the boys were laughing and smiling as they sat around the dining room table playing a board game with Gina and Drake. They looked like the perfect little family, and there wasn't a place for her there anymore.

Tears were filling her eyes, and Sydney quickly swiped them away. "Thanks for dinner. I think I should go."

Ryan lowered his head and looked her in the eyes. "I'd like it if you would stay a while. We could sit around the fire. I have plenty of wood."

She fidgeted looking unsure, and Ryan reached out to touch her arm. "Please don't leave."

Sydney looked over at him, and there was understanding in his eyes that she hadn't had from anyone else in a long time. She nodded, and he led her back over by the fire.

As she sat down on the floor in front of the sofa, facing the fireplace, he handed her a blanket. He waited until she wiggled around and got settled until he sat down next to her.

He felt her discomfort the minute he sat down. She was restless, and he knew that feeling when your own skin wasn't comfortable anymore. He put his arm around her and gave her a half hug. She leaned into him for a moment and then sat back up straight.

"I didn't mean to be so hard on you this morning about driving over to check on Darryl. The weather was horrible last night, and you still haven't replaced that tire."

"You were right. I shouldn't have gone. I just built the worry up in my head and couldn't sit there when I could easily just see if he was okay."

Ryan nodded his head. He didn't have children or even nieces or nephews, but he could imagine that he would have been worried, too. He was worried about Sydney after the fact. "He doesn't have a cell phone, Sydney?"

"He has a new number, and I'm not allowed to have it." She looked straight ahead at the fire. "There's actually a court order that says I can't have any contact."

Ryan didn't move. He figured there was more going on than she had mentioned, but that seemed a bit extreme. "A court order, huh?"

Sydney nodded and pulled the blanket tighter over her legs. "Gina pleaded to the judge, told him I was a crazy jilted ex-lover, and he believed her."

"She may be a good attorney, but I'm not convinced she could twist it enough to make me believe that," Ryan said, giving her a sympathetic smile.

Sydney buried her head in her blanket and then turned to face him quietly. After a few minutes, she whispered. "I didn't think he would believe it either, but I couldn't talk my way out of the video surveillance."

She turned her head, avoiding Ryan's stunned face.

Chapter Fifteen

Ryan couldn't think of what to say after Sydney admitted to video surveillance damning her in a court of law. What had she done? Could the little woman sitting beside him be capable of that bad behavior?

He ran his hand warmly down Sydney's arm. "I think we might need a drink for the rest of this story."

Sydney nodded and followed him into the kitchen. He pulled out a bottle of red wine from the top cabinet over his refrigerator and offered her a glass.

She'd only seen him drink beer and had pigeonholed him as one of those guys. After all, he drove a pickup truck and had a construction company. He was a walking stereotype for the town womanizer, but somehow she knew it was an act. If anyone looked closely, there was a different side to him.

He poured them each a glass, and then they went back into the living room. He gave Sydney that expectant look, and she avoided his face as she told him exactly what she'd planned never to tell anyone.

"The day Drake told me about Gina and made me leave, I was in shock. She stood right there beside him, and they ganged up on me. He said awful things about me, and she encouraged him the whole time. He accused me of being a terrible mother and wife. He said I had issues and he couldn't let me stay there. I'd had a pretty hard time after my father died, but I did my best. I couldn't find my voice. I was too stunned to fight back. I hadn't considered the fact that she would move right in or that I wouldn't get to live with the boys again. I certainly hadn't understood at the time that they weren't going to let me be a part of the boys lives ever again."

Sydney drank more wine. "I called, I kept going by the house, but they wouldn't let me in. Some days they weren't home and, of course, the locks had been changed. I don't know how many days had gone by because I hadn't been sleeping. My days were turning into nights, and they tended to run together. I was devastated. I started watching the house from across the street.

"Then one night Gina came home late and alone, and when she drove up, I jumped out of my car and confronted her. She started screaming, and Drake came running out, and they called the cops.

"When they got there, I was sitting on the curb waiting. Even though Gina cried and told them that I had threatened her, they were nice to me and let me go with a warning."

Sydney drank the rest of her wine, and Ryan poured her more. It was going to be a long night of confessions.

"They gave you a warning and told you not to go back?"

Sydney nodded.

"But you didn't listen, did you?"

Sydney shook her head. They both sipped wine and watched the fire longer.

She finally began again. "I tried to obey them. I did. I left that night and decided that I needed to see Drake when she wasn't around. I went to his office and waited for hours. When he got there, he flipped out. Honestly, he'd rarely been very excitable. He didn't have much of a personality. But she had him wound so tight, and when he saw me, he went crazy."

"Did anyone see him act crazy?"

Sydney shook her head. "That's the nutty thing. The camera's caught me breaking into his office. He kept his key hidden above the door, and all I did was climb on a chair and get it down, but still they acted as if I busted up the lock or something. Then I waited inside until he got there. They said I ambushed him." Sydney rolled her eyes. "I didn't touch him. At least, not until he shoved me into the bookcase. I was just sitting there in his chair, and he told me that I had made his life miserable and I needed to leave him alone so that he could marry his soul mate."

Sydney wiped her eyes. "I stood up and yelled at him that I was his wife and the mother of those boys. That's when he shoved me. A couple of books fell and hit me, and when he stepped back, I threw his lamp at him. It cut his forehead right here." She pointed to her right eyebrow. "I can't help the fact that I'm more athletic than he is."

She straightened up her spine and looked at Ryan. "Someone called the cops, and they showed up while we were in the middle of destroying his office. He told them that I was lying in wait and that I had assaulted him. They arrested me without question. He was the quiet-mannered doctor, after all."

Sydney poured herself another glass of wine and Ryan set his glass down. He hadn't planned to get her tipsy, but she appeared to need the courage as she told him the story.

"What happened next, Sydney?"

"I spent the night in jail. They let me out the next day, and warned me again not to go near them."

Sydney shook her hands like they were wet and then got up and sat on the couch and leaned back in the corner. She looked a little ashamed now, but she kept talking. "I didn't have anything. No money, no home. I hadn't worked in two years, so no job or prospects. My dad had died a year and a half earlier, but I hadn't sold his house or even been able to go back in there since he passed away. I just couldn't do it yet, but Drake didn't care. I met him when I was nineteen and gave up school because the baby was so young and he needed me. They all did. I worked at night so that he could be home with the baby, and I stayed home during the day so he could work and study. He used me in every way a person could be used, and then threw me out like the trash."

"You didn't stay away from them?" Ryan asked quietly.

Sydney shook her head. "Don't you understand? I was alone. I didn't have anything. Nothing."

Ryan nodded his head. He felt her pain in his soul.

"I thought about moving away, but the heartache of missing the boys tugged at me constantly. I would go to the school and watch them when they changed classes or when they went out for recess. I had no idea they had surveillance cameras there, too." She drank the rest of her wine and set the glass down on the side table. "Finally, when I couldn't take it anymore, I waited until it was Gina's day to pick them up from school. She was usually late, and that time, I let the air out of her tires so that she would be really late. I picked each of them up in carpool, and we went out for ice cream. It was like old times when I would get them from school. It was perfect."

She took a deep breath, and Ryan suddenly didn't want to know what was going to happen next. He wasn't sure he was ready to know what rock bottom looked like for Sydney. He'd lived there himself for a while, but there weren't any kids involved, and watching her relive it was heartbreaking.

Sydney didn't see the worry on his face. She was finally able to explain what had happened to her to the only person in the world that could listen with an open mind, and she kept going.

"It was getting late, and the boys realized that I didn't actually have permission to pick them up or visit them. Darryl was the only one who had a cell phone at the time, and it kept going off, but he wouldn't answer it. He just continued talking to me and telling me it was going to be okay. Finally, he said that he thought it was best that they went home. We had left the ice cream store and had been driving around for an hour or so, John had fallen asleep in the back seat, and I agreed that I would take them home. I pulled up, and there were at least ten cop cars there. I kissed each of the boys and asked them to go straight inside the house and not to turn around. I didn't want them to see me get arrested. At the time, I wasn't aware Gina had told them I might have a gun. The police waited until the boys got up to the door, and then they used a Taser gun on me. The last thing I remember was Darryl screaming, and then I woke up in the hospital."

Ryan couldn't imagine anyone considering her a threat. "The charge was too strong for you?"

"They thought it had given me a heart attack. Actually, I had started taking medication for migraines, and no one bothered to tell me to stop taking the sleeping pills. I had a reaction from the drugs that raised the serotonin levels in my body and dangerously raised my heart rate. When they shocked me, my whole system shut down. A few hours later, I was fine, and I could have gone home, but they kept me for a..."

He saw the flush that covered her face. Didn't she know that he wouldn't judge her? He was on her side. "It's okay, tell me," Ryan said, reaching out to hold her hand.

"I was sent in for a psych evaluation. Drake told them that I had signs of psychotic behavior before we separated and they believed him. They kept me for a week before they let me go. I was let out just in time to receive the court orders that I wasn't allowed to contact the boys in any way. If I went anywhere near Gina, Gina's office or car, Drake's office, car or the hospital, I would be sent to jail for a long time. It was so strict that even if I was dying, I couldn't be taken to the emergency room because Drake worked in the hospital."

Sydney avoided looking at Ryan. She wasn't crying; it was worse. She was defeated. Ryan moved over on the couch and without a word, pulled her into him and held her close. He knew what that felt like and wished he could make her feel better.

Sydney laid her head against his shoulder and chest, and they stayed like that, watching the fire die down and listening to the rain.

He thought she might have fallen asleep, but after a long while, she finally spoke. "Do you think I'm crazy, Ryan?"

"I think some people are pushed to the edge by events or, in your case, rotten people. Some don't make it back from the other side and some people, like you and me, come out of it a little bent but not broken."

"You and me?"

Ryan kissed the top of Sydney's head, and she shivered. It felt so nice to be held. She wasn't the type to sleep around like Ryan, and she wouldn't be okay to fool around with him and then watch him date the other women in town. She might not ever come back from the edge, as he called it. Still, she snuggled a little closer and inhaled his clean, warm scent. There wasn't any harm in enjoying his comfort for a while. He didn't kiss her again, but they stayed close until the fire died down to coals and he put more wood on to keep them warm.

When he walked back to the couch, he smiled at her. "It's getting late, and I know how much you like to sleep on the couch. Let me get you some blankets so that you can get more comfortable, and if you don't mind, I'll lie down there." He pointed to the rug in front of the couch.

Sydney wasn't so sure about a sleepover with Ryan, but she didn't want to go home alone, especially with the power out and the storm still lingering.

She helped him get set up on the floor, and then made up the couch the way she liked it. They both lay down in their spots close to the fire. It was the most comfortable she'd been in a long time, and even though she couldn't admit it to Ryan, it was because she didn't have to sleep alone.

Chapter Sixteen

Sydney woke to the sun beaming on her face and the smell of coffee under her nose. She jerked when she realized Ryan was close and holding a cup of coffee for her.

"Thanks," she said and took the cup to warm her hands.

"Are you cold? I can make the fire bigger."

"I'm cold when I first wake up. It's no big deal. The coffee will help," she said before taking a drink.

She smiled at him when she realized he was watching her. "The rain stopped? Are we flooded in here?" she asked, looking past him to see out.

"It's not too bad. I wouldn't drive the flooded roads in your car, but my truck could make it." He held his hand out for her and pulled her to her feet. He then opened his back door and showed her how close the water was to their back decks. It skimmed the top of the piers, and she was wide eyed looking at it. It was scary to think it could get that close.

Ryan picked up a quilt and wrapped it around her and hugged her from behind at the same time. It didn't make sense for her to be shy, but she felt exposed with most of her secrets out.

"I promise it's safe. I've been coming here since I was a kid, and I know this water. It'll recede quickly." Ryan's voice was deeper and more gravelly in the morning, and she thought about how sexy it sounded right now.

He hugged her a little tighter when she leaned back into him, and then he gently let her go. She immediately felt colder but didn't dare let him see her shiver. What was she doing?

She turned around to see him going into the kitchen to get himself a cup of coffee and then they sat down on the couch away from each other looking out at the lake. A kayak went by and then a canoe, but they didn't recognize the people in them.

"Tourists. Can't follow directions and stay out of the water," Ryan said.

He saw Sydney's eyes get bigger and he explained, "It's safe. You just have to stay out of it. People get hurt from attempting to drive through it or swim and play in it."

Sydney nodded. "My dad used to tell me that your entire car could be swept away by just inches of swift water." She shivered again, thinking about the water being that close to them, and where it wasn't supposed to be. She thought about how nice it would be if she could curl up next to Ryan, but she didn't move.

He could see she was nervous and figured the flooding was upsetting her. He reached over and patted her hand. "We're fine, Sydney."

She half smiled and nodded. "You're a pretty good person to have around in an emergency," she said.

Ryan considered how difficult being alone was for Sydney. She'd had a house full of kids, and now her house was full of silence. If you weren't used to it, that much quiet could make any small predicament or crisis seem worse.

Break-ups were different for everyone, not just how couples handled them but what type of life they had prior to the split. Some women would feel relieved while others could be devastated.

It made him want to be there for her even more. But he felt guilty since she'd opened up to him, and he really hadn't told her much about his past.

He wanted to tell her everything, especially now that she was honest and unguarded. He hadn't seen her act shy before, and although it was out of character, it was also endearing. He was so attracted to her confidence that it surprised him by how charmed he was by her vulnerability. She was complicated and passionate, and he couldn't remember ever feeling more drawn to another woman. It was unnerving since he'd been with a lot of different types of women. However, in just a few short weeks this redhead had his full attention, and he was pretty sure she didn't know it.

She set her coffee down and looked straight at him before she spoke. "I hope I didn't freak you out last night with my sob story."

"Don't make light of it, Sydney. It was real and honest. You have no idea what I've seen, trust me."

She smiled at him and then looked away. "What is it about you that makes all of this," she pointed to herself, "acceptable in your eyes? I mean, everyone, and I do mean everyone, has taken Drake's side and written me off. The judge decided in about two seconds that I was guilty and gave them the restraining order. Even the divorce judge sided with Drake."

Ryan gave her a reassuring smile. "I might be a little biased, but I think we should talk to Reagan about it."

"I don't want to bother her." Sydney was embarrassed of her past. She'd often thought about how ashamed her father would have been.

Ryan moved closer to Sydney, and her stomach did that tightening thing again. What was she going to do about her feelings for him?

"I don't think you understand, Sydney. She's one of the best divorce attorneys in the state. She has a list of who's who in her client base, and she doesn't talk about it to anyone." He used that deep voice that proved how steady and strong he was, and it made Sydney catch her breath.

She couldn't look at him, not right that second, or he would see the longing in her eyes. She felt weak, and she didn't like being vulnerable. It's what got her into trouble with Drake in the first place. She openly showed her emotions when it came to relationships. She gave everything. It would have worked if her partner did the same, but she hadn't met a selfless man other than her dad.

Ryan reached for the quilt and covered her legs before he sat down on the coffee table directly in front of her.

"It may be hard to believe, but I've had moments that I'm not proud of, too." He gave her that smirk that she was beginning to enjoy, and she stared at him.

"No kidding?"

"No kidding." His smile gave way to a more serious expression, and Sydney waited for him to explain.

"After high school, I joined the Marines. It was what I was meant to do, at least I thought it was and I loved it. I'd been an average student and hadn't really liked school, but I excelled at most things Marines."

Sydney set her cup down on the side table. She hadn't finished her coffee, but she didn't want anything to distract her. It was the most serious she had ever seen Ryan, and she wanted him to know that she was listening.

"I moved around a lot, going to training, and there was nothing that I couldn't do, but shooting was by far my talent. It was what I was known for, and I couldn't escape the fact that no one else was as accurate or as fast as me."

"Sniper?"

He nodded his head. "I went to school to be a scout sniper, and did that for a while, but later joined a special ops team. My specialties were amphibious reconnaissance and raids."

"Amphibious?"

"I'm good with water." He smiled and pointed toward the lake.

"Your home away from home," Sydney said, half-teasing.

Ryan stared into her warm brown eyes. There was comfort

there. "I was good at getting in and getting out where others couldn't. We were a very specialized team."

Sydney scooted to the edge of the sofa where her knees were almost touching his. "You did that for a long time?"

He nodded his head. "Five years." He turned to look at her. "I was in for ten."

They watched as the people in the canoe from earlier rowed back by going the other direction. He shook his head and focused on Sydney again.

"My girlfriend left me three years after I joined the Marines."

Sydney watched him, but his face was expressionless. She couldn't figure out where he was going with his story or how it was similar to hers.

"She didn't like that I was gone most of the time, so she sent me a Dear John letter. She'd been cheating on me the entire time, but she fell for a bartender at one of the clubs she went to, and got pregnant."

Sydney reached out and held his hand, but he didn't act like he needed reassuring. "Were you upset?"

Ryan shrugged. "I would say no, but I haven't gotten serious with another woman since."

Sydney understood he was explaining why he ran around with different women, but he wasn't going to out and out say it.

"Eventually, I'd had enough of military life and moved home. I lived with Reagan. I was having a hard time adjusting to civilian life. I didn't have a job, couldn't sleep, and according to Reagan, I was unstable. I got angry. A lot."

He stopped for a minute, and Sydney now understood how it must have been for him last night hearing her tell her story. Listening to his tale was painful.

"I put Reagan through hell. I would go out drinking and come home bloody from a fight or not come home for a couple of days. She called the cops several times, hoping they would find me. Eventually, I left and stayed gone for weeks. I was sleeping under an overpass when she found me."

Ryan stood up. He was restless, and Sydney understood. She followed him to the glass doors and wrapped her arms around his waist from behind and leaned her head on his back. It had given her comfort when he'd hugged her.

He turned around and wrapped his body around her. It was incredible and the most intimate moment she'd had in years and her clothes were on. She took a deep breath and took in his smell. He was all clean soap and a natural scent that was his own. She closed her eyes and for a moment didn't think about how she should put some space between them. After a few minutes, she backed away, giving him some room. This friendly relationship was going to get her into serious trouble.

Ryan smiled at her and understood they were getting close and it was too much for her. He took an exaggerated big breath and began telling her the rest of his story.

"I didn't realize that I was suffering from PTSD. My sister sat there under a freaking bridge and talked me into going to the Veteran's Hospital for some help. It saved my life. She saved my life. It took a month or so, and then I moved out here and remodeled my uncle's house that he had left us. Reagan sent a car each week to pick me up and take me to my counseling sessions and then she invested in my remodeling business. She told me she thought this was what I was meant to do, and now, three years later, I'm finishing my eighth house."

"You had PTSD from your time in the Marines?"

"Everything I did was classified," he said and stared into Sydney's eyes. She felt the weight of what he was not saying.

"You don't have to tell me. I understand."

"Two of my closest friends were killed on our last mission. I couldn't save them. I did get the rest of our team out of there, but I was wounded." He lifted his shirt, and she could see the scar that ran down the side of his body and below his waistband. She gently reached out and touched it. She could see chill bumps pop up on his skin, and she trembled. He was as attracted to her as she was to him. She put her hand down and looked at him.

"It looks really bad."

"I ended up losing too much blood. I barely made it out, and when I finally did, I was in the hospital for weeks. The doctor said he hadn't seen anyone come back from that much blood loss without brain damage. Reagan laughed at him when he told her that. She said you couldn't damage something that wasn't there. My sister, the comedian."

Sydney was biting her bottom lip and struggling not to cry. She couldn't imagine the world without Ryan Gentry in it. He was a rock. He was the strongest man besides her father that she'd ever known.

She leaned up and kissed him hard on the lips, taking him by surprise. It was more than he could have hoped for, and Ryan wrapped his arms around her and lifted her off the ground as he kissed her back.

Chapter Seventeen

Power was not restored to Sydney and Ryan's side of the lake until early evening. They spent the day talking about where they grew up. Ryan and his sister were city kids part of the time and country kids the other half when they visited their dad. Then they enjoyed lake life in the summers with their uncle, who was self-employed and had time to be with them every day. Sydney grew up in a suburb of the city and had a nice, quiet small town lifestyle.

They discussed home restoration and how much the small community meant to Ryan. Sydney had only started coming here with her kids about five years ago. It reminded her of the places her father had taken her fishing and camping.

Ryan explained how the lake community had fallen out of favor with tourists a few years back after some bad storms wreaked destruction on the area. There weren't many places for rent except for the east side of town, where Drake and the boys were staying right now, but it used to be for private homeowners only.

He loved the west side of town, where his house was built. Years ago, the area was a self-contained little town, with a grocery, a couple of restaurants, and a drive-in movie theater. He specifically wanted to give it that old time charm and bring it back into its golden era again. At least, that's what he built his business model around. Hoping families would come back in the summertime and spend their lazy days of summer here, making memories like he did as a boy.

Reagan had promised him that once he finished his tenth house, she would partner with him to redo the drive-in movie theater. The land was tied up in some legal paperwork, and it was going to take some extra time to get it unencumbered. He'd made a deal with her when he was working on his second house, and now he was close to making it happen.

"I haven't been to a drive-in theater," Sydney said, lying back on his couch as she thought about how much fun that would for her kids.

"Once our parents divorced, they shipped us off to Uncle Trey a lot. We would swim or fish most days and go to the movies at night. You could fill your car up with as many people as you wanted and get in for twenty dollars. Uncle Trey would pile us in the car, including the neighbors up and down Lake Road. Kids were hanging out of the trunk. It was great! We could fit fifteen in there if we laid a couple across our laps in the back."

"How could you see the movie?" Sydney asked.

"Once we got there, Uncle Trey would let us sit outside or on top of the car. He also bought us tons of popcorn." His fondness for his uncle was endearing. "Those were some of my best memories as a kid."

"I would love to help with a drive-in. Give it a retro fifties look. During the summer we could host a teen night around Fourth of July and help parents out. It could drum up a lot of business."

Sydney stood up and acted like she was interested in the scenery outside to avoid Ryan's stare. He hadn't asked her if she wanted to work with him on the theater.

Ryan smiled at her sudden apprehension. His confident woman needed reassurance. Just another side to Sydney that he liked. He stood beside her and gently nudged his shoulder into hers. "I think we would do a great job together with a drive-in theater. Besides, I'm the muscle and you're the brains of this operation."

Sydney rolled her eyes and pointed around his beautiful lake house. "Seriously? You and I both know you have what it takes without me, Ryan. I'm not sure why you've chosen me to help you." She kept looking at the lake, avoiding his stare. "But I am grateful. I love doing it."

Ryan wrapped an arm around her shoulders and pulled her into him. He was thrilled that she enjoyed the work, but he wasn't about to explain why he had asked her to help him. He could admit to himself that he was wildly attracted to her, but it was the thought of her going through such a difficult time without anyone to help her that had first touched his heart. It drew him to her in a way nothing else could have. She was still on uncertain ground, and he didn't want to overwhelm her.

"So you're saying you've bought into my lake restoration project? The whole thing?" he asked. He waggled his eyebrows at her. Sydney nodded, still nervous.

"I'm glad to hear it, Red. This is your first storm here, and once that water goes down, we have some clean-up to do. It would normally take weeks, but the whole town volunteers to come out and get it done. You up for that?"

Sydney put on her brave face, the one she'd perfected since she was a young girl, and nodded. The truth was that her stomach was doing flips since she woke up at Ryan's house that morning. She couldn't slow down the attraction she felt and having his arm around her made it worse. They'd spent too much time together in the last twenty-four hours, and it was starting to affect her in crazy ways. She had to put some distance between them. She should have gone to her own house.

Maybe picking up debris and physically working on clean up would give her the fresh air and clarity that she needed. After all, she came to Maisonville for a specific reason, and she wasn't going to give up on getting her boys back, not even for a beautiful man like Ryan Gentry. *Focus, Sydney.*

Early evening, as the power was restored around the lake, Ryan and Sydney worked on sending emails and handing out flyers for a community clean-up initiative the very next morning. They would gather and start work at daybreak, and Ryan added a list of tools and supplies that were needed, too.

It was early dawn when Sydney stumbled out of her house with large garbage bags and ran into Ryan in the driveway.

"Come and ride with me, Red," he said. "I've got coffee." He held up a large thermos, and Sydney followed him like he was a lighthouse and the thermos a beacon light.

She was mentally scolding herself because she had thought for a second that he'd said, "Come and ride me," and she was still ready to hurry over to him. She needed freaking caffeine like she needed air to breathe.

Ryan was talkative that morning. He appeared to have been up for hours and was perkier than the day's events warranted. Sydney was not a morning person and it took all of her self-control to not glare at him when he asked her questions. Finally, she had to stop him.

"Look, Ryan, I know that today's bad decisions aren't going to make themselves, I'm all in, but I need caffeine before I can chat about it."

Ryan raised an eyebrow at her and smirked, contemplating what she was saying. "So what type of bad decisions do you plan on making today, Red?"

Sydney laughed out loud and blushed at the innuendo of her phrase. It was something she'd said since she was a young girl and seldom had anyone questioned her on it. People usually laughed it off, and that was that, but of course, Ryan wasn't like anyone else.

"For starters, getting out of bed this early, and second, riding in a behemoth truck with a morning person. There is no telling how much worse it's going to get."

Ryan laughed at her and shook his head. He didn't talk anymore until they reached the trail head and he parked in the gravel. Sydney could see that a handful of people had already started gathering, and, of course, they were smiling and talking. She wasn't sure she was ready for all of the cheerfulness at that hour, but she had at least consumed a full cup of coffee and was starting on another as Ryan grabbed a notebook and led her over to the group.

Within thirty minutes, there were two hundred people waiting for instructions, and Ryan had signup sheets for various areas that needed work. It was incredible, and Sydney was proud to be a part of such a community. It reminded her of her hometown.

She followed Ryan everywhere he went and picked up trash or nailed up signs; whatever he was doing, she was with him. She didn't talk for the first half of the day, just simply watched and admired him. She'd thought she had him figured out and yet, here he was doing more selfless work for others. He was kind to others and a leader in the community. Most the residents in town looked to him when they had a question about what to do or how to do something. He smiled and laughed with several of the older men and made time for anyone who had a question. If she hadn't already fallen so hard for him, today would have pushed her into it. He was a force, leading the troops to clean up their town.

By lunch, Ryan sent people back over to the trail head, where volunteers were standing by with hot lunches. They had jambalaya and French bread for anyone that was hungry. He was the last to eat, and Sydney stayed by his side as he repaired a wooden fence that had been destroyed by a fallen tree. He'd first used a chainsaw to cut it into pieces, small enough to haul off, and then pulled out fence posts that were the appropriate size. Sydney helped hold them and then nailed some into place. She hadn't built a fence before and felt useful assisting him.

She sat next to him as they ate lunch on the tailgate of his pickup truck, and he threw the trash away when they finished eating. It was time to get back to work, and as she was opening the passenger door to climb into his truck, he was there to help her.

"You're the sexiest woman I've ever seen, Sydney Bell," he

whispered into her ear. Sydney lost her breath at the feel of his warm words, and then he kissed her. He kissed her right there where anyone could see.

For a moment, she didn't care what the world thought; she kissed him right back, shutting everything else out. But then she felt the other's looking at her and quickly climbed into the truck.

"What?" he asked.

She shook her head but didn't say a word; the other volunteers were watching them.

The energy between them in the truck was palpable, and neither of them spoke. They were back near the camping area next to the lake and Ryan was pulling out a shovel and handing her some garbage bags but avoiding looking at her.

She wasn't sure what was going on, but the sweet feeling she had before when he kissed her was gone, and the mood between them didn't feel right. She looked around, but the rest of the workers weren't paying attention to them. She leaned up and kissed Ryan on the cheek, making him stop and look at her. "We should get to work, Sydney."

His words surprised her. Did she upset him earlier when he kissed her? Should she have said or done something afterward? She had no idea what was going on inside his head. He gave her that raised eyebrow that he must have practiced in the mirror, and she stared back at him before she could find her words.

"I didn't mean to hurt your feelings earlier."

"You didn't."

Sydney exhaled her frustration. "I think I did, and I should explain." She had her hands on her hips, daring him to talk, and this time he kept quiet.

"I'm not used to PDA." Again he gave her the raised eyebrow. "You know, public displays of affection. I'm not used to that, and you surprised me, that's all. Drake didn't kiss me in public. It was like he didn't want people to know we were together. He didn't even hold my hand, and, well, you surprised me." She looked past him, avoiding his critical stare, and whispered. "But I liked it. I liked it a lot more than I ever expected."

Ryan stared at her for a minute, and she couldn't tell if he believed her or if he could care less. As usual, she kept talking. "I mean, I always thought it would be amazing to be so in love that you couldn't help but touch each other and show affection, no matter who was around."

Suddenly, Ryan reached over and pulled her into him tightly. He kissed her until she was breathless. His hands were in her hair, and up and down her back, and when he let her go, she stumbled. The men who she'd thought were busy began whistling and hollering, and she laughed and hid her face in Ryan's chest.

When she looked up, Ryan was grinning like she'd never seen him, and without another word, he picked up his tools, grabbed her by the hand and pulled her over to where they were working next.

Chapter Eighteen

The sunset was a deep red-orange color as Sydney and Ryan headed home for the night. They completed the fence repair and cleaned their entire quadrant designated on the map. It was a good day, and Sydney couldn't remember ever being that physically tired.

She leaned against her door and was drifting off as she stared at how beautiful Ryan was, even with the layer of dirt that covered him. It felt so natural being with him all day, and she was happy for the first time in a long while. She needed to be honest and tell him the truth about why she had moved to the lake, but it would have to wait until tomorrow after she had some sleep.

Tonight she wanted to shower the mud and muck off her entire body and crawl into bed. Actually, she would crawl to the couch, which was where she felt most comfortable.

As soon as they pulled onto their street, they could see the dark SUV in front of Sydney's house. Ryan carefully pulled in beside it, and they saw Darryl sitting on the porch.

"This isn't a good idea, Sydney."

She looked at Ryan and then shrugged. Before he could put the truck into park, she opened her door and got out, but not before she told him, "They're all I've got, and nothing else matters."

Her stomach contracted at the hurt look on his face as she shut the door. Ryan didn't look back as he threw his truck into reverse and drove into his garage.

Sydney regretted the words she'd said to Ryan as soon as they left her mouth, but she had hurt each day that she wasn't with her boys. It wasn't natural for her to not talk to them. And if one of them ever came to her needing to talk, then she would break the court order and do it. Damn the consequences.

Darryl stood when he saw her get out of the truck and hugged her tightly as she stepped onto the porch.

"Mom, I was so worried about you. We lost electricity for a few hours, but we had a generator. The water came up on our street, but I kept thinking about how close you were to the lake."

She held his face in her hands. "I'm fine, D. You don't have to worry so much about me. I'm resourceful, and I have a handy neighbor who also has a boat. We were fine over here."

Sydney had also worried about them, but Ryan had told her they were at a safer distance from the lake and had nothing but street flooding.

"I thought you would have headed back home by now. Isn't this the last day of fall break?"

Darryl avoided looking at her. "I had to know if you were okay and dad wouldn't have agreed to let me call you."

Sydney kissed his cheek and asked him to come inside for something to eat and drink. She didn't have anything except for day old donuts and milk, but Darryl was appreciative for it. He was surprised that the mother who cooked great meals for him and his brothers didn't have anything real to eat in her house.

"You don't cook anymore, Momma?" he asked with a sad look in his eyes.

"It feels a little weird to cook for just one person. One day when you boys can come stay with me, I'll cook a big meal, okay?"

"Do you think that will ever happen? It doesn't feel like it will. Especially if Gina has anything to say about it. I miss you. I'm so sick of this. We want you to come back home."

Sydney hated to admit that she could no longer imagine herself with Drake. She wanted to be with her children more than anything, but she was starting to belong in Maisonville. She wasn't certain where Ryan fit into her life, but she was happy whenever she spent time with him. As she hugged Darryl, her mother's intuition hit her square in the heart. There was more going on with him than he was letting on.

"Darryl? Do you have school tomorrow?"

He looked at her and slowly nodded his head.

Her heart sunk. "Did you drive your father's car out here from the city by yourself?"

It was at least forty-five minutes to their house across the lake.

Darryl avoided her face until she leaned over to look at him and whispered the question again. "Did you drive here from your house tonight?"

He nodded his head, and then the doorbell rang and a loud knock came at the door.

Sydney slowly went to answer it as Darryl started explaining. "You don't understand, Mom. He wouldn't have let me come if I asked him. I needed to talk to you."

Sydney opened the door to two state police officers, the local sheriff, Drake, and Gina.

It took less than five minutes for them to come inside, and determine that Sydney had broken the law by seeing Darryl. It didn't matter that he'd driven to see her or that he swore it was his idea. He was a minor, and she knew the law as the judge had laid it out for her.

As a courtesy to the town sheriff, the state police waited until Darryl was tucked inside his father's car before they handcuffed Sydney. She didn't make excuses or argue; she just stared coldly at Drake as they read her rights and then led her to the police car.

Ryan had been in the shower, and didn't hear the commotion until she was put in the backseat of a cruiser.

He ran outside attempting to stop them. "This is ridiculous. We drove up, and the kid was already here. She volunteered and worked all day by my side as part of the flood clean-up crew. She couldn't have called anyone to coordinate this. She can't be held responsible when they can't keep their child from taking a car, driving underage, and then coming to see his step-mom."

Tim, the sheriff, had been a longtime friend of Ryan's uncle and now was his friend, too. He nodded his head and put his hand on his shoulder. "I wish I could do more about this, but the truth is, Ryan, that nasty woman is a lawyer, and she's making a federal case of it. Literally."

Ryan shook his head and then ran over to talk to Sydney through the glass window of the police car.

"I'll come for you," he said, sickened over the last words they had as well as the defeated look on Sydney's face.

She nodded and then leaned back in the seat, facing straight ahead so he wouldn't see her tears.

She didn't think she could hold them in much longer, especially with him looking at her like that and acting so worried. He was a great man, and she'd mistreated him. Shoved him to the side when what he'd tried to do was help her over and over again. The shame of that behavior overrode what was happening at the moment.

Ryan watched as the police car pulled out with Sydney in the back and then Drake and Gina drove away in their SUV with Darryl in the back. He couldn't miss the tears in the young man's eyes or the glare in Gina and Drake's as they stared at him before they left.

He didn't blink as he glared back at them. Gina might be a lawyer, but he was related to one who would take her down.

Chapter Nineteen

Ryan drove straight into the city to meet Reagan. She was waiting when the officers walked in and booked Sydney. She'd made a few phone calls and talked to a few fellow attorneys for advice, but things were more complicated than Ryan knew.

It was an hour before Sydney was signed into the jail and able to talk to Reagan. Ryan was outside waiting impatiently. He couldn't believe they couldn't post bail tonight. He didn't want Sydney to have to stay there.

Sydney was sitting in a metal chair in a small room. Everything there was the same washed out gray color. It was depressing. Reagan came in wearing a smart black suit, and Sydney was more aware of how disheveled she looked in her orange jail scrubs and unwashed hair. She looked at Reagan but couldn't find any words.

Reagan went straight to her and hugged her tightly. "It'll be alright, Sydney. We've got a lot of work to do, but I'm going to fight for you."

Sydney couldn't control her emotions when this woman who hardly knew her extended kindness just because Sydney was friends with her brother; it was almost too much.

Reagan sat down across from her and reached across the table to hold Sydney's hand. "We don't have much time, but I need to ask you a few questions."

"First, is Ryan okay?"

"He's waiting outside." Reagan gave her a smile. "He's worried about you."

Sydney wiped her tears and nodded. "Tell him I'm sorry and that he was right."

"I'll tell him."

Sydney sat there for a second and then looked back at Reagan. "You can tell him everything."

They spent the next twenty minutes going over the charges, and then Sydney finally got to tell her side of the story.

Afterward, Ryan followed Reagan back to her downtown apartment and stood to look out at the city lights while she made them both a Jim Beam over ice, her drink of choice.

"Little brother, this isn't going to be easy."

Ryan didn't look at her. Instead, he took a drink of the liquor and continued to stare out the large glass view of downtown. He wouldn't live here if he were given the penthouse suite, but he could appreciate the beauty of it all.

"Tell me, Reagan."

"They are going after her hard. A few months ago, she was arrested for stalking Gina and kidnapping the boys. They questioned her mental health then, and she was held for a mental evaluation for a week. They didn't get very far. The judge did grant them a protective order against her. The judge told her that she was not allowed around any of them. She didn't listen. She continued to drive by their house and would follow them out to restaurants so she could sneak and see the boys. They had cameras and caught her. She was sent for a mental evaluation again. The judge then threatened her with jail time. Drake and Gina tried to make a case that she was dangerous, but again, the judge let her go. He warned her that if there was a next time, she would go to jail. The divorce happened, and she was screwed out of everything. I'm not certain how they did that, and I'm not finished going through the entire case yet, but they were able to kick her to the curb with nothing but a few trinkets, her car that he bought her and some clothes. She wasn't given any right to the boys and no visitation. Gina fought like a rabid dog to keep Sydney out of their lives. It looked like Sydney had an inexperienced attorney. She walked away with less than she came with, and it's amazing she didn't blow sooner."

Ryan looked at her. "She didn't blow, Reagan. She didn't do anything."

"They have a statement from the son that Sydney contacted him and told him to sneak and come see her. He's a minor, and I'm telling you, it looks bad on paper. "

"When could she have contacted him? She spent the night with me after the storm because our power went out and the water was rising. She was home for a few hours the next night, but she left her phone at my house. I picked her up at five this morning, and we worked for thirteen hours, cleaning up the community. Her phone was in my truck uncharged until she got home, where Darryl was sitting on her porch."

"He's saying something different. It's his word against hers."

"It's a lie, Reagan."

She stood next to him, looking out the window, and they drank together silently.

❦

DESPITE GOING to bed after one, Reagan was up and dressed by six the next morning. Ryan had slept restlessly on Reagan's couch and stirred when he heard his sister making coffee in the kitchen.

He looked like a wreck, and she gave him the first cup of black coffee. "I have to go into the office and have my assistant clear my calendar this morning. Sydney will be arraigned first thing, and I need to be there."

Before he could ask, she told him, "You can be in the court, but don't talk to her. I'm going to try and get them to release her, but it just depends on the judge and whether or not he thinks she's a real threat to the boys. They are going to say she's dangerous, and he might not let her out, or he could charge a large bail amount if he thinks she's a flight risk."

"I can get the money if she needs it." Ryan ran his hands over the stubble on his jaw. He knew it was bad news when he saw Darryl waiting on her porch, but he couldn't have imagined just how bad.

At 7:30, Ryan sat outside the courtroom waiting to see if he could get a glimpse at Sydney. He didn't, but he was there when Reagan came through with her assistant and another attorney. His sister was just as fierce as she looked, and although he was worried about Sydney, he knew she couldn't be in better hands.

Reagan winked but didn't stop to speak to him. She was busy talking to the younger attorney walking in with her.

Ryan went into the small courtroom to wait for Sydney. He listened to a couple of domestic abuse cases, one where the judge gave a permanent protective order against the defendant and the other where the judge gave a man a year's jail time for disobeying his restraining order on purpose.

His heart sank as he realized the judge was a no nonsense type of man and briefly listened to the accused before handing down the maximum sentence to each one.

When Sydney entered the courtroom, her head was down, and she was wearing orange jailhouse scrubs. She didn't get to shower after yesterday, and it reminded him of himself when he was homeless. His heart ached for her. She stood next to Reagan, and for a minute, it looked like the case might get thrown out because the other side hadn't shown up.

Then Gina strutted in, wearing what his sister would call her red power suit, without a hair out of place. Drake followed behind her, wearing a perfectly tailored black suit with a red tie, and Ryan rolled his eyes. It was only an arraignment, but they weren't going to let her get a break in any way.

Gina intimidated Sydney by staring her down, but Reagan

moved so she was blocking her view and instead gave Gina a smooth smile. It rattled Gina, and she dropped her folder and notes on the floor.

When the judge began talking, it sounded hopeless. He then acknowledged how unusual the situation was and asked each side questions, allowing Gina and then Reagan to speak.

Gina read a document from Drake about how scared the boys were of Sydney and how he worried that he couldn't keep her away from them.

When Gina said the boys were frightened, Reagan reached under the table and squeezed Sydney's hand.

Uncertain of how much leeway the judge was going to allow during this most unusual arraignment, Reagan pushed forward, offering up letters from Sydney's employers along with her previous neighbors showing how Sydney was a level headed loyal employee along with a considerate mother and neighbor.

When the hell did she have time to do that? Ryan thought as he sat in awe of his sister.

Reagan also took advantage of the judge's apparent leniency and explained that Sydney's ex, along with his live-in girlfriend, the prosecuting attorney, was not a trustworthy source for the boys' emotions. She added that Darryl couldn't be frightened of Sydney as he drove himself over to see her. It was more likely that they were upset over not seeing their mother.

When Gina objected with "step-mother," the judge reminded her it was an arraignment and there were no objections allowed.

Still, Sydney had broken the law, especially by inviting her son inside her house, but Reagan's tenacity in getting letters on Sydney's behalf helped strengthen her point that Sydney was not a danger to anyone.

The judge appeared to look both sides over heavily and then turned to Sydney and spoke directly to her. He didn't drop the felony charges against Sydney and set a date for trial where the boys would have to come in and give their testimony against her. He ordered a psychiatric evaluation, and tears filled Sydney's eyes.

Ryan had watched the judge hand out tough news most the morning and when he mentioned bail, Ryan was relieved that he didn't rule to keep Sydney in jail.

Gina was instantly furious at the judge, and he stopped his speech to address her.

"I rarely ask for additional information during an arraignment and I'm certain that I gave you ample time to speak," he said to Gina. "Do you have more you want to say to the court?"

Gina put her placid look back on her face and said, "No."

The judge cleared his throat and continued. "As I was saying, although bail may or may not be allowed in a criminal protective order case, I am allowing the defendant to be set free on her own recognizance.

Sydney was led out by the guard so she could change back into her clothes and then finally was released. It had taken two hours from the time she left the courthouse before she was free to go with Ryan.

The moment she walked out of jail, he wrapped his arms around her and squeezed her tight.

He drove straight home without stopping and couldn't miss the fact that Sydney didn't speak but a couple of words before she fell asleep in his truck.

When they arrived home, Sydney excused herself to go shower and change clothes. It was late afternoon when she walked barefoot to the end of her pier. The lake looked normal again, and she wished her life was, too. She sat down and held her head in her hands and cried.

Ryan watched her for a while, and when he couldn't take it any longer, he went out there and sat with her, holding her close.

"I'm sorry, Ryan. I should have listened to you. I was short with you last night, and you were right from the start."

"You don't have to apologize to me. You're under attack, Sydney. I've seen it. I saw Darryl waiting for you last night with my own two eyes. He was here because he loves you and wanted to talk with you. They out and out lied about him. They are systematically coming after you, and I want to help you fight. Those boys deserve more than Gina and Drake raising them."

Sydney shook her head. "I don't think I can fight anymore. I can't bear to think of the boys being frightened of me. Do you think any of that could be true? Do you think Darryl really said that to the police? I—I don't know what to think."

Ryan kissed her forehead and held her hand as she teared up again. "My poor, sweet boys. I've loved them from the moment I saw them, and the thought of putting them through a trial and forcing them to choose sides and hearing their father and me fight—I can't put them through that."

"At this point, you may not have a choice, Sydney. Gina plans to be their new mom."

Sydney turned her head and Ryan could see the storm in her eyes. He smiled at her. "I know it's hard to believe but she's doing whatever she can to replace you. She and Dr. Sleaze may deserve each other, but no way should they make it a crime for you to spend time with the boys."

Sydney nodded. "I'll fight."

"I know you will, Red." He kissed her forehead and held her tighter.

Chapter Twenty

Ryan and Sydney sat out on the pier for hours. When it finally turned dark, he gently pulled her up to go inside his house.

"I'm starving, and we need to eat some dinner."

Sydney nodded.

"Want to ride with me to Miss Lynn's? You can sit in the truck while I run inside and pick up dinner for us." He moved in closer to her and kissed her sweetly. "I don't want to leave you here alone." He kissed her again. "Or be away from you," he said.

"I'm fine, Ryan," she said, avoiding his stare.

He bent over, so they were face to face. "I'm not okay, baby."

Sydney stared into his eyes for a second and then planted a kiss on his mouth. He didn't say another word, just grabbed his keys in one hand and held her hand in the other.

"The whole town will be buzzing, wanting to know what happened or I would have you go in with me. Is it okay if I tell Miss Lynn an abbreviated version?" he asked.

"I've been pretty secretive the whole time I've been here. Miss Lynn's not going to understand. No one will. I didn't tell her or Olivia that I have kids. They know I have an ex, but I think they thought it was an ex-boyfriend, not husband." Sydney was frowning as she looked out the window into the dark. "I feel so foolish."

"It's going to be okay, Sydney. It gets easier with each step you take."

Sydney shook her head. "You don't understand, Ryan. I didn't learn my lesson. Not there. Not here. I moved here because the twins had overheard their Dad talking to Gina about buying a second home at the lake. I figured if I got here first then I would get to spend vacations or holidays with the boys. I had no intention of staying away from them. I was just going to be sneakier about it, possibly use a boat, and show up where they were. It was stupid to think that Drake would eventually stop pushing me away. While we were married, he didn't spend a lot of time with the boys. He didn't like to take time off work, and I thought if I waited a while, he would eventually want a break, maybe want to spend some alone time with his demanding girlfriend. Now I'm going to lose everything. I might go to federal prison. My father must be rolling over in his grave at this very moment. Sheriff Jeffrey Bell's only daughter, a felon."

Ryan pulled into the diner parking lot and took off his seat belt so he could move in closer to Sydney. "You listen to me, Sydney Bell. We've all had secrets and made bad decisions for what we thought was the right thing. I helped blow up villages trying to free soldiers. I killed people, and I have to live with that for the rest of my days. I lost my two best friends in battle, and they both had children back home. I didn't think I deserved to be the one who lived. I didn't want this life anymore."

It wasn't the way Ryan wanted to tell her, but he couldn't listen to her run herself down anymore. She needed to know that lots of people made mistakes. It was what you did afterward that made the difference.

Sydney's eyes were huge as she stared at Ryan. He couldn't see her pupils from the dark brown of her eyes. She breathed heavily as she stared at him, and his heart sunk, thinking what she must believe of him now. The next second she grabbed his shirt and pulled him into a hard kiss, and then she hugged him tightly against her body. The truck windows were fogged up when she let him go and Ryan was speechless as he caught his breath.

"I don't want to think of a life without you in it, Ryan Gentry. I can't. Don't you ever think you aren't a wonderful person. Look at what you've done for this community. You inspire others to be better people, better neighbors." Sydney kissed him again and again.

Ryan laughed when he saw Wesley walk by his truck and then heard him whistle. "Red, I need to go pick up our food. Trust me when I tell you that we're both going to need our strength, because I'm not going to let you out of my sight anytime soon."

Sydney nodded and slowly let the collar of his shirt go and straightened out her clothes. "Okay, go get some food. I'll wait here. Hurry," she said, like she wasn't going to make it long without doing that again.

Ryan laughed as he got out of the truck and hurried into Miss Lynn's. It didn't take but ten minutes and Ryan was back. He laughed, telling Sydney that most of the people in the restaurant were watching them fog up the windows. They had bets on whether or not the couple would get out of the truck and actually eat and when he walked in, Miss Lynn had already told the kitchen to put together two dinner specials to go.

"She didn't ask you what happened or why I had been arrested?" Sydney was shocked.

Ryan shook his head. "She kissed me on the cheek and told me to be good to you."

"She thinks we're together," Sydney said, looking at the restaurant.

"I'm not going to lie, Sydney, I want to be together."

Sydney's stomach tightened as she heard Ryan admit his feelings. If she were honest, she'd wanted him for weeks, but hadn't allowed herself to believe he felt the same.

They crashed inside the front door of his house because they suddenly couldn't keep their hands off each other. Ryan pulled his shirt off as Sydney unbuttoned her own. He kicked off his shoes inside the doorway and pulled off each sock, too. Sydney toed off her shoes, unbuttoned her jeans and slid them to the floor before they made it to the kitchen to drop off the Styrofoam boxes of food. Ryan grabbed one of the cups of sweet tea, took a drink and then gave Sydney one before they continued stripping in front of each other. She finished first and stood there, watching him as he dropped his skivvies onto the floor and looked over to stare at her. She smiled but didn't flinch as he looked her up and down. She just kept staring back at him, and that confidence got to him. He could feel heat consume his entire being. She was a gorgeous natural redhead with glowing soft skin, and he couldn't take his eyes off her. She giggled and turned around to turn off the one and only lamp in his living room before they collided into one another.

They dropped to the couch, and their hands explored each other as their kisses became more desperate. Sydney felt like she'd been starving for that kind of passion.

"I've never wanted anyone the way I want you, Ryan Gentry," she whispered.

Sydney was a good bit smaller than him, and Ryan was worried about crushing her since they were both in a frenzy. He just had time to get a condom before he grabbed a blanket and rolled them off the couch and onto the floor, maneuvering Sydney on top.

He pulled her lips into his and groaned when she straddled his lap. There was no way they would get enough of each other one time, and he gave her a wicked look as he turned her over for his turn at being in control.

Afterward, they lay on the floor next to each other, letting their racing heartbeats slow. Ryan kissed her several times. She lazily rolled over onto her stomach to look out his back door toward the lake. The moon was full, and she loved how bright the lake was that evening.

Ryan rolled over too and laid a leg possessively over her and an arm across her middle. He kissed the top of her head as they watched the water glisten in the moonlight.

"Want to eat out on the deck?" he asked Sydney.

"Not that hungry," she whispered. "Not for food."

Ryan leaned in to kiss her ear and nip her earlobe. "You are insatiable."

Sydney bit her bottom lip as she nodded.

"Look, naughty girl, I need some food, and then I will ravish your body again. Deal?"

"Fine," she said, pouting and making him grin at her.

Ryan grabbed his pants and pulled them on quickly, but Sydney simply wrapped the blanket loosely around her naked body and went outside with her food. She ate half her dinner and then sat there sipping iced tea.

Ryan practically inhaled his food. "I'm warning you, Sydney. You don't want to give me that sultry look sitting there all fresh and naked. I can't be held responsible for my actions now that I've had nourishment."

Sydney climbed onto the large handmade table and lay down on top of the blanket she'd brought outside. "Do your worst, Mr. Gentry."

He scrambled to remove the food containers so he had plenty of room. He planned to do his very best.

❧

THE SUN SLIPPED through the curtains in Ryan's bedroom and woke Sydney. She was draped in Ryan's arms and legs and nothing else. When she peeked out from under her wild hair, he was staring at her.

"Morning, beautiful."

She rolled her eyes but gave him a quick smile. "Good morning yourself."

"You usually sleep on your stomach?" he asked, rubbing his warm hands across her bottom.

Sydney smiled and whispered, "Not since I was younger." She knew that it was because she felt safe with him. Safe and comfortable.

Ryan whispered into her ear. "Sex or coffee?"

"Can I have both?"

He laughed at her and pulled her over to him so they could make love again before he gave her the full cup of coffee he had waiting for her on the nightstand.

After they had showered, Sydney pulled on a giant sweatshirt of Ryan's and joined him downstairs. He was making some scrambled eggs, and she wrapped her arms around his middle. "I can't believe you didn't make me go home last night."

"What?" Ryan poured eggs onto two plates that already had toast and bacon for each of them.

"Thanks," she said, picking both plates up and carrying them over to his small round dining room table. "You know, you make your women leave after sex."

Ryan shook his head. "Let's get one thing straight, Sydney Bell."

Sydney opened her eyes wide like she was giving him her full attention, and he yanked her into his lap, making her gasp.

He kissed her while her mouth was open, and she laughed at him.

"This is serious, Red. Look at me."

Sydney tried to look seriously at him, but she couldn't wipe the grin off her face.

"I don't have women. I've dated a lot of nice women, but I haven't been serious with any one person until now. I'm serious about you."

Sydney softly kissed him on the lips. "Why?"

Ryan held her tightly and kissed her breathless. "You're not a woman I could get over easily, Sydney."

Sydney's eyes watered. "I don't share very nicely," she admitted.

Ryan fed her some eggs and kissed her on the cheek. "Eat some breakfast, Sydney. After last night, you need your strength."

Sydney laughed and then scooted back over to her seat. "Hmpf, you mean after last night, you need your strength. I'm just fine."

Ryan had work to do, and Sydney tagged along. He had a checklist to complete on the Clapboard house that Sydney had decorated. It had to be ready by the end of the week for the new owners, and it was good for her to see the process since he planned to have her working with him fulltime.

Next, they headed over to what he referred to as the White House and Sydney called the haunted mansion so that he could discuss construction details with his crew. While he was going through the plans with his foreman, Sydney was sharing coffee and handing out bottles of water to the workers. She chatted with a few and laughed with others.

Who could believe that woman was dangerous? She was passionate and fought for those she loved. It was the biggest lie Drake and Gina could fabricate against her, and suggesting she was unstable was cruel on a deeper level.

There was a lot to get done at the new house, but Ryan needed more alone time with Sydney. It was a crucial point in their relationship, and he needed to be close to her. To let her know how important she was to him.

He would fight for her and do whatever it took to help her through the situation she was in with her ex-husband.

The more he learned about the divorce and charges against Sydney, the more questions he had concerning Drake's motivation. He got the fact that Drake had cheated on Sydney with Gina. He could even see that the man salivated over that reptilian woman. He was personally thankful for it because Sydney was meant to be his. However, Sydney had raised those boys as her own and was the only mother they knew. He could tell she was an amazing mother. Why would Drake hurt them that way? Lots of people divorced and shared custody of their children. With their biological mother dying tragically, wouldn't Drake want those boys to have the stability of sweet Sydney? Things just didn't add up.

He looked over and saw Sydney watching him. There was something so warm and loving about her. Those brown eyes full of mischief and her fiery mouth; he could spend the rest of his life with her.

Sydney walked over and cuddled up close to him, curling her arms around one of his. "What are ya thinking?"

"I think we should go home for the rest of the afternoon," he whispered in her ear.

He loved the smile she gave him as much as the way she inhaled and deeply exhaled when he suggested they be alone.

It was colder outside today, which was the reason they had such a terrific storm last week. But it didn't stop either one of them from shucking their clothes on the way inside the house, so they could make love in the living room again, before heading upstairs to his large king sized bed.

They spent the entire afternoon in each other's arms and were startled at four-thirty when they heard the front door open.

"Um, hello! Put some clothes on before you come downstairs, Ryan!" Reagan yelled, loud enough for them both to hear her.

Sydney's face turned pink as she whispered, "All of our clothes are on the floor downstairs."

"I think she approves of you, Sydney." Ryan laughed, thinking about his sister catching them at his house together. Reagan knew he dated a lot but hadn't actually seen him with anyone. That was going to be interesting.

Sydney jumped up and found a flannel shirt of Ryan's to put on. It looked like a sloppy dress on her, but she looked perfect to him. She went into the bathroom to freshen up, and he threw on some clothes and headed downstairs ahead of Sydney as if he could curtail some of his sister's comments, but knowing full well that Reagan had a mind and mouth of her own.

She was sitting at his dining room table, drinking out of her travel coffee mug. "Imagine my surprise when I went to your job site and they said you were gone for the day." She smiled. "That hasn't ever happened before, has it, baby brother?"

Ryan surreptitiously picked up Sydney's clothes and then his own and laid them across a stool. He then made himself and Sydney each a glass of iced tea. "I come and go as I please, Reagan. It's one of the perks of owning the company."

"I'm just giving you hell."

Ryan smiled at his sister. He expected her teasing but didn't want it to spook Sydney. "I'm afraid to ask what brings you out here so early."

"Sorry, Ryan. I need to speak with my client, and I can't discuss it with you."

As if on cue, Sydney came down the staircase, holding down the sides of Ryan's long in mock modesty. He smiled because he loved that she wasn't.

"Hi, Reagan," she said and walked over to the pile of clothes that Ryan had stacked up. She slipped her jeans on and turned around to button them up before joining them at the dining room table.

Reagan looked at Ryan, and he nodded his head in agreement. "I'll let you two talk," he said, excusing himself before he walked outside to his back deck.

Sydney was suddenly nervous and drank half her tea before looking over at Reagan again.

"Alright, our court date is in ten days. We're required to have the psychiatric evaluation done before that, so my assistant was able to get it scheduled." Reagan handed Sydney a notecard with the information and watched as Sydney's face dropped.

Reagan leaned in so that she was closer to Sydney. "You know I want to help you, Sydney. I like you, and I think you're getting railroaded. I hate when someone abuses the law for their personal gain instead of for the truth and justice for which it was intended."

Sydney nodded but was too nervous to say anything yet.

"But above and beyond what I think, I would help you no matter what you've done, simply because you make my brother happy. I haven't seen him like this before, ever." Reagan took another drink of her coffee. "I need you to tell me whatever it is that you're hiding so I can do damage control for your case. I don't want to drag you into a battle without being prepared." Reagan looked straight at Sydney. "And make no mistake, they are planning for war."

"I-I've told you everything. I swear, Reagan."

"No. No, you haven't."

Sydney stared at Reagan but didn't say a word. Sydney couldn't stop the tears forming in her eyes because of the way her new friend looked at her.

"Tell me about your mother's death, Sydney."

"What?"

"They are using that as a premise for your behavior. Gina has already planned the case against you and sent the information over to my office. It doesn't look good, Sydney. I'm certain she's hoping we'll make a plea deal. She has a psychiatrist ready to explain that mentally ill parents, specifically mothers, pass the illness to their children. Was your mother mentally ill?"

Sydney lowered her head to her hands and couldn't speak. She didn't see that coming. She hadn't thought about her mother's illness in years and years. She'd told most people that her mother had been ill before she died, and that had been the truth. It didn't feel right after twenty years to dredge up the type of illness.

Sydney nodded slowly. "I wasn't hiding it because it has nothing to do with this."

"Did she or did she not kill herself?"

Tears slid down Sydney's face. "I was only eight. I didn't understand that my mother was different. Daddy said it happened after she had me and that it would come in waves. Some waves were stronger than others. She'd had a really bad episode when I was three and she was hospitalized. He'd tried to get more help for her from her doctors, but they'd told him originally that it was postpartum depression and that it would pass eventually. It wasn't, and it didn't."

Sydney wiped her face, but the tears still rimmed her eyes. "She took medicine for it and would occasionally throw them down the sink. On her really bad days, Daddy would take me to work with him or send me to a babysitter. He didn't realize that particular day that she was having a hard time. She called him, and he was in a meeting with the city council and had left his phone in his office. She attempted to reach him thirty-one times before she cut her wrists. I was swinging in the backyard when he and the deputy pulled into the gravel driveway at a hundred miles an hour. I knew it had to be Momma, but I kept swinging as the ambulance and fire trucks got there. Daddy came outside to swing with me afterward, and I knew she was gone. He didn't say the words, but I knew."

When Sydney looked up, Reagan had tears in her eyes. Sydney had only seen her tough side and was certain that Reagan wasn't very emotional. It touched Sydney that she would care about her story.

"I'm sorry, Sydney. That must have been hard."

Sydney nodded. "It probably should have been worse, but my dad was an amazing man. Larger than life. We had some good memories of my mom, too, and chose to hold on to those."

Reagan stared into Sydney's eyes. "You need to know that your rat bastard ex is going to use that information against you. His attorney will do everything in her power to make you look crazy so their case sticks. The saddest part is people are not sympathetic to things they don't understand. And trust me, they don't understand mental illness."

"I haven't told that story to anyone. I definitely didn't tell it to Drake."

Reagan shook her head as if she'd misheard.

"I know it sounds weird, but I was only nineteen when I met Drake. He was finishing up medical school, and I was pretty star struck by him. I was raised by a cop and his cop friends who were super protective. It was the first time anyone had treated me like a grown up. He took me home with him, and we cooked dinner together for the boys, and I was infatuated. Later on I realized it was the boys I was smitten with, but it didn't matter. We eloped after six weeks, and I was in full-on adult mode from that day forward. I never got around to telling him the truth about my mother dying, and after we had been married, it didn't seem that important compared to our busy daily lives."

"You were afraid he would judge you?"

Sydney nodded. "I wasn't sure how he would feel about it, but I quickly learned that he was critical of people and their differences. I know he's a doctor, but most the time it's about the money and status for him, not helping people."

Reagan reached her hand across the table to hold Sydney's. "If you weren't sure before, Sydney, you can be sure now. He and his girlfriend are judging and using whatever they can to win this case."

Reagan squeezed Sydney's hand and then looked at her seriously. "It's the reason I have to ask you. Why? I've handled hundreds of divorce cases, high-profile custody cases and it rarely comes down to a battle unless more is going on: sex addiction, drugs, or in this case, mental illness. I'm your lawyer; I won't judge you. Is there something else that happened?"

"No." A deep voice answered. Reagan and Sydney both turned their heads to look at Ryan, who was standing in the doorway.

"Damn it, Ryan." Reagan glared at her brother. "I told you to let me talk to Sydney."

"It's okay," Sydney said quietly. "I don't want to have any secrets from him."

Ryan walked over to put his arm around her as he explained. "I wasn't trying to listen in when I realized that I could hear you two from the deck, I walked out on the pier, but it's so quiet out there that your voices carried.

"You heard everything?" Sydney asked.

Ryan nodded his head and then pulled her in tightly for a hug. He then sat down beside Sydney and held her hand. "Sydney has gone through a lot with having her children taken from her with no warning, but it hasn't broken her."

"I've done some crazy things." Sydney said.

"Picking the boys up and keeping them late after they took your rights away could be considered over the top, but not to people who know how passionate you are about those children. You're not the type of woman who meekly goes about her day without getting involved, whether it's to stand up for another person or to fight for what you believe in."

"I threw a lamp at Drake's face, and I let the air out of Gina's tires."

"Yes, and letting the air out of that woman's tires was pretty desperate, but it wasn't premeditated. It was an impulsive move, like throwing things at Drake, and after the way you were treated, it's understandable. I'm not a parent, but I know that one day when I have children, I will fight for them."

Reagan and Sydney both stopped and stared at Ryan.

"What?" he asked, shaking his head at Reagan.

"Nothing. I haven't heard you talk about kids before. I'm wondering who you are and what you've done with my brother."

"You're hilarious, Reagan. Because I'm a man, I can't talk about wanting children? Don't you ever think about having any?"

"Um, no. I don't," Reagan said, staring into his eyes. She then got up to rinse out her travel cup and catch her breath. She'd been an attorney for years, and it wasn't the first case that felt personal, but it was the first case that touched her family. She had to reign in her feelings and do the job she had perfected.

As she headed back over to the table, she paused to watch Sydney and Ryan together. He was consoling her, and Sydney did the same for him. It touched her. It was the first time she'd ever seen her brother in love.

She sat down and cleared her throat. "Alright, Sydney. I need you to think about what has happened over the last two years. No offense, but Dr. Drake Winters has the personality of a concrete wall. I can't see him mustering up the emotion to do more than going to work, much less wanting to raise four young boys on his own."

Ryan turned to look at Reagan. "I'm telling you, Reagan; I've met those two together. The attorney girlfriend is in charge. Have you looked into Gina?"

Chapter Twenty-One

Reagan went back to the city to work on her strategy for Sydney's case. She needed to hire a detective, and since she was doing the work for free, it would have to come out of her pocket. She knew her firm would take exception to it and she would have to inform the partners. She seldom had a moment when things around her weren't swirling.

"Life in the big city, Reagan," she said to no one, as she walked into her perfectly decorated apartment and got to work.

Sydney and Ryan spent the night together again.

It was amazing what a good night's rest in a bed instead of on a couch could do for a woman. And sex, lots and lots of great sex. Sydney laughed at her thoughts and walked into the bathroom to shower before she joined Ryan downstairs where she could already smell the coffee.

The conversation with Reagan still lingered in her mind as the hot water soothed her body. Reagan was definitely on to something. Sydney had been so devastated by the situation that she hadn't thought about it logically. It simply didn't make sense that Drake would fight for sole custody of the boys. Drake's true love was medicine and always had been. He spent the majority of his time learning everything he could about his job, even after his practice was successful.

Sydney rinsed the soap out of her hair as she acknowledged that Drake loved his children but rarely had time for them and even less for her. She was certain that he'd married her so she would care for the boys and he could focus on his career. She'd been married less than a year when her father expressed his concern and told her he was worried that one day she would realize she needed more in life than just being a mother.

She wrapped her body in a towel and then sat down on the side of the tub. Had her father worried that she would turn out like her own mother? Was Abigail unhappy with just being a mom? Sydney shook her head. She only had a few good memories of Abigail Bell, but she could remember that she wanted to be a loving parent. She'd had tea parties with her only child and would set up elaborate picnics for her and her stuffed animals. Whenever Abigail would have a spell and not get out of bed for several days, she would apologize to Sydney. It was the mental illness that robbed Sydney of a good mom.

Downstairs, Ryan was flipping French toast and thinking of the beautiful redhead in his shower. It felt right. He filled two plates with breakfast food. How could anyone doubt Sydney's love for her boys? To her, being their mother was a gift and the love she had for Darryl, Eli, Erik, and John poured out of her. She was so much more, too. She had enough love and compassion for her work at the diner, her new community, the design work for his renovation company, and for him. She was dynamic and energetic. He was inspired by watching her, and being around her made him want to be a better man.

"Could anything smell better than whatever it is that you're cooking?" Sydney asked as she walked down the staircase.

Ryan winked at her. "French Toast and bacon?"

"And real maple syrup?"

"Of course."

Sydney walked right into his arms and planted a kiss on his

lips. Would he ever get used to that? He pulled her in tightly and felt her wrap her body around him.

"Are you working at Main Street Grocery today?"

"I am," she answered, rubbing her body against his. "But I'm starving right now."

Ryan laughed at her flirting but wasn't going to allow her to head off for the day without eating.

They sat down together in what was becoming one of his favorite times of the day. They discussed their schedules for the week, their current project, and what time they would see each other later. He hadn't even realized how much he wanted that in his life until he wanted her.

Before Sydney could hurry out the door for the diner, he pulled her in for another kiss and hugged her tightly. "You sure you don't want to quit the diner and work for me exclusively?"

Sydney laughed. "Miss Lynn needs me, and how are you going to miss me if I'm with you all day and night?"

He nipped at her bottom lip. It might be too soon to let her know that he wouldn't tire of her. Besides, he enjoyed the way people in their little town had fallen in love with Sydney, too.

"Alright, I'll share you with Miss Lynn for now," he said and reluctantly let her go.

She blew him kisses and waved as she pulled out onto their street, and he waved back, knowing he would do anything for her.

As soon as Sydney walked through the door of the diner Olivia and Miss Lynn were beside her.

"She looks good," Miss Lynn said.

"Of course, she looks good," Olivia agreed. "I told you Ryan would be great for the right woman."

"Hello. I'm standing right here," Sydney said, interrupting them and laughing.

"We were worried about you, dear," Miss Lynn said, extending a hand to her.

Sydney reached over and let the motherly woman hold her hand. "Thank you, Miss Lynn. I'm fine."

"Why didn't you tell us about your children, dear one?"

Sydney looked at Olivia and then Miss Lynn. "I didn't think I could discuss it. I missed them and still miss them so much, and if I had talked about it, then I would have cried. I get crazy emotional whenever I speak about them like they were just in my past. I can't think of my future without them."

Miss Lynn leaned in and hugged her and then when she let her go, Olivia hugged her, too. It was incredible to think that the worst time in her life had sent her to that wonderful place with these loving women. She'd only had her mother for a short amount of time and after she passed away there were rarely any women in her life, and it hit her how much she needed them.

The comfort and compassion from women could level out her world, and here these two amazing women were, standing there, opened armed just for her.

Sydney wiped her eyes and then told them what had happened.

Olivia gave Sydney a sympathetic smile. "When I had to split custody with my ex-boyfriend, I thought I would die. It's hard to be away from them even if they're loved by the other parent because you want to be there when they experience life."

Miss Lynn reached over to hold Olivia's hand, too, before she started speaking. "Of course you do. You both need to know those children understand how much they are loved. It's not the amount of time but the quality of the time that you have with them. You make the most of it, and your babies will know it."

Sydney nodded at Miss Lynn and Olivia. They both understood her, and Sydney wanted to admit everything. "Because of some of the things that I did, Drake filed a protection order against me. I'm not allowed to be within a hundred yards of any of them."

"What?" Olivia gasped.

"Well, that's just not right, baby," Miss Lynn said. "Is that why you moved here?"

Sydney shook her head. "My twins told me that Drake and Gina wanted to buy a second home at the lake. It wasn't fair because we used to vacation here. I thought if I bought a house here first, then it would look like I was moving on with my life and they would stop freaking out when I ran into the boys. I hoped to ease back into their lives, at least when they were out of school on vacation. The protection order was temporary. I'd hoped Drake would ease up because Maisonville is small and we would easily run into each other. I was going to make sure it easily happened a lot."

"I would help you make that happen," Miss Lynn said.

"In a heartbeat." Olivia winked at her.

Sydney's heart hurt over their sincere friendship. She loved these two women.

"My oldest son came to see me, and that's why I was arrested. Drake and Gina are attempting to get a permanent restraining order against me and are saying that I'm dangerous for the boys. I could go to prison."

Miss Lynn's eyes filled with tears. "There must be more we can do."

Sydney shook her head. " I was great at problem-solving before the divorce. I used to handle difficult situations more logically, but I'm so emotional over the kids. I can't do anything right."

She wiped the tears from her eyes and put on a strong face for her new friends. "I don't know if there is anything anyone can do, anymore. I think Ryan knows that, too. We talked to Reagan last night, and I could see it in her eyes. She's doing what she can to help me fight this, but Drake and Gina are making me look mentally unstable. They pieced together videos of me and taken out of context; I look like I'm casing their house or creeping around the school playground. I would be scared for my children if I saw someone acting like me in those videos."

"Video doesn't tell the whole truth, Sydney," Olivia said.

Sydney had already thought this over. "I know, but at what cost do I put my boys through more of this? I've already had two psychiatric evaluations in the past year, and they are sending me for another one. I think they're going to keep doing it until one comes back telling them what they want to hear. Next, they plan to interview the boys. I think maybe I have to love enough to let them go."

Miss Lynn wiped the tears in her eyes. "You have to fight. You can't let them put you in jail for something that isn't true."

"Trust me; I'm going to do everything I can to not go to jail. My father was the sheriff in my hometown, and if he were alive, this would kill him. I think Reagan could make a deal with them. They might drop the case if I would offer to move far away and stop interfering with the boys. It's a long shot, but it might work."

Olivia shook her head. "We're not going to let you go."

Then she and Miss Lynn, both, wrapped their arms around Sydney, slightly squeezing her.

"I-I can't breathe," Sydney squealed, and then they stood there together smiling at one another until they slowly let go.

Sydney felt the same way they did, she didn't want to leave Maisonville or Maisonville-Lafitte Lake, but there was no reason to discuss any of it further.

She didn't have to like the situation. She would do what she had to do for her boys and suffer the consequences, personally. It's what most mothers did for their children.

It was getting late, and Miss Lynn hadn't unlocked the front door for the breakfast crowd, yet. She headed for the front as Sydney and Olivia put on their aprons and set out condiments for each table.

Sydney paused. "Please don't say anything to Ryan, just yet. I have that evaluation and depending on how it goes; I'll make my decision. He's been through so much, and he shouldn't have to worry over any of this with me."

Miss Lynn nodded, Olivia stopped and crossed her arms in front of her chest. "I understand why you want to protect him and even why you think you can, but Ryan doesn't miss much. If he even suspects you're going to raise the white flag, he's liable to blow a gasket."

"Then we'll just have to make sure that he doesn't," Sydney added, knowing that she wasn't going to allow him to get hurt because of her.

The morning and lunch shift passed quickly with customers coming and going steadily. It was time for Sydney to get off as she served the last piece of Miss Lynn's famous strawberry pie.

Only one customer was left in the diner when she heard the bell on the front door jingle and Olivia greeted a customer and seated her at Sydney's station at the bar.

When she turned around, it took all of Sydney's strength not to run. Sydney had been court ordered not to get near her, so why would that woman show up there?

Sydney managed to stop visibly shaking before she spoke. "What do you want, Gina?"

Chapter Twenty-Two

Sydney couldn't believe her ex-husband's girlfriend was waiting for her at the lunch counter. After the lying, cheating, and meanness that Gina had shown her, they hadn't had a conversation that didn't include Gina slamming the front door of Sydney's old house in her face. She was wicked but hadn't been this brazen before. Sydney looked around, and they were alone. Her last customer was finishing up his dessert, Olivia was in the back room, and Miss Lynn was preoccupied, cleaning out the coffee pot.

Gina leaned in like she had a secret. "I'm pretty sure you don't have anything else that I could want," she said, and then sat up straight smoothing out her fitted blue sheath dress, and wearing a smug look on her face.

Sydney was rarely without words, but Gina had the advantage. Sydney was already vulnerable because of her feelings for Ryan and the thought of having to leave him and her new home. She hadn't expected Gina to come here to gloat. Instead, Gina had perfected the wounded girlfriend routine, and this arrogance was out of character. Then again, if Sydney had paid attention, Gina behaved erratically when it came to her.

Sydney took a step back and quickly closed her mouth, which

had been hanging open in shock. It took all of her willpower to make it look like she wasn't afraid of the bony woman.

What could the evil witch want with her now? And why couldn't Sydney say what she wanted and then rip Gina's freaking hair out of her head?

Gina adjusted the giant diamond ring on her finger. The ostentatious ring that Drake must have given her. Then she raised her eyebrows at Sydney. "Cat got your tongue? That's surprising. In fact, I'm a little disappointed in you, Sydney. I've heard so much about your mouthy little opinions. Those damn boys wouldn't shut up about you. Not until I threatened them with boarding school."

I will not jump over the counter and kill the anorexic cheating ho-bag, Sydney was chanting inside her head, struggling to keep her composure, when Olivia slid in to stand beside her and put an arm around Sydney's waist. Sydney wasn't sure if Olivia was hoping to give her strength or attempting to keep Sydney from blowing her temper, but she was thankful just the same.

Gina rolled her eyes as Miss Lynn joined them, too. She stood on the other side of Sydney with enough anger in her eyes to validate a call to the coroner for Gina.

"Isn't that sweet? You have little friends. Hope they can visit you in prison."

"What. Do. You. Want?" Sydney asked through clenched teeth.

Gina smirked and shrugged her shoulders as if she were modest. "Honestly, I have all I could possibly want." She batted her fake eyelashes. Her real ones must have fallen out from the lack of nutrition. "At least soon I'll have all that I want, but Drakey wants a house here at the lake. Not just any house, but a Gentry home. A nicer one than yours, of course. We've picked it out; it's the largest one on the west side, and that freaking arrogant builder won't sell it to us. You should talk to him. We might be persuaded to lessen the charges if we get what we want."

Olivia leaped toward Gina and Gina fell out of the barstool as she yelped. Sydney and Miss Lynn both grabbed Olivia before she could touch her, but it scared Gina. The fear in Gina's eyes was unmistakable, and for once Sydney was relieved to see that the woman wasn't invincible.

"You should be on a leash," Gina said to Olivia as she stood out of reach. When she was certain Olivia wasn't going to come after her, she scooted closer to the bar to pick up the purse she'd dropped. "You heard what I said, Sydney. It's the only shot you've got and the only offer I'm going to make." With that last sentence, she turned and stomped out of the restaurant.

Olivia visibly exhaled. "What a wicked witch. There's a good chance someone will drop a house on her and your troubles will be over."

Miss Lynn laughed and then so did Sydney, but Sydney knew her troubles were far from over. She couldn't possibly ask Ryan to give up one of his houses to them, but especially not his beloved White House. They were works of art and a part of his soul. The houses rarely went on the market but rather sold by word of mouth and sometimes ended in a bidding war. He cared about the people who got to live in them and wanted to feel like they loved the property. Drake and Gina wouldn't make the cut.

Olivia poured Sydney a cup of coffee and then flopped down on a barstool. "It's pretty far-fetched that this was about a lake house, Sydney."

"No way." Sydney shook her head. "All this time I've mostly blamed Drake, but he's an idiot. A brilliant doctor, but still an idiot. Until just now, I didn't realize that this was between that she-devil and me. I just can't figure out why." Sydney looked up at Miss Lynn and Olivia. "That lake house they want is just the cherry on top."

RYAN WORKED on the White House with his construction team for most of the morning to keep things on schedule. Then he drove by the diner to make sure that Sydney's car was there before he headed to the long bridge that would take him into the city.

He was halfway across the bridge when his phone rang. It was Reagan.

"What are you doing, Ryan?"

Did she have him under surveillance?

"Are you watching me?" He laughed, understanding that it could be true, knowing his sister.

"Should I be watching you?"

"It wouldn't matter if you did. I would still do whatever I wanted, and you know it."

"And that's why I'm calling you." She paused for a second, but before he could speak, she began again. "I could tell last night that you weren't happy with the conversation over Sydney's case, but it had to be said. It's not like I had a choice; she needed to know what they were planning against her. I am her attorney."

"You were acting like an overprotective sister."

"Possibly, but I have my reasons for that too," Reagan said.

He knew her reasons. His ten years in the Marines made her worry, but the first one hundred twenty-three days after he became a civilian kept her up for days at a time. Those four months that he referred to as the dark days were imprinted on his brain. It caused him pain when he thought of the heartache he had caused his sister, his first best friend. He'd loved his time in the Marines, but after his friends had been killed, he couldn't handle that life anymore. He couldn't go back. He wouldn't let the dark swallow him up again. His sister needed him, too. He was stronger now than ever before and able to help Reagan and Sydney.

"Reagan, you know that I'm good, right?"

"Every time I visit you and see how well you are, it makes me feel better." Her eyes softened. "But Ryan, I'll always worry a little about you. It's my job as the big sister."

Ryan laughed. "You're not big. In fact, you look like you

haven't been eating enough, Reagan. Should I be worrying more about you?"

Reagan laughed. Unlike her brother, she didn't have anyone in her life, not even an occasional date in over a year. Becoming partner was taking all she had, and she wasn't sure if she cared about anything else anymore. She hadn't been good at relationships. Her brother was her closest friend, and she didn't share her problems with him. After their parents divorced and then died within a couple of years of each other, she'd learned to pick herself up and keep moving forward.

"Stop changing the subject, Ryan. You know why I'm calling you. Sydney's situation hit a new low yesterday, and after you niggled your way into the conversation and Sydney allowed you to hear the details of what they were planning, I could see you were ready to kill someone and bury the body."

"So what's your point?" Ryan asked, keeping the smirk on his face out of his voice.

"Very funny, Ryan. I know you want to protect her. I'm just skeptical that you can, and before you give me that ridiculous line, *I know people who know people who kill people*, I want you to understand that you need to stay out of this."

"That's not a line; I do know people," Ryan said.

"Listen to me, Ryan. I've got this under control," Reagan said firmly.

She couldn't tell him the truth. She'd already hired a detective to look into Doctor Winters and his girlfriend. They were both credible in their fields and had character witnesses. Sydney hadn't worked in several years since the doctor started his practice, and Reagan couldn't find anyone to stand up for her in court except the women she worked with at Main Street Grocery. Unfortunately, they hadn't seen her as a mom. The only socializing that Sydney did was with other mothers and not one of them or even a neighbor would let Reagan put them on the stand. The caddy women were spreading gossip about Sydney and making it near impossible for Reagan to find the truth. Reagan was more concerned than ever that Sydney was a selfless wife and mother, and the only thing she'd have to show for it was a cheating husband whose lover helped him frame her and put her in jail.

"I'm not going to let anything bad happen to her," Ryan said.

"I knew you were going to cause trouble with this case. I knew by the look on your face last night."

"Well then, you were right, sister. You should have called me and told me how to help you with the investigation. We could have worked together on a plan."

Reagan was furious. She had to make him understand. "You are so damn hard headed. As my brother, you cannot be involved in this case."

"Good to know," Ryan interrupted. "You make sure Sydney gets a fair doctor, and I'll do my own thing. You should know, I'm convinced this entire investigation will begin and end with Gina."

"I have no control over the psychiatrist; the court appoints him, and you stay away from Gina. She's out to burn Sydney, and it's way more than jealous girlfriend behavior."

"Loud and clear, Reagan. Call ya later."

Reagan heard the silence before she could say another word. She wanted to strangle her brother. Ryan had an incredibly sweet heart and would fight to the death for those he cared about. He could unintentionally ruin Sydney's case, and she wasn't sure she could stop him.

Instead of hanging up her phone, she quickly dialed her firm's senior partner. Terrence had a huge crazy family, and he was pulled into multiple cases every year defending one of them. She needed help and planned to run things through him before she made another move.

Chapter Twenty-Three

Ryan slowed down after he got off the phone with Reagan. Gina's behavior toward Sydney didn't make sense, but he couldn't interfere with the case. His sister was right, and he needed to stay away from Gina. His idea to follow Gina around and check up on her was foolish. He'd acted impulsively. He wasn't a detective. He wanted to help, but he didn't want to compromise the situation.

He had already taken the mid-city exit and traveled several blocks when he turned his truck around deciding to head back home. At least the drive helped clear his head. *Strong caffeine could help, too,* he thought as he saw the Bean Gallery coffee shop ahead.

He was stirring sugar into his black coffee when he heard a familiar voice behind him.

"Is Mom okay?" Darryl asked, looking at him.

Ryan took a drink of his hot coffee before he answered. "Darryl? Right?"

Darryl nodded nervously, looking around. "Can we talk?"

Ryan had been focused on Gina's office and hadn't realized how close he was to St. Peter's Academy or that it was time for school to let out for the day. He should have noticed the kids in uniform walking around, but he'd been preoccupied. Now the situation he'd planned to stay out of had reached out and pulled him in.

For a moment he thought about simply walking out the door, but he recognized the desperate look on Darryl's face. He'd felt the same way when he was a boy. His father wasn't much of a role model, but his Uncle Trey had been there for him. Sydney's boys needed someone, and surely listening to them in a public place would be okay.

Darryl motioned Ryan over to his table where Eli and Erik were sitting. There was no mistaking them for Darryl's brothers. Other than the fact that they were younger and a little smaller than Darryl, they looked just like him. After brief introductions and handshakes, Ryan sat with the boys and waited for them to start.

"Little John is at soccer practice," Darryl said. "We hang out here to do homework until he's finished."

Ryan could see he was stalling but didn't want to rush the young man. He could see in his eyes that this was difficult for him.

"We overheard Gina talking to Dad about the charges against Mom. Gina said Mom has a psychiatric appointment in the next couple of days, too. She's making it look like Mom had mental problems and even has Dad writing down stuff that could fit into her story. Gina told him it was the right thing to do because it ran in Mom's family."

Erik whispered loud enough for them to hear. "The only psycho is Gina."

"He's right," Eli added. "It's one thing to track our cell phones. Most parents do that, but that woman watches everything we do. She has surveillance on us inside the house."

Ryan's eyes got bigger as he drank his coffee and let the boys talk. They clearly needed to divulge this information to someone. Erik and Eli continued telling him about Gina getting brochures for boarding schools for all four boys. At first she said it was to give them each a better educational foundation, but lately, she'd been threatening military academy for discipline.

Darryl had remained silent as Erik and Eli told their stories. He finally set his cup down and admitted to Ryan and his brothers what he hadn't told anyone until now.

"Gina told me that the judge is going to interview all four of us. She said he would ask us about specific situations and then ask for anything else we think is important. She gave me a list of things she wants me to say and some for Eli, Erik, and John." He looked down as if he were ashamed. "She said we have to do it. If I don't get my brothers on board, then she'll send us to military school before Christmas break."

"Darryl? Why didn't you tell us?" Eli asked.

Erik just dropped his head into his hands.

"We're going to stop her, boys. Alright? It's going to take some work, but we're going to figure out a way to do it," Ryan said. The boys looked defeated, and he had to give them that reassurance.

"I don't think anyone can stop her," Erik said quietly. "She's the meanest person I've ever met. She got rid of our family dog, Beezus. We got him when he was a puppy. She'd only been there a week when she said he got sick. We were at school, and she took him to the pound. One night when I was upset and missing Mom, Gina got mad at me and told me she wished she could take me there, too. Then she laughed and said not to worry; they don't keep anyone long; if you're not adopted after a week, they euthanize you."

Eli had tears in his eyes. "Why didn't you tell us?"

Erik just shook his head, and Darryl patted his brother on the back.

Eli wiped at his eyes. "He was a great dog. Maybe he was adopted. He was a golden retriever, and a lot of people want them."

"It's true. He could have been adopted," Darryl agreed.

Ryan watched as the young men consoled each other, and it made him even more determined to help them. He finished his coffee and set his cup down on the table. "Look, men. We're going to stop her, but you're going to have to be smart about it. You can't use your phones because she's reading your texts and tracking your calls. You're going to need to gather intel and turn it over to the authorities, your school counselor, or possibly a social worker who can intervene on your behalf. Darryl? Do you still have the list that Gina wrote out for you on your mom? You need to make a copy of it, too, so you can give the authorities proof. Can you do it at school?"

Darryl nodded his head, and for the first time, he had a glimmer of hope in his eyes.

Ryan smiled. "Good. Now you three need to write down any information that you can on Gina, things she's said to you or you've overheard her say. Write down the date and time it happened. My sister is your mom's attorney. Her name is Reagan, and she's going to do what she can to help your mom. She's really good at what she does, so don't worry."

The boys were much calmer than when they had started this conversation, and Ryan knew it was time for him to leave. He stood up and looked at each of them as he spoke again. "I want you boys to know that you're safe and that your mom is being taken care of, too. When you get your information together, you can turn it into your school counselor, a social worker, or even the judge, and they will know what to do with it. In the meantime, if you ever feel like you're in danger, you call 911."

"Can we call you?" Erick asked.

"I can't be here as fast as the police, but I'm not going to tell you boys no. Here's my number." He handed them his business card. "If you really need me, you can call."

The boys looked relieved, and Ryan gave them a nod before he turned and left.

Ryan got back into his truck, feeling anxious about helping the boys get away from Gina. He'd been thinking the whole time how awful Sydney had been treated, but it hadn't crossed his mind that Gina would be mean to the boys, too. It made him angrier than before and more determined than ever to find a way to help them.

He waited until Drake pulled up in front of the coffee shop and the boys piled into the SUV before he pulled off and headed toward his sister's office. She would be angry at him at first for talking to the boys, but there was nothing Reagan got worked up over more than kids being mistreated in the middle of a divorce or custody battle. It would set her off when she heard that it was still going on after the divorce was final. She would know exactly what to do to help him protect those kids.

Chapter Twenty-Four

Reagan sat on the edge of Terrence's desk as her brother explained to both attorneys what the boys had said. She heard his words, but she also watched as Ryan sat for a few seconds at a time and then paced the floor as he talked about Sydney's boys. She learned as a kid to watch people's body language if she wanted the whole truth and the truth was, he was upset over what he had found out.

"The strangest thing was listening to a fifteen-year-old and two fourteen-year-olds sound like they were twenty. I'm pretty sure they haven't told their father what's going on. It's hard to tell whether they're being mistreated or are just really unhappy with that women's behavior. More than anything, they're worried about Sydney. I'm concerned for them. I'm not sure what to do because I don't want to keep this information from Sydney, but if she finds out, my little redhead is going to flip out."

He finally leaned against the wall and stopped talking. Reagan nodded in understanding. He had called Sydney his. Reagan ached to keep her brother safe, especially after what he'd been through, but he was going to get his heart broken. Things were a mess on an epic scale, and there was no way Reagan could see it ending any other way but badly. She'd been a part of a lot of colossal fights during divorces, especially with custody battles. She was an expert. However, her brother being involved with the boys put her in a precarious position. She had to do the proper thing for her client, but then again, she had to do what was right by those boys, too. She looked at Terrence, and he nodded his head, agreeing with her unspoken words.

Reagan got up, hugged her brother and then excused herself. "Terrence will need to advise you from here," she said, exiting the office and leaving the two men alone.

It was one of the hardest things she's had to do as an attorney. She trusted Terrence and knew he would call social services if the boys needed help. She also believed he could advise Ryan so that he wouldn't cause trouble for her or Sydney.

It was overwhelming, and the only thing that ever soothed Reagan was work. She hurriedly closed the door to her own office and went directly to her computer, plucking away furiously on the keyboard.

She was getting a clearer picture of what Gina was capable of, and Gina was a lot worse than she had originally thought. She received a message from her detective that included pictures of Gina and Drake as college students. According to the notes, Gina and Drake Winters had met each other as undergrads. Gina dropped out for a while, and it looked like they lost touch. Drake then met and married his first wife and had children.

Reagan printed the pictures the detective had sent. She sat there staring at the grainy photos of a very young Gina and Drake together at what were likely fraternity parties. Then a few pictures of Drake with his first wife, the boys' biological mother.

She was startled by another message from the detective. She read it out loud: "Gina was put into foster care at the age of fourteen. She wasn't adopted and stayed in the system until she aged out at eighteen. Her last foster parents were an older couple who couldn't have children, and they paid for her to go to private school and then for her college, including law school."

She quickly typed another message to him asking him to look into the records and find out what happened to Gina's bio parents and why Gina had left college her sophomore year and finished her degree somewhere else.

Reagan studied the pictures for a few more minutes and then put them into her case folder. Gina's background was becoming more peculiar. Surely that information would give them the answers they were searching for. At least for her new friend and client, she hoped that was true.

Reagan paced her floor for a moment and then looked down the hall to see if Ryan had left Terrence's office. He was standing at the elevator and gave her a nod.

Reagan walked over to him and hugged him.

"Sydney didn't do anything to deserve this, Reagan," he said.

Reagan nodded but didn't speak. She didn't want him to see how much the case worried her. The stakes were higher now, and she couldn't afford to overlook even the smallest detail.

"She grew up in a small town, right outside of the city. It was quiet and family oriented, a place where most the town knew each other. Sydney said other than her mother's illness she'd had a nice childhood. They didn't have a ton of money, but her father was the town sheriff, and most people loved him and helped him take care of her."

Reagan smiled. "So, sort of like Maisonville?"

"Yes." Ryan grinned back at her. "She hasn't said much about it, but I know she's worried about meeting the psychiatrist tomorrow morning."

"She'll be fine, Ryan. I'll get the report from the psychiatrist before we go to court, and we'll have a plan ready. It'll work out. You'll see. Not my first picnic."

Ryan kissed his sister on the cheek and then got into the elevator. He couldn't stop thinking about the boys and then having to sit with Terrence as he called a social worker to make sure their local office had the boys on their radar. He understood Terrence was a great attorney, but it was uncomfortable discussing private matters with someone other than his own sister. Still, he trusted

Reagan. She was brilliant when she put a plan into action; he just wished it didn't involve Sydney. He was comforted because Reagan worked on a different plane than most other people, and he hoped that big brain would work to Sydney and the boys' advantage.

It was dusk when Ryan pulled up at his house and saw Sydney's car in her driveway. He knocked on her door, but when she didn't answer, he figured she must be out running and decided to go inside and take a quick shower.

He was sitting on his back deck, watching the sun set, when he heard her back door close. Still in her running gear, she spotted him and gave him a sheepish smile. He understood. He missed her today, too.

He stood up and reached over to help her leap over to his side. When she made it across, she reached around him and hugged him tightly. She smelled like fresh air and sunshine, and he kissed the top of her head several times.

"You okay?"

She nodded but kept her arms around him and her face buried in his chest. After a couple of minutes, he lifted her chin up to look into her eyes. "What's up?"

He watched as she took a deep breath and then reached over to take a long drink from his beer. He grinned at her and then offered to get her one, but she shook her head and handed the bottle back over to him.

She then sat in a chair and propped her feet up on another one as she leaned her head back to look up at the sky.

"Nothing. How was your day?" she asked, still avoiding looking at him.

"Alright. Busy. Yours?"

"It was alright," she said, but her voice cracked, and he sat up straighter.

He was sure there was more going on with her. She didn't hide things well and usually didn't hold anything back. So why would she not tell him what was on her mind?

"Are you sure?" he asked and reached over to tug her hand into his. She immediately smiled.

"Sure. Just tired."

"Let's go get takeout food and go to bed early tonight," he offered.

Sydney nodded and then stood up, taking her hair out of the ponytail holder that was holding it tightly on top of her head. "Give me ten minutes to shower?"

He agreed and then watched as she took a running jump to her side of the deck and hurried inside. As he sat there, he wondered if something had happened today with her or if it was his own guilt distracting him. He didn't like keeping secrets from her, and his was a relationship-breaking kind of secret. He was certain of it. Still, he couldn't tell her what was going on with the boys. Terrence had warned him of the repercussions. If he could just get through the next few days until Terrence gave him the green light, then he could tell her everything.

He finished his beer and wondered if he could keep her preoccupied with work and in bed until then.

SYDNEY QUICKLY UNDRESSED on her way to her bathroom and left a trail of clothes along the way. She usually was neat, but at the moment her mind was in overload, and she couldn't think about anything as insignificant as picking up her clothes.

Keeping her day a secret from Ryan was eating at her, and she didn't think she could handle it for very long. She didn't keep even little things bottled up, and just being around him made her want to spill the truth.

He would flip out if he knew that Gina had come to Miss Lynn's today, and she couldn't handle upsetting him. It would hurt him even more if he found out that Gina and Drake wanted his prized new house. She couldn't possibly let him do it. Not for her. Not that way.

It wasn't in her nature to surrender. Her father would tease her and tell her that generals would admit defeat before his feisty daughter. She wouldn't admit it, but it was true. She was passionate about the things she believed in and fought for them with vigor. Sometimes to a fault, like with the custody of her boys and the stalking, but her heart was in the right place. She got that from her father. It was in her DNA, and she couldn't deny it.

The ball of fire she had building up inside her stomach right now made the idea of dinner impossible. How would she fake her way through a meal without Ryan noticing? They had a silent understanding between them. He could read her better than anyone; this was one of the things she liked most about him. It might also be the thing that was her undoing.

She quickly rinsed her hair and body and jumped out of the shower, still consumed with her secrets. Gina wanted the White House for Drake, but Drake would've settled for her to move far away from here. It's what he'd told her when he kicked her out. No matter what, she was going to lose Ryan.

Sydney threw on a navy shirtdress and tied the belt. Then she grabbed a brush and ran it through her hair. She couldn't think about all of that a minute longer, or Ryan would read it on her face. He was smart enough to ask Olivia or Miss Lynn, and both of those women loved her enough to tell him exactly what was going on. She smoothed on lip gloss and then braided her hair before she rushed down the stairs to meet Ryan for dinner.

If they went to bed early, she could lose herself in him tonight and forget about her troubles until morning.

Chapter Twenty-Five

Sydney sat in the waiting room chair, crossing her legs for the tenth time as Reagan looked over at her. They smiled at each other, but neither of them spoke here in the small space.

Reagan had warned Sydney that her body language would be evaluated just as closely as the words she used during the appointment as they made their way over to the doctor's office. That wasn't the way either of them had planned their morning, but after an impossible discussion with Ryan, both women gave in and went to the appointment together.

Sydney replayed the previous evening in her mind. Ryan had showered her with affection, and they didn't get to sleep until the early morning hours. She'd worried that he could tell she was upset and was certain after making love that he would get her to confess. Instead, he kissed her and held her tightly, and before either of them could speak or fall asleep, they were at it again. They couldn't get enough of each other.

She smiled and felt the warmth cover her face. Ryan was a generous lover, and in the light of day, she wished she deserved him.

Sydney had woken to a hot cup of coffee, and when she got out of the shower, she discovered that Ryan had left her a warm towel. He did whatever he could to make the morning easier on her until she told him that he couldn't come with her to the doctor's office.

She wished she could have taken it back. The wounded look on Ryan's face slayed her. He recovered fast, but she wouldn't soon forget how deep the pain seemed to penetrate him. Then he proceeded to ignore her decision until she threw a monumental fit. She braced for the fight, but it never came. He ran his hands through his hair and over his face and then backed her up against the kitchen counter and kissed her senseless.

It almost worked.

She stopped herself from giving in and letting him go with her, and from telling him about Gina and her threats. She was more certain than ever that he would give Gina and Drake the house they wanted in order to save her, and she was not going to let that happen.

The longer she could keep them away from Ryan, the better. She would figure another way out. The love he had put into those houses, especially the Haunted Mansion, was palpable. He'd wanted that particular house from the very beginning. He then worked tirelessly to earn enough money to buy it while he talked the owner into selling the property. Gina and Drake didn't deserve to live there. No way. No how. Not as long as she had a breath in her body.

She just had to keep the information from Ryan long enough for the judge to pass sentence on her for these new charges. Sydney could handle anything Gina and Drake did to her as long as no one else suffered.

Reagan reached her hand over and placed it on top of Sydney's. Sydney hadn't realized she'd been shaking until the warm hand covered her own. She looked up and saw the concern in Reagan's eyes.

"I'm fine," she whispered where only Reagan could hear.

Reagan gave her a slight nod, and Sydney admired the quiet confidence on her attorney's face. It was the same look Ryan gave her most of the time, including that morning as he drove her across the bridge. She'd told him he was not going with her on the appointment and he'd told her that she was not going alone.

She knew that if she drove her car that he would follow her. He wasn't a man who asked permission. He finally gave in and told her he would drive her into the city so that his sister could accompany her. And just like that, they both got what they wanted.

Sydney jumped when she heard the doctor's door open, but when she saw Gina walking out with him, she visibly gasped. Reagan reached over to squeeze her hand that time. It was reassurance, but also a warning. *Get it under control, Sydney.*

They watched as Gina wiped the corners of her eyes and smiled shyly at the doctor. No doubt she was reeling him in with her act. She could win an Oscar with her performance, and Sydney rolled her eyes.

As soon as the doctor could no longer see her, Gina's cold smile covered her face. She looked over at Sydney and gave her a wink.

It was definitely on.

Sydney went to stand up, but Reagan put her hand out and stood up first.

"Seth?"

"Reagan." The doctor smiled.

Sydney was certain she saw a gleam in his eyes that wasn't there before.

"I didn't realize..." Reagan stopped mid-sentence when the doctor reached out to touch her hand.

"How long has it been?" Dr. Young asked, not taking his eyes off her.

Reagan shook her head, and for the first time, Sydney watched Reagan stand there with nothing to say.

Reagan shrugged her shoulders and smiled as Seth leaned in and whispered, "You look great, Rea."

She suddenly felt ten years younger and bit her lip to stop

herself from grinning like a fool. The world stopped spinning as Reagan looked into Seth's golden brown eyes. Then she felt the pain of her teeth pinching her bottom lip. His words fell on her like a brick to the head.

What the hell was she doing? She had a job and purpose here. She had a client sitting in the room that needed Seth's utmost professionalism. That behavior wasn't professional for either one of them.

Reagan pulled her shoulders back and gave Seth her best lawyer smile. "Dr. Seth Young, I would like to introduce you to my favorite client, Sydney Bell."

Dr. Young stared for a moment longer, and Reagan noticed the tightening around his eyes as her words sank in. It had been five years since they had seen each other. Five long years and neither of them had bothered to call or reach out to the other. Reagan was climbing the corporate ladder at her firm, and Seth had been offered a great position with a practice in Tennessee. Their careers came first. Reagan remembered the conversation where she kissed him goodbye and explained that it was nice to end things on a positive note, where they both accepted the relationship had run its course.

She meant it when she said it, or at least she had wanted to mean it. Looking at Seth now, it took concentration for her to pretend again.

Thank goodness, he turned away from her and looked over at Sydney.

"Hi," Sydney said, standing up.

Dr. Young smiled her way, and Sydney reached out and shook his hand.

"Ready to get started?" he asked.

"Sure."

"This will take about an hour," he said, turning back toward Reagan. "You're welcome to stay here, or there is a coffee shop across the street."

"I'll wait for you here, Sydney," Reagan said, avoiding Seth's face as she smiled at Sydney.

As soon as he closed the door between them, Reagan paced. *What was she going to do?* This case was already the worst she'd had in years. She didn't like the personal connection it had to her little brother, and it was affecting her judgment. Watching Ryan fight his way back from death, and then witnessing him lose his will to live, after he discovered his closest friends had died, was the hardest thing she'd ever been through in her life. He was stronger than anyone she'd ever known, but she understood how vulnerable love could make even the strongest man. She saw broken hearts and broken families all the time. It was a casualty of the job she loved. The job she was gifted at and was born to do, except this freaking case.

It was keeping her up at night, and she already didn't get enough sleep. The psychiatric evaluation was a normal request of the court, and she hadn't made too much of it until Gina walked out grinning like a school girl at the doctor. Why would she have made an appointment with him? This case was as bazaar as Reagan could handle. Until she saw the psychiatrist and felt it might actually be more.

How in the name of all that was holy was the doctor Reagan' ex, Dr. Seth Young?

Reagan sat down and looked at her phone; fifty minutes to go. She pulled out a notebook from her briefcase and started making notes. It helped her organize her thoughts when she had a particularly hard case, and she needed it today more than ever. She believed Sydney was innocent, but it didn't make sense that her ex-husband would set her up to go to jail. He'd already won. He'd successfully kicked her out of his house, and life, with only her clothes and a luxury car that she had to sell to support herself. She didn't even have visitation rights to the boys. The boys that he let her raise as her own for years. Why wasn't it over? Financially and emotionally, he had beat her. What else was there? It didn't make sense that everyday something new and disturbing was coming up or being discovered.

Reagan stood up. What was going on with this case? And when did Seth even move back to town?

She checked her phone again and saw that time had crawled along; she now had thirty-five minutes left. She couldn't take counting minutes and gathered up her things to go across the street for coffee. She would drink caffeine while she waited in Seth's lobby and mowed through the other case files she'd brought along with her. She certainly needed all the distractions she could muster until Seth finished with Sydney.

Buried in her work, Reagan was surprised when the interior door opened and Seth stood there, smiling down at her.

"Sorry we ran over a bit," he said.

Reagan quickly scooped up her papers and put them away as she stood up. "Not a problem. You good, Sydney?" she asked, looking her client over for any signs of distress.

"Fine," Sydney said.

"Do you need anything else from us?" Reagan asked Dr. Young, but at the same time she was opening the outside door, so she and Sydney could get out of there.

Seth stepped closer to Reagan and put his arm out blocking her exit and causing her to look up at him finally.

Sydney smiled as Reagan blushed. It was obvious those two had a history and Sydney was thankful she was already in the hallway. She winked at Reagan and then headed outside so that the handsome psychiatrist could have a moment with her alone.

Reagan stared into Seth's eyes and then looked away. He gently lifted her chin up. "Why can't you look at me, Rea?"

"I'm working. Sydney is my client. I need to be with her to discuss our case." Her eyes turned to slits, and she gave him a sly smile. "Unless you can tell me what your professional consensus will be and if it will be in her favor."

Seth laughed. "You know I can't do that, Reagan. You wouldn't respect me if I did."

"So you think I respect you now?"

Seth leaned in closer. "Why don't I cook you dinner tonight, and we can discuss it?"

"I don't eat," Reagan said, as she reached out and moved his arm from in front of her.

"I'm not giving up," he said as she stepped out of his reach.

"You should."

He ran to open the outside door for her, and when she turned around to thank him, he handed her his business card.

"My cell number is on there, too."

Reagan didn't say another word, took the card and then headed to meet Sydney at the car.

RYAN KNEW he couldn't wait around at Reagan's office for Sydney to finish with her doctor's appointment. His sister knew they'd had a disagreement and assured him she would get Sydney home. He'd hesitated at first, but her office made him anxious.

His sister believed it was the stuffed shirts that she worked with at the firm and confronted him about it two years ago. But Ryan laughed it off explaining that the dark, wood clad walls they were so proud of in that fancy office reminded him of a coffin. Reagan didn't laugh at his joke, and he felt guilty making her think of how close he came to dying.

The truth was that her quiet, widowed secretary hit on him whenever he came around. It wouldn't normally be a problem, he appreciated flirting and had gone out with women older than him before, but Reagan's secretary was sixty and had the most vulgar mouth he'd ever heard on a lady. The first time he'd met her, she caught him off guard, and she made him blush. He was a Marine and couldn't remember ever being embarrassed, before that moment.

He did all he could to avoid her after that day.

This morning he was just going to walk Sydney into Reagan's

office, but she jumped out of his truck and ran inside without him. Sydney glanced quickly at him before she bolted and he worried she would skip out on Reagan, too.

Frustrated, he parked his truck and went inside to make sure she wouldn't go to the appointment alone. She was the most stubborn woman he'd ever met besides his sister. He worked at reigning in his temper as Sydney bolted into the restroom when she saw Ryan walk into the lobby. He sat there and waited until she went into Reagan's office before he left. He'd called Reagan earlier, but he already knew she'd be there because she was in her office at least ten hours a day.

He didn't understand how she did it. He would have felt like a caged animal. He needed the fresh air. Reagan needed work. She was the perfect person to escort Sydney.

While Reagan and Sydney were together, Ryan headed back across the bridge to work on the White House. He grinned thinking about Sydney referring to it as the Haunted Mansion. She was something else. She made him laugh, she made him frustrated, and she made him happy, but most of all, she made him feel whole.

Everything was also going well at the new project house. Ryan marveled over the progress of the house and wasn't sure he would be able to part with it. It should go to a family, but he'd dreamed of that house for so many years. He'd once thought about living in it himself, but with Sydney next door, he knew he wouldn't move away from her, but still the house was his dream.

He worked for an hour, but couldn't get his mind off Sydney. He wished he could have stayed there with her or even waited at Reagan's office. He decided he needed a break and so he headed to Miss Lynn's place.

Miss Lynn waited on him at the counter and told him to have a seat so he could taste her homemade donuts. He ate two in a couple of minutes and Miss Lynn laughed at the powdered sugar on his lips and chin.

"Was Sydney okay this morning before her appointment in the city?"

"Yes, ma'am. Reagan went with her."

Miss Lynn reached her gently aged hand across the counter to pat Ryan's arm. "I'm sure she didn't want to bother you with sitting there in a doctor's office. Besides, don't you think she needed to tell her lawyer about that visit yesterday from you know who?"

Ryan's eyes turned to slits and Miss Lynn smiled at him.

"She didn't tell you what happened?"

"She was pretty upset last night when she came in," he said, hoping Miss Lynn would fill in with what actually went on at the diner.

"We were pretty shaken after that lying, cheating, man stealing, sorry excuse for an attorney finally left. My Uncle and cousin, you know Wesley's father and brother, are attorneys and wouldn't have done anything to hurt another person. She shouldn't be allowed to practice law."

Ryan nodded his head and kept a mad look on his face to match Miss Lynn's, but listened as she continued. "Of course, I didn't see her at first. Then it was like the whole room went cold and I looked up to see Olivia running over to stand with Sydney. Bless her heart, Sydney looked as white as a sheet."

Ryan kept his composure as he listened to Miss Lynn's account of the events. He knew Gina didn't believe Sydney was mentally ill. The fact that she was brave enough to confront Sydney aggressively certainly proved that. He'd thought she was a snake before, and after hearing the boys' side of the story, he knew she was capable of anything, but until now she'd kept her nasty side hidden. Was she unstable?

He felt Miss Lynn's hand patting his and his eyes cleared as he focused back on her.

"I thought I lost you there for a moment." Miss Lynn smiled, but the look on her face was one of concern.

"Of course, Miss Lynn. I was thinking about what you said.

What would make a woman like Gina finally let down her guard? Arrogance?"

Miss Lynn shook her head. "More than arrogance. That one is a calculating she-devil. She must think she's already won."

Ryan thought of the boys. Anyone evil enough to hurt the family pet was capable of anything. Isn't that how most serial killers started out? He worried about the boys, but by now the social worker would have contacted them. He hoped that would be enough. They had his number too, but he worried that Gina was ramping up her attack. He decided to call Terrence about his concerns. If nothing else, Terrence could call the social worker to verify they were all good.

He paid Miss Lynn for the coffee and donuts and then gave her a hug. He needed to go back into the city.

Chapter Twenty-Six

Sydney sat quietly as Reagan drove them back to the office. She realized that Reagan was preoccupied from the moment she ran to catch up with her at the car. Sydney was certain it had to do with Dr. Young, but she didn't ask Reagan about him.

"I need to drop off some notes for my assistant, and then I can drive you home," Reagan said, still not looking over at Sydney.

She was professional and distant, and Sydney understood. Something had gone on between those two. They both acted surprised and a little excited to see the other.

Did they date each other? Did he break her heart? Reagan didn't act like the type to get attached. She could've broken his heart. She seemed to love her job. Perhaps it was a work thing?

"Are you coming?"

Sydney smiled when she saw that Reagan had parked her car and had already grabbed her briefcase and opened her door.

"Sure," Sydney answered and quickly hurried behind Reagan into the building. It had been nice to be preoccupied over someone else's story for a change.

They were both surprised to see Ryan sitting there in the lobby with Nancy leaning over him. She was giving him a cup of coffee but had her shirt unbuttoned past her cleavage.

He quickly stood up when he saw Reagan and Sydney standing in the doorway. His face was flushed. Reagan acted as if nothing was wrong, but Sydney was certain the older woman had said something to embarrass him.

"Nancy. Hold my calls for the next half hour," Reagan said and held her office door open until Sydney and Ryan followed her inside, and then she shut it firmly.

"We need to talk," Reagan said.

"Yes, we do." Ryan stared at Sydney, and then over at his sister.

Reagan's mouth formed a straight line, and Sydney wasn't about to say anything. That woman was aggravated, and she hoped it wasn't at her.

"What the hell, Ryan?" Reagan snapped.

He sat down and then told Reagan all he had learned from Miss Lynn at the restaurant.

"I can tell by the look on your face that Sydney hasn't mentioned anything about Gina visiting her at the diner."

"She hasn't had a chance, now, has she?" Reagan defended her.

Sydney didn't want to be the cause of a fight between them and figured this was the time to come clean. "He's right. I wasn't going to tell him or you. At least, not until I met with the psychiatrist." Sydney took a deep breath. "To be honest, you've both been good to me and I wanted to spare you from having to deal with Gina as long as possible. She's caused havoc in my life and with those who I care about."

Ryan reached his hand out to hold Sydney's. "We're tougher than we look."

He sounded like Miss Lynn with her clichés, making Sydney half smile. Actually, they were the toughest two people she'd ever known other than her father.

"She came to the diner to threaten me but then asked for the impossible, Ryan. She told me that she and Drake wanted the

Haunted Mansion and if you sell it to them at a deal, then they'll drop the charges."

Reagan's left eyebrow raised about an inch as she stared at Ryan. He answered, "The White House around the bend that we loved as kids."

Sydney spoke up. "I know you love that house and there is no way you can let them have it. I won't let you do it."

"There is no way that I'm going to let them put you in jail for something you didn't do, Sydney. It's just a house."

Sydney's eyes filled with tears as she shook her head. "I should have been honest and told you both what she said. I was hoping the meeting today with Dr. Young might go in my favor. I just don't have a good feeling about it, at all. Seeing Gina there putting on her emotional act, well, I might be hard headed, but after three times of going up against her, I know I can't win. She's always a step ahead. I'm done fighting her. I'll plead guilty, and this will be over. They can't have your house, and they aren't going to hurt anyone else that I care about."

Reagan cleared her throat. "Am I invisible here or what? Do you both know what I do for a living?"

Ryan looked at his obstinate sister. Sydney stared at the family resemblance.

"Yes, we know, boss. You're a lawyer," Ryan said.

"No," Reagan said, as she stood up. "What I do is win. I win ninety-nine percent of my cases. I win for this firm, and I win for my clients. And the other one percent are cases that are dropped out of the system for one reason or another."

Ryan half laughed at his sister until she shot him a threatening look that made him instantly stop.

"Do you have something to say?" she asked, looking at her brother as she tapped on her desk with her perfectly manicured nails.

"No, ma'am."

"Then it's time for us to put our heads together and figure

out what Drake and Gina are doing because I have no intention of giving up. We'll start with all of the truths. Ryan?"

Ryan didn't say a word but kept staring at his sister.

Sydney swallowed hard and her mouth went dry as she felt like the oxygen in the room had disappeared. The tension from those two was staggering, and she held onto the arm of the chair as she stood up.

"I've told you both all that I know. I swear. I have no idea why they're after me. You have to believe me; I don't have any more secrets."

Reagan looked away from Ryan and smiled sweetly at Sydney. "Don't worry. I believe you, babe." She then turned back toward her brother and cleared her throat.

He glared at Reagan and shook his head. He had been advised to keep his information to himself. Wasn't that the whole reason she made him meet with Terrence?

"She deserves to know," Reagan said. "I've talked with Terrence and he agreed. I'll explain later."

Sydney cut her eyes at Ryan. "Who's Terrence?"

"Sort of my attorney."

"What?" Sydney's stomach twisted. "What are you not telling me?"

Ryan took a deep breath. This wasn't how he'd planned to tell her. "I didn't want to upset you."

Sydney sat down and put her head in her hands. That was exactly what she'd been afraid of happening. She was miserable without her boys, but they were safe. The only way Drake and Gina could hurt her now was to cause trouble for her new friends. She dreaded the thought of anyone new in her life being hurt by her past. It was more than she could stand.

Ryan leaned over and kissed her on top of her head and rubbed his hand down her back. "It's going to be okay, Sydney.

When she looked up, she had tears in her eyes. "You don't have to tell me anything that you don't want to," she whispered.

"I don't want to come between you and your sister. My troubles are not yours."

Ryan tenderly placed his hands on each side of her face to make her look into his eyes. "Reagan and I are fine, and we are both here for you. We aren't going anywhere." He saw the vulnerability in her eyes and pulled her into his arms. "I was hoping to protect you, but I was wrong for keeping information from you. I won't do it again, Sydney."

She sat up and wiped her eyes. She held her head up, showing him she was ready for whatever he had to say.

Sydney waited as he looked over at Reagan again. She nodded as if encouraging her brother to speak.

It made Sydney more nervous. "Ryan? Please tell me. Whatever it is, I can handle it."

"Promise me, Sydney. Promise both of us that you'll listen to what I have to say before you react."

Sydney put her hand on her stomach. It felt like she was in an elevator that had just plummeted twenty stories. She faintly nodded.

"I came here, into the city the other day, to The Bean Gallery coffee—"

Before he could say another word, Sydney gasped and put her hand over her mouth.

"The boys are fine, Sydney," Reagan interjected. "Ryan, you can't start a story about her family without prefacing their health status first."

He smiled and rolled his eyes. "Alright, let me try this again. Your boys are great kids, and they are fine. When they saw me, they asked me to sit down to talk with them."

Sydney smiled at him, but he could see the light tears fill her eyes again. The longing for her family was constantly there.

"We had coffee. Everyone but John. He had soccer practice. The older three had a lot to say about Gina. She's been threatening them. Threatening them if they talk to you, and she told them she'd send them away if they didn't lie to the court about you. She is trying to force them to falsely testify against you."

Sydney took a deep breath and then stood up to walk back and forth a few times before she leaned against the wall and looked at Ryan. "They looked good, though? I mean, healthy? Did they say how they're doing in school? Or mention anything about what they've been up to?"

"They looked good, Sydney. They're tough young men. They're worried about you. Did you hear what I said about Gina forcing them to testify against you?"

Sydney nodded. "It's okay. You have to tell them that it's going to be okay. I'm not going to let her send them away. And they won't have to testify because I'm going to plead guilty. Can you tell them that for me?"

"Sydney," Reagan said, looking soft for a moment. "I know you're worried about them, but you can't just let her win."

"She's already won. I can't put my children through anymore. Their lives are there. I want them to grow up in that beautiful house where I mostly raised them. Drake and I aren't together, but he'll make sure they have what they need. They deserve to be happy there with their neighborhood friends and Beezus. To keep playing at the same park and graduate prep school with their friends. I can't let their loyalty to me be the reason those things don't happen."

"She took their dog to the pound," Reagan said firmly.

"What?" Sydney's voice was a whisper.

"She told the boys and Drake that the dog was sick and he died. But later when she was mad at Erik, she admitted she had taken the dog to the pound," Ryan said.

Sydney turned toward the wall and slapped her open hand into the wood paneling as she gritted her teeth and spoke. "If I'm going to have to go to jail, then I should at least do something to deserve it! Don't you think?"

She turned around to see Ryan and Reagan watching her. Ryan eased his way over toward her. "Calm down, Sydney."

"I am calm. I'm calmly going to kill her." She wasn't emotional and didn't have tears in her eyes anymore. Instead, the pupils in her brown eyes looked like black saucers. She was focused and angry. The heat of her temper poured out like heat from a furnace.

"My dad gave the boys Beezus the first Christmas we spent together. He was a tiny pup, and the boys loved him. They grew up together, and he was a part of the family. He was smart and loyal." This time, tears fell down her cheeks. "I loved him so much, too."

"He might have been adopted," Reagan said, and Sydney looked over at her and tried to smile. She could tell Reagan didn't believe it either, but it was sweet of Reagan to give her hope.

Sydney didn't have any hope left.

Ryan wiped Sydney's tears with his thumbs. "You don't want to go after Gina, Red. At least, not yet."

Sydney gave him that incredulous look, the one he was getting used to receiving from her whenever she didn't agree with whatever he said or did.

"Reagan has her detective looking into Gina. He's getting close to something."

Reagan nodded to agree with Ryan. "That's right. He's looked back to her college days. You didn't tell me that Gina was an undergrad with Drake."

"What?" Sydney asked.

"You had no idea they went to college together?"

Sydney shook her head and then slid down the wall until she was sitting on the floor. *When was this craziness going to end?*

Ryan sat on the floor next to her and reached out to hold her hand. Sydney leaned her head on his shoulder.

"Are you sure?" Sydney asked. She was restless and stood up, then she walked over to sit back down in her chair, opposite Reagan's desk.

Reagan nodded. "I saw the pictures."

Ryan followed Sydney and sat back down in his chair beside

her across from Reagan. Sydney was lost in thought, and the room was quiet until she finally spoke.

"It makes me feel a little bit better. I mean, you hear of men leaving their wives for someone younger, but I was the younger wife. I was really good to him. When he first moved me out of the house for her, I half thought he would get her out of his system, then things could go back to the way they were, but it didn't happen. I can at least understand a little more that they had history and what, were rekindling a lost love?"

Reagan pulled the email information up from her detective and then turned her computer screen so Sydney could see it. "According to Jerry, my detective, Gina dropped out of school and off the planet for a couple of years. During that time Drake met his first wife and got married. So, it doesn't sound like he and Gina were too serious."

"He might not have been serious, but she went after him like her life depended on it," Sydney said. She looked embarrassed but pushed on with her explanation. "I read his email and text messages from her."

How did you do that?" Ryan asked.

Sydney avoided his face. "He cheated on me. He kicked me out of my home and took my boys away. Believe me, there are plenty of programs out there that let you catch your ex having cyber-sex."

"I don't even know what cyber-sex is," Ryan said. "Sounds painful."

Reagan and Sydney both laughed at him.

"Shut up, Ryan," Reagan said and then looked at Sydney. "So you caught them online with each other?"

"That was after he'd filed for divorce. I was at my lowest point and then ended up in a chat room with some hardcore jilted lovers. There I was, struggling to figure out how I would ever win in a divorce against a doctor and his attorney lover when this guy explained how he caught his wife sexting and turned it in as evidence during their divorce. He told me about some software that would let me go back and read text messages and emails. I knew Drake didn't delete anything on his computer. The evidence would be on there. I had no idea I would stumble onto naked pictures that Gina sent him. She did whatever she could to get and keep his attention. She was relentless. I told my attorney, but he scolded me for spying on them and told me not to tell anyone I'd done that or I could get into more trouble. So there I was, losing my case, and I couldn't unwatch the videos of her or unread the sexting messages. I did find out that they had been fooling around for a few months. In the beginning, he'd lied to her a couple of times, too. He would tell her he was working instead of that he was having dinner with us or watching TV with the boys. Clearly, naked pictures won."

"I want you to forward me the things you have on them, Sydney." Reagan started writing down notes. "We might be able to use some of that information."

Sydney grinned. "You sure? I mean, you won't be able to unwatch or unread any of it, either. Some of it's rough."

Reagan laughed. "I have famous clients who have sex tapes on the World Wide Web, Sydney. That won't shock me."

Reagan stood up and walked to the door of her office. "I've got some other cases I need to work on, and I'll let you two know when I hear from Jerry. He thought he'd figured out Gina's high school and then he was going to find out why she was in foster care. We could use a break in this case."

Ryan and Sydney stepped out of Reagan's office when she quickly closed the door behind them and startled them. Was she in a hurry?

Reagan's secretary was at lunch, and Ryan took advantage of the empty office. He cornered Sydney, and she could see he was concerned about something.

"So was the naked picture thing usual for Drake? I mean, do I need to worry about naked pictures of you floating around on the internet, Sydney?"

Sydney grinned as she slowly shook her head. "Not a chance."

Ryan kissed her forehead, nose and then lips. "Thank God," he whispered. "Technology isn't my thing. I wouldn't know where to begin to find and eradicate them. I barely use email. " He held out his phone. "I just learned how to text with this thing."

Sydney kissed him and then headed to the elevators after she said, "It could be because you're a caveman who still uses a flip phone."

Ryan shrugged his shoulders, and she couldn't miss his smile as he grabbed her hand.

Chapter Twenty-Seven

Ryan and Sydney spent the next morning working together at the White House before she had to be at the diner for the lunch shift.

It was the perfect schedule since it allowed him time with her and then the entire afternoon to finish the custom cabinets he was building for the kitchen. He needed the feeling of accomplishment he'd have by completing the job, mainly because he felt ineffective with helping Sydney and the boys.

The look on her face when he had to tell her about his conversation with the older three kids upset him. She was concerned for their wellbeing, and he understood more than ever why. After all, once he'd heard their story he'd wanted to check on them nightly too. And he'd just met them. Terrence assured Ryan the call he'd made on their behalf would take care of things. Ryan wasn't the type of person to wait around for someone else to come to the rescue. He couldn't rest easy until he knew for sure they were okay. He definitely needed the distraction of work.

He'd assembled most of the cabinet boxes and had them installed, but as he was finishing the last of the cabinet doors in the garage, a familiar SUV pulled into the side driveway.

He wiped his brow as he watched Darryl, Eric and Eli get of the vehicle and walk over to him.

Ryan promptly met them half way across the drive. "You boys okay?"

"Sorry to just show up without calling," Darryl said.

"Did something happen?" Ryan asked.

Eli stepped forward to look directly at Ryan. "You said we could talk to you."

Ryan ran his hand over his face and hair and tried to get a handle on the situation. "I don't want to jeopardize your mom's case or get you boys into trouble. I'm guessing you don't have permission to be here?"

Darryl shook his head and then started walking back toward the SUV. Eric and Eli watched him and then slowly followed.

"Wait," Ryan said and caught up to Darryl before he climbed into the driver's seat. "Didn't you go to your school counselor or talk to a social worker?"

"The school counselor isn't there for us, man. As soon as I walked into her office, she picked up the phone and called Dad," Darryl said, staring at Ryan.

Eli spoke up. "I guess you called the social worker? She came to the school and called us down to the office. Do you know how hard it is to keep news like that secret in a private school?" Eli rolled his eyes. "She wanted to sit outside in the courtyard and discuss what was going on."

"Yeah, we weren't doing that," Darryl said. "We told her that we had no idea why anyone would call her."

"That was lame, man," Eli said, shaking his head.

Eric stood there looking disappointed but didn't say a word.

Ryan stepped forward and put his hand on Eric's shoulder. "I didn't call the social worker, but a lawyer friend of mine did call her. He thought it would help. It could have if you boys had given her a chance."

"We've already trusted too many people," Darryl said. "Look where that's gotten us. Let's go, guys."

"Adults suck," Eric whispered as he jumped in to the backseat.

Ryan knew he was at a crossroads, but the path had already been chosen for him. He remembered what it was like to not be able to talk to his own father. His Uncle Trey had been his only confidant, and he couldn't imagine his life or Reagan's without his guidance. "Now and then we do suck, but it's because we're trying to do the right things for you."

He put his hand on the door and looked at Darryl. "Come on, I've got some bottled water and Gatorade in my cooler. You guys can explain how you got your Dad's SUV today and then drove across the lake without anyone catching you."

All three boys nodded their heads at the same time. They followed Ryan up the driveway to his truck and then sat on the large tailgate as he passed them cold drinks.

Darryl started talking first. "I got my license and Dad lets me drive to school. We thought about calling you to come meet us at the coffee shop, but Gina's off work and she's paranoid. She shows up at random times, just hoping to catch us doing anything wrong. I know how to unhook the GPS tracker in the SUV and we put our phones into John's soccer bag after school. We didn't want to take any chances."

"After we walked John to soccer practice, we headed straight here. Figured we had enough time to get back by 5:30 to pick him up," Eli said.

Ryan looked at his watch. It was four, and he knew it took a smooth forty-five minutes. They must have hurried.

"How's Sydney?" Erik asked, but before Ryan could answer, Eli whacked his twin brother in the back of the head.

"You can call her Mom when psycho woman isn't around," Eli said.

"Stop it, you two." The oldest brother scowled. "How's Mom doing?"

Ryan smiled. "She's fine. Mostly, worried about you boys."

Eli nodded. "She's the reason we came today." He handed over a notebook. "We know we can't call her, but we wanted her to know how much we missed her. We all wrote her letters inside there. Could you give it to her?"

Ryan nodded his head as he took the spiral notebook.

"That's not the only reason we came," Darryl said, looking at his brothers for reassurance.

Eli took over. "We figured out a way to get information on Gina. First off, she's a nut, and I know we've said that before, but you should have seen her. We waited until dinner and told Dad we had to each write a paper on our parents, and I wanted to ask him and Gina questions. She practically flipped out. I mean, even stranger than normal."

"Yeah, but Dad talked her into it, and Eli interviewed her at the dinner table while Dad was there, so he's still alive to tell about it," Eric added.

Ryan smirked at the funny teenagers but wasn't sure if they meant to be funny. He watched Erik take a deep breath and laugh. It helped ease the tension, but it was difficult to watch the pressure the young men were under. They'd had a perfectly normal life before Gina came into the picture.

"We wrote out a list of questions to ask so it looked like a real assignment. Then when Eli started talking to Gina, I didn't look her in the face. You know in case she tried to turn me to stone like Medusa," Erik said.

Ryan stared at him, trying to figure out what he was talking about.

"Sorry, Erik still likes those Percy Jackson books, you know, about Mythology and stuff. I told him her heart was cold as stone and since then he's been calling her that." Darryl shook his head as he explained.

"Got it," Ryan said. "Could I see the answers?"

Eli pulled the papers from his book bag and gave it to Ryan. "They're all in there," he said. "She grew up close to the city and was raised by her mother. She doesn't go back to her small town because her mother died a couple of years ago and it makes her sad."

"One strange thing," Erik added. "She let it slip that she used to be called Regina Watkins, not Gina Watts. Dad was surprised by that, too. He'd known her first name was Regina but didn't realize her last name was shortened, too. She told him that it sounded more professional.

"Strange thing. She did it right after high school, not college. Weird, huh? She was angry after she told us that, and we didn't get any more information."

"I think she's part of the witness protection program with the FBI," Eli said. "She could have been part of a mob family and changed her name to get away."

Darryl rolled his eyes. "Sorry, Eli doesn't read. He watches movies and is obsessed with some mob trilogy."

Eli smirked. "How many times do I have to tell you, it's *The Godfather*?" He used an exaggerated New York accent that made Erik and Darryl both laugh at him. He was a smart kid and had a strong personality that Ryan was certain Gina didn't like.

He grinned at the boys. "She's not part of the witness protection program, but something weird is going on. I'll give the information to the lawyers and see what they can figure out."

Darryl added, "She acted weird after she talked to us. I ran into her in the hallway, and she was arguing with herself." He paused to look at Ryan directly. "I mean, like really having a full blown conversation, and there wasn't anyone else around."

"See, she could have had a hidden microphone or spy gadget and was talking to an agent," Eli said, and Darryl gave him a serious look that made him stop.

"Whatever," Eli said and then pulled a notebook out of his book bag. "I wrote down all we could think of since she moved in with us."

Ryan could see Sydney's influence in everything the boys did, including their humor. "You're just like your mother," he said to Eli. Then he looked the three of them over and said, "All of you are."

The boys smiled at that comment but were interrupted by a

beeping noise coming from Darryl's watch. "I set an alarm for when it was time to leave, so we wouldn't be late to pick up little John."

"Quick thinking." Ryan told him. "Please be careful driving back home. The traffic will be heavier this time of day."

Darryl gave him a thumbs up as they each climbed into the SUV and buckled up.

Ryan leaned in to speak to them all. "I want you men to know how proud I am of you for stepping up and taking charge like this." He held out the notebook and loose pages they had given him. "I'm going to pass this on to the attorneys, and they will take it from here."

They nodded their heads and smiled at Ryan, which made it harder for him to have to tell them to stop. "That is, you fellas need to sit back and let the attorneys take over. Don't put yourselves in a difficult position with Gina anymore. No more questions or making her uncomfortable. And although you're welcome anytime, don't drive over here without anyone knowing where you are, okay?"

Darryl agreed but looked a little disappointed.

Ryan cleared his throat to make him look his way. "You did good, man."

"Thanks, Ryan," Darryl said before he started the car and headed around the circle driveway to the road home.

As soon as the boys were out of sight, Ryan walked back to his truck. He prayed he'd done the right thing and then called Terrence.

IT WAS early evening when Ryan picked Sydney up from work. According to Terrence, Ryan shouldn't discuss the case with Sydney. However, he'd already made the decision to tell her the truth, at least about them coming to see him. He would wait until they were eating and then tell her that they snuck over without permission. Before she got too upset, he would surprise her with the notebook containing notes from each of them.

It had been a difficult week for her, and he'd hoped the notes would be enough to cheer her up.

Things were going as expected with Sydney grilling him over seeing the boys while the two of them ate dinner. He'd omitted everything except the letters to her and how much the boys missed her. He'd told her that he'd called Terrence and that he was allowed to tell her. She didn't question whether there was more to it. Instead, she curled up on the couch with Ryan to read the notebook a second time.

There was a knock at the door. Ryan gave Sydney a quick kiss on the cheek, reassuring her that there was nothing to worry about as he headed to answer the door.

It was Reagan.

As soon as Sydney saw who it was, she hurried over to greet her.

"I know it's late for you lake folks, but I needed to talk to you, and it couldn't wait."

Sydney nodded, but Ryan could tell she was on edge. She'd been quiet since he picked her up, and they hadn't had time to discuss it.

They moved into the living room. Reagan took the chair, and Sydney and Ryan sat together on the couch. He wrapped an arm around Sydney's shoulders, and Reagan smiled at how natural it was for them to be together.

"Did you get the report back from the doctor?" Sydney asked.

Reagan's eyebrows knitted together as she shook her head. "No, sorry. I expect it any time now. I stopped by because my detective gave me some information today, and I needed to talk to you about it."

Sydney's shoulder's tensed, and Ryan pulled her in tighter next to him. "So what did he find out?"

Reagan shot him that big sister look she'd perfected over the last thirty years and then turned to Sydney and spoke. "I know you said that your mother was in the hospital several times before she..." Reagan paused, attempting to use a gentler tone. "Before she died, but do you remember the name of that hospital?"

Sydney shrugged her shoulders. "No. I'm sure I could figure it out, though. My dad kept lots of records, and I kept his stuff. I have a couple of boxes over at my place if you want me to look for it."

"No, that's okay. While she was there, do you remember meeting anyone, like her roommate, or friend? Possibly another patient who she did group therapy with and their family?"

Sydney shook her head. "I was really young, and it was a scary place for me. I didn't understand mental illness, but I knew my mother was in a hospital because she was sick. It made me nervous, like if I got sick, they would take me away from home and put me there, too. When I told my dad, he only let me go a couple more times."

"And you're sure you don't remember anyone from there? Or your dad ever mentioning a case he might have worked there? You said he kept records, maybe a journal? Did you read information about it?"

Ryan was staring at his sister now, but she kept watching Sydney and talking only to her.

"I'm not following your questions. I don't remember the hospital much. I don't recall anyone from there. I haven't read anything about it either. But my father put my mother in that hospital, Reagan. Is that what you're getting at? I mean, I thought that was understood. He had her committed because she was a risk to herself and by neglect, me. That's all I know."

Reagan reached her hand out and patted Sydney's knee. "No, I understand that, Hon. I just needed to know if you remembered anything specific. The hospital was called Greenbrier, and it was thirty minutes away from your hometown, but another woman from your town was also placed there at the same time. She was older than your mother, but since you were from the same small town, I thought you might know a Ms. Sarah Watkins."

Ryan stood up and went into the kitchen to make a cup of coffee. After speaking with Terrence, he purposely hadn't discussed what the boys had told him about Gina. He also wasn't sure if Terrence had shared the information with Reagan, yet. He was feeling guilty keeping it to himself and had to escape the moment. He poured three cups of coffee as he listened to Sydney and his sister continue to talk.

"I don't remember Mrs. Watkins; should I know her?"

"I had a hunch about some information that Jerry gave me today. Sorry to act like I'm cross-examining you," Reagan said. She stood up and headed to the door.

"Wait, can you tell me what's happening? Should I be worried? Should I have known the answers to those questions?"

"Try not to worry, Sydney. I don't quite have all of the information, but as soon as I do, I'll explain everything." Reagan winked at Sydney as she took the coffee cup from Ryan, and stood on her toes to kiss him on the cheek.

"Get some rest and I'll call you in the morning to let you know what time tomorrow we're meeting with Drake and his counselor."

"Oh. Tomorrow? I didn't realize it was going to happen so fast," Sydney said. "I'm not sure if I'm ready."

"I've got this, Sydney." Reagan reassured her. "I have one more stop tonight, and then things will be set for us to close this case."

She didn't say another word, but turned and swiftly headed out the door as quickly as she had blown in.

Ryan held Sydney's hand; it was going to be a long night.

Chapter Twenty-Eight

Ryan figured last evening could have gone one of two ways. Either Sydney would decide to go home to work out the new information alone, or she would spend the night and discuss it with Ryan.

He wanted her to know how much he hoped she would stay. Within minutes of Reagan leaving, Ryan took Sydney to bed and made love to her thoroughly. Afterward, they lay there naked, and he explained what the boys had told him. He'd decided before Reagan left that he owed the information to Sydney. She was heading to a face to face negotiation with her ex and Gina. She deserved to know as much as possible before wrangling with them.

Once she learned Gina's real name, things started clicking in her head. Gina's mother had to be Sarah Watkins. Did Gina remember meeting Sydney there as a child? It didn't make sense because Sydney would have been four or five years old and Gina a teenager. Did Sydney's mom mistreat Sarah? Or was she mean to Gina? Sydney couldn't remember her mother ever being cross with anyone except her dad, but she was too young to know for sure. Could this whole thing have been about Sydney's mother?

The next morning, Sydney was drinking coffee out back when Ryan woke up. She usually slept well whenever they were together, and he worried that she hadn't slept at all. Without getting a cup of coffee for himself, he went straight outside to check on her.

"Hey," she said, barely above a whisper. She was wearing his t-shirt from last night, and he smiled at her messy red hair. He thought she was the most beautiful in the morning before makeup or even a brush. It meant she had slept the night with him and it made him feel like they belonged to each other.

He kissed her on the forehead and then sat next to her. "You okay? Did you sleep?"

"Just a little."

"Reagan will call us as soon as she knows the meeting time. You sure you don't want to go back to bed and get some rest?"

Sydney shook her head. "I've had three cups of coffee. I keep thinking of the times I went to visit my mother in that place, but I don't remember much about how it looked. I remember it smelled like floor cleaner, and there was usually a person mopping the hallway, but that's it. I can remember some of the times that my mother would sit in a chair while my dad and I would talk to her, but she acted like we weren't there. She would just stare straight ahead and leave her mouth open like she was sleeping without closing her eyes. Those times scared me the most."

Ryan hugged her. "You were too young to remember a lot of it. I think that was the point Reagan was making last night, or at least that's what she was verifying with her questioning."

"You know, it's hard for me to remember my mother's face. I forgot her voice years ago, but now I have to look at pictures to even recall what she looked like. I didn't want to forget her, not altogether, just the bad parts."

Ryan felt the shiver run through her body as she discussed her mother. He grabbed Sydney by the hand and pulled her inside the house with him. "I need a cup of coffee, and then we both need to shower. I know Reagan didn't sleep either and trust me, she's a bear when she doesn't sleep. She'll be ready to pounce on Drake and Gina this morning."

Sydney stopped and looked at him. "Most of the time, I thought Drake had just cheated on me. It was about him and Gina. I thought they both were selfish jerks. I never guessed it had anything to do with me. You think Drake even knows?"

Ryan couldn't think about that right now. It killed him to think about Drake as a victim when he disliked the bastard so much. "I don't know, but Reagan was definitely putting the pieces together last night. Your answers helped her, and I have no doubt she'll have it sorted out before the meeting today."

Sydney kissed Ryan. That last comment made her feel better. She'd prayed for so many things over the past year and half, but getting closure now was at the top of her list.

They didn't discuss the impending meeting anymore. Instead, they methodically showered and dressed for the day. Ryan and Sydney finished at the same time when Reagan's assistant called. They had two hours until they were supposed to meet in the city at Reagan's office. It was more than enough time, and they even went to the White House to drop off supplies for later.

"The Haunted Mansion is looking good," Sydney said, as she jumped down out of Ryan's truck.

"Babe, you have to stop calling it the Haunted Mansion. You're scaring off my day laborers."

Sydney laughed as Ryan wrapped an arm around her shoulders and pulled her into him. She loved how casual he was with affection. He usually touched her or gave her random kisses on the lips or forehead. She felt like she belonged with him, and she avoided thinking about the meeting later that morning that might change things.

"I'll admit that it doesn't look as haunted now as it did before, but those new giant French doors they're installing in the dining room look a little suspicious."

"That's because they came from a real haunted house in Biloxi. Mario got them when he was working on a place with his brother in Mississippi."

"Ooh, tell me more."

Ryan kissed her on the lips. "You can ask him yourself this afternoon when he gets here."

Sydney stuck out her bottom lip. "I might not be here this afternoon."

"You can ask him tomorrow." he said as he carried his tools out to the garage to stow them until he returned.

"You sound so sure."

Ryan nodded his head. "That's because I am." When she didn't say anything, he turned around to look at her. "Come here, Sydney."

She walked right into his arms and let him hold her tightly. They didn't talk about anything else that might happen. Instead, they held each other. The truth was things could go terribly, but for that moment, they were together.

REAGAN HAD the conference room ready and was reading over some documents when Ryan and Sydney got there. Her assistant brought in coffee along with bottled water, and Sydney smiled when she noticed the older woman checking Ryan out. He was wearing a dress jacket over a tight button down shirt but still had on his jeans. He looked great to Sydney, and it was obvious what's her name approved, too.

"Where are the others, Reagan?" Ryan asked, ignoring the unwanted attention from her assistant, Nancy.

"They'll be here in thirty. I wanted to have a few moments to go over my notes with Sydney before they arrived."

Sydney nodded and sat down at the conference table next to Reagan.

"Could you stay with me?" she asked Ryan. He'd assumed he would wait in the lobby until the meeting was over. He didn't want to put any added pressure on Sydney and had avoided asking her. He was relieved she asked and thrilled to stay.

He sat next to her, and she was as ready as she was going to get about facing Gina. It was hard to explain since she didn't understand herself why Gina rattled her so much. Sydney didn't have a hard time speaking up for herself in situations, but she found herself without words or comebacks each time that women verbally attacked her.

Reagan explained how she wanted things to go, and the best part was that she didn't want Sydney to say a word. Basically, she wouldn't speak unless Reagan either nodded that she could answer the opposing side's questions or if Reagan herself directed a question to her. That was it. She wouldn't have to respond to Gina or even Drake personally.

Before she could get too comfortable, the hair on her arms stood up, and a shiver ran through her. Gina was close. She looked up to see Gina staring through the plate-glass wall as she and Drake followed Nancy into the conference room where the rest of them waited.

She was wearing a black pencil skirt along with a black silk blouse. If she turned sideways, she would have looked like a straight black line. Sydney turned, avoiding Gina's stare.

After they were offered and then declined coffee, they sat down. Gina pulled out her paperwork, looking like the professional that Sydney knew she wasn't. Drake adjusted his chair four times and wiggled in his seat. He clearly was uncomfortable and looked confused over Ryan being there.

Reagan leaned back in her chair and looked Gina over and then Drake before she slowly unveiled the truth.

"I'm glad you both could make it on such short notice. I believe you both know my brother, Ryan, and there was some interest in one of his homes that we need to discuss. Sydney already agreed that he could be here. I assume it's fine with both of you since we are negotiating this ourselves and avoiding court?"

She waited until Drake and Gina nodded before she continued. "I thought it best to have this private meeting to spare your children the discomfort of hearing this information in a court room."

Gina's eyes sparkled as she grinned primly. She had been waiting for her chance to speak. "We want to thank you for sparing our boys. We've been through so much already with the divorce, and we want Sydney to get the help that she needs."

Drake had a sad look on his face as he nodded over Gina's comment.

Ryan reached under the table and grabbed Sydney's hand. He wasn't certain Drake knew how serious he was about Sydney, but he could feel her trembling next to him.

"I'm glad you feel that way because I have a few more people who I feel are necessary to join our discussion."

They watched as Reagan pressed the button on the intercom and spoke, "You can send them in now."

Dr. Young, another stockier man wearing scrubs and a man in a suit walked down the hall and came into the room. Dr. Young had a seat, but the other two men stood behind him. Sydney was more nervous than before as it dawned on her what the men were doing here. Her father was a police officer, and she understood the suit with the firearm attached at his side was some form of law enforcement. However, she'd only been around people who looked like the other man when her mother was in the hospital. Was he a nurse or an orderly who worked with Dr. Young?

Sydney had trusted Reagan, but what was about to happen to her?

Gina kept smiling, but Drake appeared to be miserable. It didn't make sense.

"Gina and I have already verified with our clients that it's okay for Dr. Young to discuss his findings as long as the information stays in this room. Sydney has already signed a document that Dr. Young can disclose his information as it pertains to the case. The gentlemen with him have also signed a confidentiality agreement about today's meeting, along with Ryan Gentry. Since you met with Dr. Young separately Gina, I will need you to also sign a separate form that he can release that information as it pertains to this case. I have another one for Dr. Winters to sign."

Reagan handed a document over to Gina, who strangely only glanced at it, but quickly signed. She was eager to get things started.

Drake took longer, reading the form and then signed.

"Okay, Dr. Young, you've met with both Gina and Sydney. Correct?"

"Yes," Dr. Young said.

"Please tell us your professional opinion on Sydney and then the case."

"Alright. When I met with Sydney it was clear that she was concerned over this situation and the verdict. However, she was much more concerned about her children and how they would be affected by the outcome, whatever that may be. She discussed what the boys had been through since she and Dr. Winters had separated, and how devastating it was for them not to be allowed to speak to each other when she and the boys hadn't been apart for even a day during the entire marriage."

"They're not your children," Gina mouthed silently to Sydney.

Ryan gently squeezed Sydney's hand, and she kept silent as she daydreamed of jumping over the table and ripping Gina's hair out.

Dr. Young continued. "I feel like this is where I need to explain. The chances of a child inheriting mental illness from a mentally ill parent is higher than a child of a non-ill parent."

"What?" Sydney said with a gasp. "I'm not mentally ill."

Reagan whipped her head around and stared at Sydney, but Sydney stayed focused on the doctor. Dr. Young looked sympathetically at her and, instead of speaking to the group, spoke directly to her. "I'm sorry, Sydney. I wasn't trying to imply—"

"Hold on," Reagan said, firmly interrupting Dr. Young. "Sydney, listen a moment. Dr. Young, please pick up where you left off with children inheriting their parent's mental illness."

Gina was still smirking at Sydney, but only Ryan and Reagan were paying attention to her.

Sydney, along with Drake, were focused on the psychiatrist.

"The chances of that child becoming mentally ill is even higher the longer they are raised by the ill parent. The reason for this can be abuse or behaviors the child learns by placating that parent. The child may have the same disease like schizophrenia, but they may also have other conditions like paranoia or depression."

"I believe you told me that these kids have a ten percent chance of getting the disease as opposed to one percent of the general population?" Reagan asked, clearly leading Dr. Young in the direction she wanted him.

"Yes, but even though a child has a higher chance doesn't mean they will become ill. After all, if a child has a higher genetic risk, then raising them in a low-risk environment is important. Those environmental factors can be just as important to raising a mentally healthy and stable adult."

Sydney finally smiled for the first time since the meeting began. "My mother was very ill, but the illness didn't show up until after she had me. Once my father realized how sick she was, he minimized the amount of time I was with her, plus she was in the hospital a lot of the time. She passed away when I was very young, and I was raised in the best environment with my dad. I had a great childhood."

"I don't see how that matters, Sydney. We have documented proof of your behavior," Gina said, shoving a piece of paper toward Reagan and Dr. Young.

"This is interesting," Reagan said, looking over the sheet. She looked at Dr. Young and then back at the paper. It was a signed statement from Darryl dated yesterday that listed odd behaviors he had witnessed while Sydney lived with them.

Gina added, "You also have the police records where she was arrested for stalking me and Drake and the boys."

"I have a document, too," Dr. Young said, and then he pulled out a piece of paper that was also signed by Darryl. That form said Darryl had been threatened by Gina and forced to make false claims about Sydney. It was signed that very morning.

Dr. Young gave a copy of the form to Reagan and one to Gina.

"That is a lie. Darryl is at school."

"Darryl came to see me this morning. He cut school and then called his dad for permission to talk to me."

Gina stared at Drake, and so did Sydney.

"What?" Drake said, "My son needed to talk to a doctor."

"I would like to add something here, Sydney," Dr. Young said. "It does matter that your father protected you from the environment around your mother and that he gave you a safe, healthy and loving home to grow up in afterward. Many times, when children are forced to be the primary caregiver to a parent who is suffering from severe mental illness, it can affect them in several different ways, such as emotionally detaching from others or displacing grief or anger. I see adults who haven't developed the disease struggle with self-loathing issues, too. Occasionally, they have combinations of all those things, plus self-blame and denial. I've had survivors' exhibit signs of Post-Traumatic Stress Disorder, PTSD, because it can be like growing up in a war zone."

"I'm confused as to why you brought us here to discuss Sydney's mental health if Dr. Young isn't going to side with us," Gina said without any emotion. "You realize that we still have a case against her for not adhering to the protective order filed against her. She was warned before, and this time we will have her put in jail. Unless that is why your brother is here today?"

"My brother is here so that you and Drake blackmailing him for his property in order for you to drop the charges against Sydney are now on record. I have a court psychiatric physician, a police officer, a nurse's assistant, and my secretary as witnesses."

"Wait. What?" Drake stood up. He didn't get motivated often, and Sydney was surprised to see him physically moved over the shock of Reagan's statement.

Gina patted him until he sat down.

"We don't know what you're talking about," Gina said.

"It's obvious that he doesn't know what I'm talking about, but we have a document here with signatures from Olivia Dufrene and Lynn Calhoun that they heard you threaten Sydney. You told her that you and Drake would drop the charges if Ryan Gentry would sell you his large white house on Moss Cove that he showed to you for a deeply discounted price."

Drake took the sheet of paper that Reagan was holding out and read it. "I had no knowledge of this happening, before, during, or after it occurred," he said.

"Drake." Gina was starting to unravel. She inhaled loudly and held her breath until her face was red while the others in the room stared at her.

"You might need a moment to calm down, Gina," Dr. Young said softly.

"I don't need to calm down."

"Are you sure? Dr. Young's not done with his assessment," Reagan said.

"Whatever." Gina's eyes darted to each one of them and then she turned around for a second and looked at the wall. She was shaking her head slightly as she unbuttoned the sleeves of her blouse. She looked disheveled and no longer like the attorney she was when she walked into the room.

Dr. Young began once again, directing his stare more toward Drake. "I've been worried since last week when I met with Gina and Sydney over some information, but then once I talked to Detective Jerry Howard and finally to Darryl this morning, I'm pretty sure I've put things together properly."

Gina slammed her pen down on the table. "If you think we're going to dismiss our case, then you are wrong. We may not have enough information to have Sydney committed, but we do have all we need to put her in jail for stalking. It'll be a felony this time, and she's looking at a hard year."

Dr. Young tilted his head at Gina as if he was studying her closer. "I've been practicing psychiatry for twelve years, and I rarely come across cases like this, but it has happened. I've been called into investigations where the one pushing the case becomes the case or patient."

Sydney put her hand over her mouth, but she couldn't hide the shock on her face.

"I can assure you, Doctor, that I'm not the problem here, nor is my mental state up for debate," Drake said. His eyebrows were pulled together, and the stress of the meeting was getting to him.

"He's not referring to you, Dr. Winters. He's talking to Regina," Reagan said.

Gina stood up and slammed her fist onto the table, causing the orderly and the policeman to both move toward her. She glared at them as if she would singe them with her anger if they touched her. Drake reached for her so she would sit down, but she shoved him away. She glared at Sydney, but after a couple of minutes, she strangely smoothed down her blouse and then skirt before finally taking her seat again.

"I don't know what type of fairy tale Sydney has been spinning, but this is all certainly fictional to me." Gina plastered that fake grin back on her face, but it was too late. The others in the room had already seen her true nature. She was the only one who still believed she was well.

"In the years that I've been doing this, I've only had one accuser and one prosecuting attorney come see me first before I had a session with the defendant. Ironically, in both of those cases, the defendant was acquitted, and the gentlemen I counseled were both admitted to the hospital."

"So you can imagine his surprise when you, Regina, insisted on seeing him the same morning he was scheduled to meet Sydney," Reagan said.

Dr. Young added, "I was surprised by that, but again, it has only happened twice. I believed Gina could have needed my help since she was also allegedly being stalked. It took about ten minutes until I realized that you, Gina, were suffering."

Gina squinted her eyes at Dr. Young, giving him that confident smirk that she used mostly for Sydney.

He continued, "It started making more sense when you let it slip that you grew up in the same hometown as Sydney, and when I saw that your mother was hospitalized five times in the same place that Sydney's mother had been. Unlike Sydney's mother, your mother came home after many short stays and mostly raised you on her own. It wasn't until one of your school teachers called Sheriff Bell to check on you that he discovered how sick your mother was. He's the one who called the hospital and finally saved you. She was severely ill by that point, and you had been taking care of her for years, even though you were a young teenager."

Gina glared at the doctor and then turned to stare at Sydney. "He didn't save me." She snarled.

"According to my detective, your mother and Sydney's mother were in the same hall. It was during her mother's last stay there that you saw Sydney and her father visiting. That's where you saw Sydney, right?" Reagan asked.

Gina didn't answer Reagan. She kept her eyes on Sydney. "You look just like her," she said as Dr. Young tried to talk to her.

"Regina? It wasn't your fault. Your mother was very ill, and you'd taken care of her the best that you could, just like she did her mother."

"You don't understand, Dr. Young." Gina said the doctor's name through gritted teeth. "My mother and I were doing just fine. I didn't ask anyone for help and that Sheriff wouldn't take no for an answer. He bullied his way into my house and in a few minutes made the decision that my mother needed to go to the hospital again."

Gina stood up slowly, and everyone in the room watched her carefully.

"Just because his little wife had postpartum depression, he was suddenly a mental health expert. Imposing his will and defying my mother's wishes. I promised her I would take care of her, and he took that promise from me."

"Regina, she'd had it most of her life, and her records said the medication wasn't helping her."

Gina finally looked at the doctor. "I was helping her!" she screamed. "Me!"

Drake backed away from Gina when she stood up, and when she screamed, he moved toward the door. Sydney was visibly trembling but slowly walked around the table beside Gina. Gina started patting her face and hair then ran her hands down her skirt as she watched Sydney curiously stand in front of her.

Sydney had tears in her eyes as she reached out cautiously to hold Gina's hands. "Your mom died in that place?"

Gina nodded. "Y-year before last."

The others watched silently as Sydney hugged her, and Gina sobbed in the embrace.

After a few minutes, Sydney was able to coax Gina to sit down as she sat beside her, holding her hand. "No one understands what it's like to have a mother who can't care for you. I was young, but I still wanted her to protect me and then I wanted to protect my mom. I loved her so much."

Gina nodded and wiped at her tears. Sydney watched as her eyes darted to the side wall at no one and then back to Sydney. She'd seen that behavior before, too.

"You know Gina; my mother didn't have postpartum from childbirth. She had schizophrenia and heard voices. She wouldn't take medicine regularly, but when she did, she was able to live a normal life."

"I didn't know," Gina whispered.

"Most people didn't, and after she died, my dad and I just told people she was sick." Sydney leaned in and whispered, "Just because we carry our mother's genes doesn't mean we're going to turn out just like our moms. You aren't necessarily going to stop responding to medication."

Gina looked at her. "You don't know that."

Sydney shook her head. "No I don't, but I think you can trust Dr. Young."

"Do you hear the voices, too?"

Sydney's heart hurt, knowing that Gina was referring to the voices in her head that only she could hear. Sydney encouraged her further. "No, but I know that you can, and you need to tell the doctor about it, okay?"

Dr. Young walked around the table and held his arm out for Gina. She allowed him to help her stand up and escort her out of the room. The orderly and the policemen followed them out of the office.

Chapter Twenty-Nine

Reagan couldn't believe how things had turned around. She thought she had it figured out, but she had no idea that Gina was mentally ill. It explained Gina's behavior toward Sydney and the boys more clearly.

Ryan had been on edge the entire time that Gina watched Sydney. His adrenaline pumped harder when Sydney let go of his hand in order to walk over and comfort Gina.

He'd moved closer to Reagan, ready to step in if needed, but now, as Gina simply walked out of the room with Dr. Young, he couldn't move. It was beyond his wildest thoughts. And after his years of military service, he thought he could no longer be surprised. Then Drake walked over to Sydney and hugged her.

Reagan grabbed her brother's arm and made Ryan stand still.

Drake kept his arms loosely around Sydney when he spoke to her. "I had no idea that Gina was crazy," Drake said.

Sydney wiggled out of his arms and looked at Drake. "You're a doctor. Don't call her crazy."

"You're right. I'm just in shock. I don't know what I'm saying or doing."

"Hmm, you love her, right? I mean, you told me you were head over heels in love and that she was your soul mate."

"Oh, Sydney. Don't be so dramatic. I was wrong. I can admit when I'm wrong. I need you back. The boys need you back."

Sydney rolled her eyes, and Reagan muffled a laugh. Ryan was about to explode, but his sister kept an arm around him to keep him centered.

"What do you want, Sydney? For me to grovel and tell you we can't live without you? Do you want a new car? New clothes? I can see you need new clothes. I'll give you anything you want."

"My attorney is right here. Will you put that in writing?"

"God, Sydney. Fine. Whatever."

"I want joint custody of the boys. And I want you to visit Gina in that hospital and bring her flowers. Pay for whatever she needs, so she knows she's not alone," Sydney said. "Did you get all of that Reagan?"

"Sure did, Nancy's typing it up on her tablet," Reagan said, and they watched Nancy until she finished typing. When she was done, she handed the tablet over for Reagan's approval.

"Please go get Terrence to witness this for me," Reagan told Nancy.

They sat down around the boardroom table, with Reagan, Sydney, and Drake on one side and Ryan still on the other. Not a word was spoken until Nancy returned with Terrence. Terrence read the form and then signed it with the stylus that Nancy handed him before giving it to Drake.

"Once you read it, you can sign right there at the bottom, Dr. Winters," Reagan said.

He looked at Sydney. "And you're going to give us another chance?"

Sydney looked into Drake's eyes. Her old life was right there in front of her, and all she had to do was reach out and take it. It was all she'd wanted for the last year and a half. She'd fought for it desperately.

She turned to look across the table at Ryan, but he had slipped out the door, and she watched as it closed behind him. He'd left her there with Drake.

Drake reached over and turned her face back to his.

"I know you miss the boys and honestly, I can't keep up with the things you did for them. They need you home, Sydney. I'm missing a ton of work because of their schedules, and we can't handle it all without your organization." He grinned like he knew exactly what to say to her. "Besides, you decorated every corner of that house; you belong there."

Sydney took a deep breath and straightened her shoulders as she stood up. Drake got to his feet, but this time when he leaned in to touch her, Sydney took a step backward and held up her hands. "You're right. I do miss the boys every minute of every day and with all that I am."

"Alright then," Drake said and reached out to sign the tablet.

"Stop, Drake," Sydney's heart thundered in her chest as she said his name. "I can't, I mean, I won't go back to the way things were. I would love nothing more than to raise those boys, and I think we could do it together amicably if you would be willing to share them with me. But we can't go back to the way things were. Things are not the same between us. You have Gina to think about and I- I have another life."

"At the lake?" he asked.

It was that condescending tone that she needed to hear to remind her how much she liked her new life without him in it.

"Absolutely," she said. "It's not that far, and I can come pick the boys up for the weekends, during school breaks and holidays. If it would help, I would be willing to have them during the week sometime and drive them into school, too. We could make this work."

Drake was shaking his head and looking at the form he hadn't signed yet.

Reagan looked at Terrence and then stood up, taking a step closer to Drake. "I handle tons of divorce cases, Dr. Winters. It's easiest on the children when the parents are agreeable."

"I understand that you have conferences that you need to attend, and I would be happy to take the boys while you're out of town," Sydney added. "I can also hire you a housekeeper that can keep things tidy for you in the house. I know it's too much for you to have to keep up with it."

"You would do that?" Drake asked looking at Sydney.

"Yes. If you sign the form."

Drake signed the form without another word.

Terrence cleared his throat. "I believe there is still a restraining order on Sydney and a violation of the restraining order case that needs to be cancelled."

"I'll call this afternoon and get the restraining order removed and drop the charges," Drake said.

Reagan walked Drake to the door and down the hall to the elevator.

Sydney flopped down in a chair and leaned her head back. She kicked off her shoes and breathed deeply. All of her problems from the past year and a half had ended in a one hour meeting.

Reagan returned whistling as she walked back into the room. "What did I tell you before this meeting?" she asked, smiling at Sydney.

"What?" Sydney asked, confused.

"What do I do?" Reagan grinned as she raised that eyebrow at her new friend.

Sydney laughed at her. "You win, Reagan, you win."

"Then what are you still doing here? Go home. Celebrate. Ryan texted that he's downstairs waiting in the truck."

Sydney smiled at Reagan and then jumped up and gave her a hug. "When do you think I can go see the boys?"

"I'll let you know when the judge signs off on the custody papers. It takes a little time." Reagan said. "Hang in there; you won."

"Finally," Sydney said with tears rimming her eyes. "It's over."

Reagan smiled bigger than Sydney had ever seen. "By the way, Jerry found the boys' dog. He was rescued by an elderly couple who fosters golden retrievers until a permanent home could be found. He picked Beezus up this morning, and was going to drop him off to the kids after school."

Sydney nearly knocked Reagan over as she hugged her fiercely. "Get out of here," she said, with happy tears in her eyes. Sydney kissed her on the cheek and then picked up her shoes to walk barefoot out of the office.

Just as Reagan had said, Ryan was sitting in his truck when Sydney walked outside. He gave her a half grin when she climbed in, but he didn't speak. It had been a crazy meeting with an even crazier ending. It was too much to process, and they both were exhausted as they headed home.

When Ryan pulled into his garage, Sydney finally spoke. "I think I'm going to go home and shower. Do you mind? I just need a few minutes."

"You okay?"

She nodded and gave him a quick kiss on the cheek before she jumped down and headed over to her house.

Ryan felt it in the pit of his stomach. Sydney Bell was the woman he wanted, and he wasn't sure she still needed him. He felt sucker-punched by the whole day. He'd consoled her and promised her things were going to go well today. He couldn't have imagined that on top of getting her boys back that she'd also get her husband. It would be like the last year and half of torture for her hadn't happened. She could go back to her life, the life she had before Gina aimed to destroy it.

He slammed the truck door and went inside his quiet house. It felt empty without her in it and would for a very long time if she moved back to the city. Whenever he pulled into his driveway, he would see that stubborn redhead. She'd be wearing her green slicker coat and boots, waving her hands at the giant moving truck. When he sat on his deck, he'd be reminded of her doing yoga or eating donuts. Driving around the lake he'd certainly think about that old Subaru wagon broken down on the side of the road, and the beautiful hardheaded woman trying to change a flat tire. She'd be in his thoughts constantly.

Ryan went to take a shower, but as he passed his bed that Sydney made up and decorated with large navy throw pillows, he shook his head. What the hell would he need throw pillows for without her? He knocked them on the floor and then went to take the hottest shower possible.

It had been an hour since he'd let her walk away, and Ryan angrily packed a bag with some clothes and took it downstairs with him. He was numb as he grabbed two beers and headed out to his deck. He looked over at her house, but there wasn't a single light on over there. He wanted to check on her, but she had been clear about needing some time alone.

Was she struggling to figure out how to tell him she was going back to the asshole doctor? He couldn't blame her. She missed those kids and if she could walk back into the life she had before, the life that she loved, then why shouldn't she?

He finished his first beer, hoping she would join him and drink the second one.

She didn't, so he opened it. He drank more than half of it when he heard her clear her throat.

"You're rather stingy with those drinks," she said.

He looked up to see her beautiful smile. She'd showered and scrubbed her face makeup-free. He thought she looked incredible that way.

She sat down next to him and that close, he could tell she'd been crying. Her brown eyes were rimmed in red, and it hurt him. Was she hurting over having to tell him goodbye? He would do anything to keep her, but he wouldn't stand in her way if she wanted to go. Above everything, he wanted her to be happy. If there was anyone who deserved to be happy, it was that little redheaded woman.

He'd never been more proud of anyone. Watching her reach out and help the one person who wanted to destroy her, showed more character than he'd ever witnessed in another human being. When her ex-husband attempted to distance himself from the woman who'd cheated with him, she wouldn't stand for it. Instead, she demanded he treat her with care. It was amazing.

"I'll go get you another one," he offered.

Sydney shook her head and reached over to take a drink from his bottle and then handed it back to him. "Nah. I just needed a sip."

She leaned into him and then laid her head on his shoulder. He shouldn't have, but he wrapped his arm around her and pulled her closer to him. He couldn't be that close and not touch her.

"Are you hungry?" he asked.

She shook her head. It's chilly out here tonight with the wind blowing. Why don't we go inside and I'll light the fireplace?"

She reached for his hand as they went inside his house. While he started the fire, she grabbed a quilt and pulled the pillows close so they would be comfortable.

"Crazy day," he said, avoiding the question he needed to be answered.

Sydney sat up and looked at him. She smiled, and then tears filled her eyes. He couldn't stand not knowing. Then again, he didn't think he could handle it if she said she was moving back home. He pulled her into him and held her tightly.

After a few minutes, she gently pushed away so she could look at him. "I didn't expect things to go the way they did today," she said. "I prepared myself for the worst, but Reagan's confidence and then yours had me thinking it might not be so bad."

The tears rolled down her cheeks, and he thought he would rather take a bullet than watch her cry. He felt helpless watching her hurt.

"I know it's been a difficult day," he said.

She swallowed back her tears and wiped her eyes and nose before she gave him a nod. "For the last year and a half, I've been so angry with Gina and Drake, but mostly Gina. I've wished her ill so many times for taking my children and then today when I saw Dr. Young and his helpers; I was scared thinking they might be there for me. I never guessed it was for Gina. She's really sick, you know." And the tears were back again.

Ryan couldn't take it another minute, he pulled Sydney into his lap and held her. "It's okay, Red. It's going to be okay."

Sydney pulled herself together again and nodded. "She hears voices." She looked Ryan in the eyes. "I think she hears them most of the time. It was like I was five years old again and alone with my mom. She would get angry and grit her teeth and then she would calm herself down, but I would see her eyes darting around like she was looking at or for someone. It was the voices getting her attention. It's our very own nightmare, Gina and me. The secret club we didn't ask to join, kids with mentally ill parents. Most of us are scared we might turn out like them or be even worse than them. I've read stories about it happening, and then medical reports on the probability of it happening. I finally stopped obsessing when I met Drake and the boys. I was too busy to think about mental illness. Figured I was safe from it since I hadn't cracked from the stress of being an instant mother of four. Gina brought it back for me today."

Ryan kissed her forehead. "Dr. Young will help Gina. Reagan says he's one of the best."

"She's going to lose her job, though, and it doesn't seem like she has anyone except Drake," she said, shaking her head.

"I think you're the one he wants, Sydney. He offered you your old life back, to pick back up where you left off at your home."

Sydney pushed up and off Ryan's lap, and when she stood up and got her balance, she pointed her finger at him. "For your information, Ryan Gentry, I didn't leave off anywhere. I was removed, kicked out with a capital K." She put her hands on her hips and shook her head. He could tell her fire was just getting started, but he couldn't hide his smile as he slowly realized that she was staying in Maisonville.

"Can you believe that jerk? He was so in love with her that he couldn't see straight when he kicked me out of the house. I know she seduced him, but he was more than a willing participant. He put me through hell with the divorce and the custody fight over the boys, choosing life with her over me. She's sick, but what's his excuse? I couldn't believe he didn't have an ounce of sympathy for her, not one ounce. And she was good to him. Even though she was ruining my life, she was making his life better. She paid his debt down and paid for him to join the fancy country club he wanted." She lowered her voice when she said, "Don't ask how I know all of that, just trust me when I say that I know."

Ryan nodded his head. She was so cute when she was angry.

"He hurt me, but I know more than ever that I only really loved the boys. I didn't care about him like a husband, but Gina did. I'm going to make sure he helps her. She deserves to have someone look after her for once in her life."

She sat on the coffee table in front of Ryan. The steam of her words finally cooled.

Ryan leaned over, placing his hands on either side of her. "You deserve to have someone look after you, too, Sydney. I'm that person."

Sydney stared into his eyes and then kissed him lightly on the lips. "I'm going to get to see my kids again." She smiled. "They can come over regularly, and I can call them whenever I want. You going to be okay with that amount of noise? I mean, I know you like things quiet, and four boys are into lots of things, but quiet isn't one of them."

Ryan rubbed his nose against hers and grinned. "If we're going to have four boys then we may need to think about adding a few little girls to even our family out."

"Our family?" she asked, and Ryan nodded his head.

Sydney stared into his eyes. "Ryan, you need to think about what you're saying. You heard what the doctor said about there being a ten percent higher chance for me to turn out like my mother and then my babies could have problems."

Ryan raised his eyebrow as he listened to her. He then moved in closer, so they were a breath apart. "I heard him, and I'm not worried about a measly ten percent because there is a one hundred percent chance that I'm going to love them, just like I love you, Sydney."

"You love me?"

He nodded his head, and she cut her eyes at him. "Then why do you have a suitcase packed?"

"I figured if you were going back to the city that I was going to have to move across that freaking lake, too."

"You were going to leave Maison-Lafitte Lake for me?"

"I told you, Red. I'm going to look after you, and that means wherever you go, I'm going to be there."

Sydney threw herself into his arms and kissed him over and over again. "You've been doing that since I got here. I think I've loved you ever since the day you went down that hill to fetch my tire."

"You did call me a genius," Ryan said and watched as Sydney's face turned red. "What? Are you saying you didn't mean it?"

He laughed and held her tighter.

"Oh, I meant it alright," Sydney said and then started laughing, too.

"Well, since we can agree that I'm a genius, tell me you'll marry me, Sydney."

"You'll marry me, Sydney." She smiled and then whispered, "I love you, Ryan Gentry."

The End

Fall Again
BY LISA HERRINGTON

Seth shook his head. The conversation about leaving New Orleans with her would always go round and round. His Louisiana girl was never going to leave her hometown.
"I would've stayed for you, Rea."
"I would've never asked."
And that was the crux of their problem. He loved her. He wanted her, but he needed to hear her say she needed him too.

Want to learn more about the mysterious, ambitious Doctor, who moved back to town for love? Read on for the first chapter of FALL AGAIN, part of the suspenseful, romantic Renaissance Lake Series.

Fall Again
CHAPTER ONE

REAGAN GENTRY, DIVORCE ATTORNEY to the stars, had already put in three solid hours of work at her office, and it was only eight in the morning. She needed to keep occupied until she met with her friend, Amber, to share her big news. Amber had recently taken a job with the city attorney's office and moved back to town. It was perfect because they could plan spur-of-the-moment coffee breaks or even lunch once a week.

After graduating from law school and working in different cities, Reagan and Amber had picked their friendship right back up where they had left off. That's what great friends did when they got together, acted like no time had passed between them.

Reagan waited in the busy cafe, happy that Amber had moved back to town and she now had someone to confide in other than her brother. Ryan was busy with his booming business and even more preoccupied with his new fiancée, Sydney.

Reagan had spent a few hours with Ryan and Sydney over dinner the night before in Maisonville. The couple had recently finished renovations on their largest flip home and were glowing with happiness. Reagan sat back and watched as they talked about the property with each other as if she weren't there. They whispered and laughed over private jokes, and she knew it had less to do with the fact they worked together and more because they were in love.

Reagan drank the rest of her iced tea as the couple kissed each other again, and then she grinned over her private thoughts. *Newly engaged couples shouldn't be allowed in public. They weren't fit for the company of others, especially single friends and family members.*

Their waitress, Olivia, stopped back by the table and refilled their drinks, but Ryan and Sydney hadn't noticed. Olivia leaned in conspiratorially to Reagan, "Sucking face in public should be outlawed. They need to get a freaking room."

Reagan laughed at the smart-mouthed waitress. Olivia was always foul and funny. Truth be told, Reagan didn't mind the couple's public displays of affection. Five years ago, she couldn't imagine her brother happy again. His injuries from his last deployment with the Marines had stolen every ounce of the little brother she'd known, and therapy along with a job he loved had only brought a portion of him back.

The redhead sitting next to him had done the rest.

Watching them together helped fade the difficult memories and hard times they each had conquered in order to claim their happiness.

Reagan shook her head. Maisonville lived up to its nickname with the locals, and even her analytical side could not argue with it sometimes. They called it Renaissance Lake. It was easy to see the new beginning Ryan and Sydney were living. Maybe there really was a little magic in the town.

Ryan and Sydney finally finished their desserts, something Sydney always insisted on and then slowly walked Reagan out to her car. In the middle of the parking lot, Sydney unexpectedly stopped as she tried to talk Reagan into spending the night and more time at the lake.

Reagan made the usual excuses about work and being too busy to slow down because she didn't like spending too much time alone at her lake house. The house was perfect and brought back memories of the only fun times she had during her childhood, spending days at the lake with their uncle, but it also reminded her that she was single, very single. And she was pretty sure the local charm of the lake wasn't going to fulfill any fantasies for her.

She'd had her shot five years ago and had thrown herself into the relationship the best she knew how, but it wasn't enough. Dr. Seth Young had been building his psychiatric practice and surprised her when he decided to move out of state to take over for a retiring doctor. Her heart turned inside out when he left, and she pulled herself together by focusing even more on her career. Recently he'd surprised her again by moving back to the city. She spent a good bit of focus avoiding him at all her regular places, but she wasn't going to stay at the lake to avoid him. She liked the city. She found comfort in the bright lights and crowds of tourists. The hustle had a beat all its own, and it gave her singledom comfort that she didn't want to explain.

Ryan and Sydney tried harder to talk her into spending the night, and she'd looked back at Miss Lynn's diner and shook her head. Those two were trying to lure her into lake life with good company and comfort food, but she couldn't handle the relaxed atmosphere for too long. The slower pace made her antsy.

Reagan loved them, but she'd left Maisonville as fast as possible, and while waiting on Amber in the early light of the cafe, it was clear that she was where she belonged. It was packed with people and humming with conversation. There were young and old professionals, college students, and soccer moms everywhere. The eclectic crowd had character, and it always made her smile to see the various types of people coexisting happily.

Harmony wasn't something she'd had growing up or saw very often in her career as a divorce attorney. However, she did strive for it in her personal life and at the office. She was a successful divorce attorney and had earned her nickname because when one of the famous football or basketball players decided to get a divorce, she was the one they called. It helped her become one of the busiest lawyers in the city and her firm. It was also the reason she was celebrating with Amber.

Reagan had received word that she would officially make partner in two months, and she immediately called Amber to meet for coffee. Reagan was wearing a tight-fitting red dress with a matching blazer and three-inch stilettos, making her petite frame look longer.

She stood up to greet her friend when she heard Amber's laugh before seeing her. "I bet you're making partner, hot little mama," she said, looking Reagan up and down before she hugged and kissed her.

Reagan wiggled suggestively, and then they both laughed again. Finally, the waiter came over and took their orders. "How did you guess? Can you believe it's finally happening?" Reagan asked as her friend adjusted her larger frame into the uncomfortable metal chair.

"There was no mistaking your excitement over the phone, and you deserved that promotion a year ago," Amber said with conviction. She was a curvy woman with flawless mocha skin. Amber was tall, and *Housewives of Atlanta* attractive. She had more dates than anyone Reagan knew, including the men, and she never stayed home on a Friday or Saturday night. Her confidence drew people to her, and Reagan loved to watch Amber in action, working a room, or controlling a conversation.

Reagan had started her career and was still at the same law firm, Williams, Morrison, and Weisnick, and loved it. It was the coveted spot everyone in their graduating law class had wanted, and she was a perfect fit. Amber had started at another law firm in Baton Rouge but was happy to be back in New Orleans with her closest girlfriend and working for the Mayor's office.

While Reagan was the family attorney to the stars, Amber was helping advise the Mayor, the Council, and other city offices and boards. She specialized in reviewing city contracts and documents that created any legal obligation affecting the city. She was brilliant but sometimes misjudged because of her looks.

"So, how goes it with Alexavier Regalia?" Reagan asked, accentuating the single mayor's name suggestively.

Amber rolled her eyes, and they both laughed again. "He's trying to kill me with the whole let's-modernize-this-city-government-for-the-people-initiative. I swear if he applies for one more federal grant in order to keep his reelection promises, I may jump out my office window."

"Oh, Amber. You know those windows don't open, babe," Reagan said with a straight face.

Amber laughed so loudly several people turned around, but before they became a complete spectacle, the waiter came with their coffees and pastries.

"I thought I heard he was advocating for that new health center?" Reagan asked.

"In case you haven't heard, he's an overachiever."

"Oh, I've heard alright. The mayor has gone out with almost as many beautiful people as you have," Reagan winked at her friend. Alexavier Regalia was of Italian descent and had the beautiful face and thick dark hair to prove it.

"If you ever want to be set up, let me know. He's asked about you before, you know?"

"Um, no thanks. My clients are in the news enough. I'm not looking for my picture to be in the paper, too," Reagan said.

"Then you probably shouldn't wear tight little dress suits that accentuate your ass, girlfriend," Amber said loud enough for the Mayor and his two male companions to hear as they walked up.

"Ms. Gentry. Amber. Good morning," he said with that politician grin that got him mostly what he wanted.

Reagan kicked Amber under the table.

"Good morning, Mayor Regalia. So, you do remember my friend, Reagan?"

"Of course," he said and then introduced the head of his technology department and a member of the city council to them.

He didn't linger, but he didn't take his eyes off Reagan while he was there. As he said goodbye, he leaned in and said, "It is a pretty great dress," making Reagan bite her bottom lip as he turned and then disappeared inside the crowd.

"I'm going to kill you, Amber," Reagan said, cutting her eyes at her friend.

"Your ex is back in town, and a little competition would do his ego some good."

Reagan shook her head. She had no intention of dating the mayor or her ex-boyfriend, but there was no reason to argue the point with Amber, who would never agree with her.

The friends finished their coffee and then headed to their respective offices, a block and a half away from each other.

Reagan walked into her office and was greeted by her assistant's strange smile. Nancy was efficient, but she wasn't friendly and rarely smiled unless it was at a good-looking man. Reagan cut her eyes at Nancy as she handed her the mail like she held in world secrets. Then, without a word between them, Reagan walked into her office, reading the return addresses on the envelopes before settling on what to open first.

She looked up just in time to dodge a large bouquet of red roses sitting on the credenza. "What?" she said and backed up, avoiding the card. That's when she felt the second floral arrangement jutting out from her desk and turned in time to grab it before they tipped over.

As she carefully stepped back to take in the room, there were five large floral arrangements, each with a dozen long stem red roses taking up all the extra space in her office.

Reagan closed her eyes and took a deep breath, trying to clear her mind, but the scent of fresh roses surrounded her. Finally opening her eyes, she reluctantly grabbed a card off one of the vases. She knew the flowers were from Seth. He'd tried to get her attention for the last month since she ran into him at his office with Sydney.

Sydney Bell had needed legal help to get joint custody of her stepsons and to help fend off an attack from her ex-husband's new girlfriend. It was challenging but helped Reagan and Sydney become close friends. During that time, Sydney needed to meet with a psychiatrist, and Seth had surprised Reagan when he walked in the door as Sydney's doctor.

Since then, he had done everything he could to get Reagan's attention. He called her office. He called her home. He left handwritten notes on her car. He sent fruit baskets and a singing gram. Every week he had surprised her with something. The roses got her attention. He'd sent five dozen long stem roses to her office for every year they had been apart.

She shook her head as she looked at her calendar. It was the anniversary of the day they had met.

Reagan sat down at her desk, still holding her briefcase and the mail. She wasn't going to see Seth or talk to him because she might have to admit that she loved his attention. In fact, she was fooling herself by pretending she didn't still think about him. After he moved, she had taken off for a week and hidden away from everyone so she could cry alone. Then after seven days, she didn't allow herself to shed another tear. She'd hardened her heart, and it made her a better person. Well, it made her a stronger woman than ever before and the best family attorney in the area.

She was about to make partner. The only way she could keep up the hours it would take to keep her status at work would be to forget about beautiful Dr. Seth Young.

Nancy knocked as she stood in the open doorway.

"Come in," Reagan said.

"Looks like that fella isn't going to give up."

Reagan looked at her assistant but didn't reply to her comment. "Did you need something, Nancy?"

Nancy gave her a knowing smile. She was twenty-five years older than Reagan and still an attractive woman. She certainly had her share of older male attention. "I wanted to make sure you saw your messages before I left for the assistant's office meeting."

"Thanks," Reagan said, giving Nancy a look that told her she was sorry she had to participate in the mundane monthly meetings. Even though Nancy worked exclusively for Reagan, she still had to pay her dues to the head of the secretarial pool. The assistant's meeting was meant to keep everyone on the same page in the office regarding employee events, changes to employee policies, or even building rules. But, what could have been handled in a single email was always drawn out into an hour-long gathering by the head partner's secretary, Betsy. She'd been with the firm and worked for Terrence for only two years but had somehow appointed herself as the office assistants' boss. And she loved to wield her power over the underlings.

Reagan laughed to herself, thinking about how Nancy would torture Betsy. It would be subtle. Probably a sneak attack. But above all, it would be the end of that twenty-somethings career at the firm, and no one would be the wiser. After all, it was why she had the job in the first place. The previous assistant had been a snitch, and Nancy wouldn't put up with anyone tattling on her for anything, including parking in the partners' parking places on their days off. Reagan sort of admired Nancy's rudeness. She had style.

॰

Seth walked his patient out and locked the office door. He had a short schedule and wanted to make sure he got to Reagan's office building before being locked out again. He knew she'd still be there after hours because she worked all the time, but her office was locked up tight at six.

It hurt him to see that she didn't have a life outside of work. He had moved back to town and prepared to win back her heart. He knew she was single but had no idea she was determined to stay that way, dedicated to her job and nothing else.

Sure, she loved her brother and his girlfriend, but she barely saw them. They would come into the city and have dinner with her most of the time because she couldn't take off to go across the lake to visit with them, and he'd heard she had a house over there.

Seth had been patient. He'd watched her from afar. But,

honestly, he had spent weeks devising a plan to see her and couldn't have planned it better when she'd walked into his office with a new patient for him.

Being that close to her was all it took. Memories of Reagan in his bed flooded his mind as soon as he smelled the vanilla fragrance on her skin and the almond shampoo she used on her hair. It was a punch to his gut when he saw her that day, and he couldn't wrap his arms around her. She was the most incredible woman he had ever met. He still remembered the red dress she wore the first night he'd met her.

His old professor had invited him to a party for the candidate for Mayor. A member of her law firm was hosting the event. She was holding a glass of whiskey, and every time she took a sip, the thin gold bracelet she wore would slide up her arm delicately. He'd felt hypnotized by the action and stared shamelessly at her until she made eye contact.

They didn't run out of conversation all night, but it took him months to get her to go out with him. "I can buy my own drinks," she would tell him. "I can pay my own tab, and when I'm done, I'll call my own Taxi," she'd said, not wasting any time letting him know she could take care of herself. It really did something to him.

The first night they spent together, he let her know that he respected her independence, and although she could do everything on her own, he wanted to take care of her. Seth tried like hell to prove it over the next few years and thought he'd gotten through to her. She'd finally told him that she loved him. Although it was New Year's and she'd been drinking, he knew it was true. They made love until the sun came up. She never said it again.

He'd tried to force her hand and get her to move to Tennessee with him, but she'd thanked him like he'd been her personal concierge or something. She congratulated him on the opportunity and told him good luck. If that wasn't a kick in the pants enough, she finished it with *it's nice to have an adult conversation when a relationship has run its course instead of some emotional breakdown and argument.*

Seth didn't know what to say but had felt the blow in his core. He felt like someone had died as he went through the motions of packing and moving. It was the hardest thing he had ever done.

Reagan didn't speak to him again.

It took him a year to realize there was no taking a girl away from New Orleans.

He worked day and night building his practice in his new state, but the success felt hollow. He knew he would never accept Memphis as his home if she wasn't with him. His career would never be as important to him as Reagan Gentry. He had built a considerable practice and fortune in Tennessee, but after five years, he sold his business without a blink of an eye just to get back to her. She had to give him a second chance. He wasn't going to take no for an answer.

He'd tried subtle. He'd been sweet. But the time had come for him to confront her.

About the Author

LISA HERRINGTON is a Women's fiction and YA novelist, and blogger. A former medical sales rep, she currently manages the largest Meet-Up writing group in the New Orleans area, The Bayou Writer's Club. She was born and raised in Louisiana, attended college at Ole Miss in Oxford, Mississippi and accepts that in New Orleans we never hide our crazy but instead parade it around on the front porch and give it a cocktail. It's certainly why she has so many stories to tell today. When she's not writing, and spending time with her husband and three children, she spends time reading, watching old movies or planning something new and exciting with her writers' group.

Connect with Lisa, find out about new releases, and get free books at lisaherrington.com

Made in United States
North Haven, CT
13 July 2023